WARSHIP ARES

CAPTAIN'S FATE BOOK 1

Written by: Skip Scherer

Cover by Skip Scherer

ISBN 978-1-7359075-0-5 (paperback)
ISBN 978-1-7359075-1-2 (ebook)

www.skipscherer.com
www.lionknight.us

For the Love of my mom and dad, you made me all that I am.
For the Love of my wife, you are the balance I always need.
For the Love of my daughter, you are my sunshine.

This book is for you.

It takes a village to raise a child, it also takes one to write a book.

Thank you to my family who pitched in to make this happen. Especially my wife, without her typing skills this book might still be nothing more than scratching on a piece of paper. My mom, for her eternal support, and whose spelling skills I wish I had inherited.

To Ryan and Nath. Whose feedback was so valuable, that I consider them my personal Rat Pack. While others helped critique my initial work, you two went above and beyond. So much so that you are now a part of this world forever.

To my editor Kathryn Farmer of Kits@twenty-six (https://www.kitstwentysix.co.uk/) editing services. You somehow found a way to take my jumbled thoughts and make them readable. Your feedback has increased my knowledge of writing and shown me how much further I need to go. I look forward to working with you in the future.

To all those not listed, I thank you all.

CONTENTS

You'll probably think this story is about me, but you'll be wrong.
This story is about survival.

CHAPTER 1

INDIANA

When Jax was a little girl, her father would often talk about how he didn't think we were well prepared to explore space. That Earth's expanding exploration of space was a fool's errand. He had a saying about being prepared for the worst and that Earth just wasn't. She couldn't remember exactly how it went, and right now, she didn't care; she couldn't see it.

Harumi "Jax" Brandt was Captain of the United Earth Ship (UES) Indiana. Just the thought of it made her smile. She adjusted her white Captain's uniform, a metal sheen glistening off it. The double-breasted suit was tailored to her, but it still didn't seem to fit right. The hat that matched the suit sat by her side; she never wore it unless someone was touring the bridge. Sitting in the Captain's chair, chai tea latte in hand, she took a moment to let it all sink in. She was young for a Captain. Not the youngest ever, she had missed that mark by about six months, but she was okay with that. She still had what she had always wanted. This had been her dream since she was a little girl, and now here she was, living that dream.

She had been hired right out of Captain's College for this post, leaving other potential candidates standing by the wayside. Captains with more experience. Captains with actual space miles. She was proud. By the abyss, she was ecstatic. She had made sacrifices, pushed herself to study, even though she hated studying. She had done her internships on little rust buckets running back and forth between the Earth and the moon. She had worked as a junior bridge staff, a pilot, doing nothing but running people around Mars. Never taking vacation, never missing a shift, gaining those hours needed to be accepted into Captain's College. Some thought she was too young, and some thought she only got here because of her parents, but she didn't care because she knew better. She had earned this by the sweat of her brow, and she was happy.

Captain was the only title on a modern starship that really mattered, Jax mused. Mr. this or Ms. that were the only other formalities used. Military titles of old were long gone, a thing for the history books, except for the Captain. All ships, as far back as people had sailed ships, had always needed a Captain. Even in space, that tradition continued. And she was Captain. She took a sip of her tea, the smile wide across her face.

Jax ran down the specs of the Indiana as she nestled into the command chair. The UES Indiana was a multi-function ship that carried both supplies and people. It was a great place for her to start her career. It could travel from Earth to almost anywhere in the galaxy. Its saucer section was outfitted for crew and families, and it had all the modern amenities a long trip could ask for, a gym, pools, full VR rooms. A gantry off the back of the saucer section held pods for transportation. Water, crates, mail, all of it was expertly packaged for a space flight.

She was in a whimsical mood as she brought up their destination. Highguard Station. Jax's smile grew wider just thinking about it. Highguard was further out than humans really had a right to be. A space station built to honor some long-ago anniversary of space exploration. Jax didn't remember which anniversary, she was always horrible about remembering those things. A few politicians had thought it important enough and made it a point to celebrate it in the grandest way they could imagine.

The standard space exploration regulations were overlooked. Planets worth exploring were bypassed. Highguard was built in a part of space that humans would not have reached for at least another two hundred years. This was a completely dangerous way of establishing a station in space, but, of course, everyone wanted to go there. *Count me in*, Jax thought.

Jax's ultimate goal was to explore deep space. Getting hired to Captain one of the premiere exploration crafts, taking it beyond where anyone had gone before. She dreamed of exploring the cosmos on a Universal Cruiser. Of being the first Earth-based vessel to discover intelligent life on other planets. Of being the first human to set foot on an alien world. She shook her head at her childish dreams, but who really knows what the future holds?

Her train of thought was interrupted by Mr. Daniel Trucker. Mr. Trucker was a bridge employee, but not an overly ambitious one. He was hired to head the scans station on the bridge. He always seemed happy where he was, and since he was exceptionally good at his job, no one ever seemed inclined to push him into advancement. He was slightly overweight but was well groomed. His dark blond hair was shorter than the long style that was currently in vogue. He wore the standard bridge crew uniform of a buttoned white shirt and trousers, no metal shine on those. He called her over.

"What have you got, Mr. Trucker?"

"I noticed these blips on the long-range scans." His voice was kind of monotone as he laid everything out matter of fact. "At first, I didn't give it much notice, since it's at the edge of our sensor range, but over the last half hour, I've noticed that they seem to be matching our course a little too precisely."

"This route is a pretty common one out to Highguard Station. Maybe another supply ship heading our way. Did you check for flight info from Earth Command for matches?"

"Yes, Captain. First thing I did. No flights should be anywhere near us right now. All ships in this area are either stationed at Highguard or on routes into uncharted space."

"Can we get eyes on it?"

"I've been trying, but look here… Whatever is out there, it's dark. Colored to blend with empty space. You can see some light blocked in the background, but not enough to get a good image profile. At least, not at this range."

Mr. Trucker brought an image up on his view screen. He was lost in thought while he studied the information.

"There have been rumors of ships disappearing on these deep space routes. Strange craft doing flybys. Mysterious happenings." The Captain and Mr. Trucker both jumped as the second-in-command, Henry Rickson, joined the conversation. Behind his back, everyone else called Henry Rickson, "Mr. Hide". Being second in command meant he was in charge of staffing on the ship, so he tended to move around a lot, showing up when you least expected it. He was skinny with dark auburn hair down to his shoulders. The Captain found his habit of showing up without being noticed a little unnerving, if she had to be honest.

"Let's get a better look at it, then. Ms. O'Connor, please launch a pathfinder probe to the coordinates that Mr. Trucker is sending over."

"Yes, Captain," came the mousy voice of Reason O'Connor, who was stationed at Navigation. A shy girl who was still getting used to her position on the bridge. Her bright blonde pixie cut had little wisps of hair that stuck up on the left and right sides, adding to the mouse affect. "Probe away," came moments later, her voice a little stronger this time.

Do I sound like that? Jax wondered. *I'm just as new to my position.* She and Reason O'Connor were becoming good friends because of it. Together,

4

they were the newest staff on the Indiana, plus both of them were pilots. The rest of the staff had been on the Indiana for a while, they already had their niche groups. *You have time, so start with one and then get to know the others. We're all new to each other. I need to make sure I don't sound that new, however.* She made a mental note to project confidence with her voice as she waited for the probe to make its way.

Jax was giddy as the probe launched. She didn't think she would get to use this little toy on this trip. Only the deep space vessels used them nowadays.

The Pathfinder accelerated faster than any human occupied ships could. Used in uncharted space, Pathfinders carried advanced imagery and scanning equipment. Ships charting new sections of space could carry a small fleet of these probes. Once entering a new area, they would launch hundreds of them at a time, charting whole regions of space in the fraction of time a single ship could. In the early days of space travel, they were instrumental in building star charts. They became standard issue on all ships, whether they were headed outside the Earth's solar system or travelling already charted space.

The pathfinder made it into range and started its work. It had only just begun to relay the transmission when the screen flashed, and everything stopped.

"What the—?"

"—The probe is gone." Shock came into Ms. O'Connor's voice as she interrupted the Captain.

"Let's get those last images back up." The Captain jumped on the command pad and started punching in commands to retrieve the pictures. Still new to the Captain's chair, she often did things on her own rather than letting others work their jobs. It was a habit she was trying to break. She recognized the mistake but pushed on. "Here is the time frame before the probe exploded. What is that?"

Mr. Rickson leaned into the screen as he asked, "EVE?"

"Yes, Mr. Rickson?" the ship's onboard computer responded in its usual chiming voice.

"Can you enhance this image, so we can get a better look?"

"One moment, Mr. Rickson. I will be happy to help."

Mr. Trucker moved back to gaze at the sensor panel with Ms. O'Connor while the Captain and Mr. Rickson stayed focused on the enhanced image EVE was displaying.

"What the abyss kind of ship design is that?" Henry Rickson said.

"EVE, please identify that ship?" The Captain inquired.

"No matches in any United Earth databases, Captain."

"You know, my father used to build models of old Earth history battle ships and I would swear those look like gun ports," Mr. Rickson said, pointing at the screen. The ship looked like a starfish or squid with too many tendrils trailing after it. Mounted above and below on its port and aft sides were the "guns" that Henry was talking about.

"Nobody puts guns on a spaceship. That's crazy," the Captain said, trying to continue, but she was interrupted.

Mr. Trucker and Ms. O'Connor spoke as one. "Captain, they are closing on us!"

"Well, that's ominous," the Captain whispered before seeming to regain her voice. "Helm, increase speed; I think it would be best if we could keep our distance."

"Increasing speed to three quarters qave drive," came the deep bass voice of Mr. Camp, who may not talk much but was always heard. Seated next to Reason O'Connor at the helm station, the Pilot had the frame of a runner, his skin tan as if he spent a lot of hours in the sun. His long weave of dark hair brushed his shoulders as he made adjustments on his consul. On the main view screen, the Captain saw the speed increase, an on-screen meter ticking upward.

Qave drives or engines were the modern marvel that made space travel possible. A quantum wave engine could bend space and time and propel you forward, pushing the ship faster and faster till it broke and continued past the light speed barrier. Once past that barrier, the more energy you put into it, the faster you could go. A warping of physics and time protected you from the velocity and time dilatation.

The technology also provided a completely safe and renewable source of energy. The invention of this technology had changed the human race. For the Captain, it was even more personal; every time she thought of qave tech, her mind formed an image of her mother. All these years after her death and Nayomi Brandt's theories on qave engines were still being explored to make spaceships achieve the previously impossible. *Thank you, mom.*

"If we assume that was a gun that hit our probe, then all these areas on that ship could be potential weapons." Mr. Trucker brought an image on screen as the Captain turned back. It lit up with 12, no 16, no 18... *What was happening?* Jax's mind raced as more spots kept highlighting.

"Captain, they're still closing!" Reason O'Connor's voice was a controlled scream. Both the Captain and Mr. Rickson had shock on their faces as they turned together. They stared wide eyed at the screen. The unidentified craft was creeping closer. Mr. Rickson moved closer to Reason as if to double check the information.

"What? A ship that size should not be able to keep up with us at these speeds." Mr. Rickson gasped the words.

"Someone forgot to tell them that. Helm, give me full power on the qave drive and let me talk to the engine room."

A quick moment later a pleasant-sounding chirp sounded on the bridge and a voice came on. "This is Ms. Imes in engine control, what the abyss are you guys doing up there?"

The Captain tried to picture Ms. Imes' face. She was a shorter woman with dark cropped hair, but it was hard to imagine. The engine room crew tended to keep to themselves. Jax rarely saw them. *I'm still getting to know the bridge crew, it's a long trip, I've got time.*

"Ms. Imes, we have an emergency situation. We're going to have to push the engines for a while, can they handle it?"

"I guess so. We ran an upgrade on most systems before we left. How long do you think you need?"

"I don't know, possibly a long time, so I need you ready."

"Well, if we go for a long time, we might get some leaks, minor radiation, some overheating, maybe blow a—"

"—Can you handle it?"

"Oh, sure, I'll have everyone suit up into emergency gear. It'll be fun for them. We don't ever get to wear that stuff. Might want to have someone from medical come down just in case we need some quick care. But no problem, Captain, we got it."

"Thanks, engine room. Captain out." *Oh, crap,* Jax thought, *I wasn't thinking about safety proce—*

"—Captain, they're still closing." Reason O'Connor once again interrupted the Captain's thought pattern.

"How can that be? That ship is half our size."

"Make that ships, Captain; there are three more behind, all closing."

"We can't go any faster," Mr. Camp offered up, his deep voice shaking.

"Maybe we're overreacting. Could this be some kind of joke?" Mr. Rickson was mostly talking to himself.

"Well, I'm not laughing, so unless someone wants to volunteer to get in a shuttle and go check it out, I don't think we can make that assumption. Helm, be prepared for evasive maneuvers. If they fire on us, you move, don't wait for my command."

"Yes, Captain. Will do, Captain," Mr. Camp said.

"Ms. O'Connor, find me a planet, moon, an asteroid, or something we can make it to before they catch us."

Jax's mind raced as she issued commands. Her stomach lurched, tying itself in knots. *Not now,* she thought, and forced herself to remain calm.

She had forgotten something. What else was she thinking about? *Safety. Safety comes first.*

"Mr. Pearson!" The Captain scanned the bridge, looking for the short stocky man. The head of security should be monitoring from the bridge at this hour.

"Uh?… It's actually Reilly, Captain. Mr. Pearson and I switched shifts so he could prepare for his wedding and—"

"—That's fine, Mr. Reilly. We need to get the passengers to the lifepods without causing a panic. Any suggestion on how to do that?"

Mr. Reilly pushed his hands through his long hair as he thought for a moment. The moments ticked on. Reason had her nose glued to the screen while Mr. Reilly kept running his fingers through his long hair. Jax's patience was about to blow. Finally, something broke.

"I guess we could run an emergency evacuation drill. Long flights like this are supposed to do them. I can't remember when the last one was actually done on ship, space flight is safer than riding a bike so there is never any need, but I think that would work."

"Great. Sound the drill. EVE, please give me ship wide announcement."

"Absolutely, Captain. Ship wide announcement ready, Captain."

Jax didn't know what the actual regulation was and there was no time to look it up. *It has to sound official. No panic. Keep everyone calm and safe. When this is over, I'm going to find the protocol for this and make sure we practice. Deep breath, you can do this. You're going to have to improvise, make it sound good.*

"This is the Captain. Due to regulation 4242 of the commercial space flight code we are conducting a mandatory evacuation drill. This is only a drill. All passengers and non-essential crew are required to report to lifepods. Security personnel will be around to check that all procedures are followed. After the drill you will be allowed back to your normal activities. Again, this is only a drill and we apologize for any inconvenience."

"Mr. Reilly, please make sure everyone is stowed away." The Captain turned without waiting for a reply or to see Mr. Reilly leave. "All right, I need to see where the ships are and, Ms. O'Connor, what have you found for me?"

"Putting the ships on the main screen, Captain." Mr. Trucker said.

Jax's heart dropped; they were catching up so fast. "What's the red circle around their ships?"

"I added an estimate of their firing range from when they shot down our probe, plus a couple hundred yards just to be safe."

"Good thinking, Mr. Trucker. Ms. O'Connor, what do you have for me?" Jax put hopeful eyes on the young navigation specialist.

"A comet, Captain. Here."

The main screen image zoomed out to show the comet's location. It seemed so far away and the oncoming ship so close, but if they could only reach it in time, it looked like it would provide some needed cover and a bit of time. Now she just needed something to do with it.

Jax took to the command chair and started to work a plan. It was like being back at Captains' school when they throw you a hazardous situation at random. Most of those involved engine failures or some crew member getting hurt. The stakes here were a lot higher. *Who plans for getting attacked in space? Work the problem.* she told herself. Jax used the command chair to lay out her plans. It automatically started to relay information to the appropriate stations, the projected screen in front of her moving as fast as her fingers could fly.

Thankful for something to focus on Reason O'Connor and Jonathan Camp instantly went to work. Mr. Trucker, seeing his commands, turned a confused eye at Mr. Rickson. The second-in-command turned in disbelief to the Captain. "I'm sorry, you want us to do what?"

"Just do it, Henry."

Henry Rickson and Daniel Trucker both shook their heads. "This is crazy."

The Captain barely heard it, she was not even sure who had spoken. "Slow it down a little, Mr. Camp; we want them a little closer. Half qave drive. Keep us at light speeds until I give the order to drop back to normal space. Cruising engines only then." Jax tried to force a level tone into her voice.

As the ships closed in on them it was like watching water boil. The red line Mr. Trucker had provided inched painfully closer to the image of the Indiana. The flight line for their course was mapped out ahead of them. It was all guess work at this point. Life or death. Modern space flights were not supposed to be hazardous. Jax swallowed a lump in her throat. *Don't lose focus, just work the problem.*

"Clear to make our turn, Captain." Mr. Camp's voice cut through the deathly silence that had enveloped the bridge.

"Cut to sublight, give me three quarters cruising speed. Hold on the turn, wait for it, wait for it …" The Captain sank into a whisper as she watched the red line moving "…nearer. Closer. Just another few seconds and—. Now, Mr. Camp! Full power, hard turn. Turn! Turn! Turn!"

Jax kept talking, more to cut her own apprehension than to supply any useful statements. Her fingers gripped the chair, knuckles turning white. The Indiana lurched hard like it had run into a wall.

"Beam from the lead ship hit us, Captain!" Mr. Rickson roared. "Grazed the starboard side. Outer hull damaged but intact."

As the Indiana dipped behind the comet, Jax's mind continued to race. *Lucky. Lucky. Please just let our luck hold. Please. Please.* The first ship was coming around the comet now. It was almost on top of them. Within minutes, they would have another clear shot. All about timing. Jax's knuckles turned white as she gripped the arms of her chair. *You can do this. Work the plan.*

"Mr. Trucker, eject now!"

"Safeties disengaged. Pods away!"

Outside the Indiana, container pods 9, 10, 11 and 12, all full of fresh water bound for Highguard Station. Nearly one million cubic meters of water were ejected into space. The maneuvering thrusters, designed to make unloading the pods easy, had been quickly reconfigured. Instead of drifting away from the accelerating ship, the pods begin to rotate and move back in behind the Indiana. It wasn't beautiful, they were careening, but would it work? The bridge stopped. All eyes were glued to the screen. No one was breathing.

The lead pursuer came around the comet and hit the first pod at a slight angle. A ripple in space sent it tumbling off. Jax's heart sank. *They have some kind of defensive shield.* Her thoughts turned to despair. *This isn't going to work.* That's when the pursuer slammed head on into the other pods. The crew of the Indiana watched in disbelief. A spectacular event unfolded in front of their eyes.

The craft rushing to catch up came speeding around the comet; barreling into the dense pods and exploded. Water contacting the cold vacuum of space created a massive wave of crystals. The shimmer around the ship seemed to flash and then pop. Through that maelstrom, one of the containers smashed the front the vessel. Like a brick through a window, the front of the craft exploded into space. Blown off course, the ship tumbled away from them.

The bridge of the Indiana erupted into cheers. All except for Jax.

"There're three more coming!"

The Indiana bucked and was thrown off its axis. The bridge crew went flying. The blast had torn through the number four engine, sending the Indiana hurtling to its port side. EVE enabled emergency stabilization and righted the ship. The Indiana was hobbled. The bridge crew started picking themselves off the floor. Cuts and bruises riddled them all.

"Is everyone all right?" Jax called out as she rubbed her jaw. She had hit the floor face first on the initial blow. Her chai tea had splashed down the right side of her uniform. The Captain's hat rolled freely across the bridge. Calls of, "okay", and, "fine", echoed in from around her. It was obvious they had all suffered from that jolt. They shook it off. They had to get to work. *Safety*, Jax thought. *I keep forgetting safety.*

"Everyone lock yourself into crash positions. This is not a drill." Back in the Captain's chair, her harness secured, Jax called out, "Where are the other ships? Give me an update."

"Two of the last ships are coming around and I've lost the…" The port side of the bridge detonated around Mr. Trucker before he could finish his sentence. He died as the mass decompression plucked him and others into open space. Jax watched helplessly as Mr. Reilly and a science technician whose name she didn't remember were all swept out into space. *What is happening? This shouldn't be happening.* Her mind raced in a panic. *Who was that? Why can't I remember his name? Why did Reilly come back to the bridge? Why weren't they strapped in? Why? Why? Why?* All in a split second, they were gone as the air was pulled from the bridge. Jax's lungs burned. The air rushed from them. The emergency breach shields kicked in and sealed the fissure. Air flowed back in. She could breathe. Turning to ask navigation to take the helm, she saw Reason O'Connor slumped in her chair, a piece of shrapnel piercing her neck. *We must get out.* The thought whispered in the back of her head.

"Abandon ship." The command squeaked out of her. "EVE, sound abandon ship. Abandon ship!" Each time she said it just a little louder.

"Yes, Captain. Sounding abandon ship. All passengers and crew should proceed calmly to their nearest Lifepod Bay. All lifepods are ready and clear for launch. Have a nice day."

As EVE's cheery voice grated on her nerves, she hit the release on her harness and screamed. For the first time, she realized her left arm was a bloody mess and something was burning on her leg. Nothing was on fire, but scorch marks ran from her knee to her ankle. The burning would remain. Nothing she could do as she stumbled up. That was when she saw it.

The alien. Even in her mind, she had a hard time getting her head around it. The craft settled in front of her. It seemed so close, nestling just outside the breach like a hawk eyeing its prey before closing in for the kill. Time slowed for Jax. Her perfect day. Her first time as a Captain. It would all end here. Nothing to do as despair became acceptance.

"Come and finish it, you—"

Her world exploded.

Chapter 2
Escape

A binding flash and Jax fell back as if struck by a blow. Her mind raced. She was alive! The menacing ship in front of her had disintegrated in a flash of light. Her heart pounded. In its place, another ship slid into view, like a hunter coming to check on its prey. Confusion, fear, pain and adrenaline all raced through her body. Where the other ship had reminded Jax of a prickly squid with its strange protrusions and external weapons, this ship was all shark.

She had always enjoyed the shark holovids as a kid. The sleek lines and intimidating presence of the creatures had captivated her. In the blink of an eye, her mind took it all in; it had more angles than a real shark and its three dorsal fins looked more like gun mounts or were they missile tubes? It was hard to imagine guns on a space craft. The colors of this space shark shifted slightly like it was trying to blend with its background. Was it looking at her?

"What the abyss do you want?" She shouted into the ether. It came at her. She stumbled back in fear, catching herself on the command chair. Instead of ramming the ship, it flew directly over them. Off to look for another victim.

A hand pulled her around, another shock to her system, and there was good old Mr. Hide, shouting in her face. *Great*, she thought, *just what I don't need; something else scaring the crap out of me.*

"Captain, we need to get out of here!"

"What about the rest of the staff?"

Jax hadn't realized how loud it was on the bridge. Her senses were in overload. She could barely hear as they shouted back and forth.

"Ian, Paul, Daniel and Linda all went out the breach, Captain."

Paul? Oh, the science technician, I remember him now. How could I have forgotten? Her stomach knotted up like a punch to the gut. She hadn't seen the two interns, hadn't even thought of them. *Ian and Linda gone just like that.* She shivered.

"I pushed the other two interns off the bridge. They should be on their way to the lifepods. Captain, we need to go!'"

Jax thought of the last two interns, Max and Janel. *Some good news,* she thought, as her mind tried to process it all. Mr. Rickson continued to yell at Jax while he pulled her along.

"Right!" she belted out, willing her body into motion, focusing her mind back to the task on hand. They left the bridge running. As they reached the escape bay reserved for the bridge staff, Jax pulled up short.

"Wait. EVE, has the Indiana been evacuated?"

Henry Rickson looked at Jax and gave a nod of support. EVE began to speak. When the shipped bucked again, her voice skipped and stuttered, but it finally came out clear enough for them to understand.

"All passengers and staff not listed as deceased have been evacuated, Captain. Only you and Mr. Rickson remain. Would you like a casualty report?"

"No, EVE, that will be all."

"Thank you, Captain. Have a good day."

Jax was starting to hate EVE's perpetually happy demeanor. She gave a sigh of relief. Passengers and crew had made it off the ship. They were safe. Or were they? Would the aliens leave them alone? Worries started to rack her brain.

"Good call on the safety drill, Captain."

"At least something went right with this whole thing. Shall we go, Mr. Rickson?"

16

"Yeah, let's get the abyss out of here."

Jax turned and opened the door to the Lifepod Bay. Jax stared into the void. Before her was a hole reminiscent of the one on the bridge. The safety fields were in place, protecting them from the harshness of space. "Oh, come on!" she bellowed.

There was nothing she could do about the lifepod issue, but now there was a whole new problem to solve. It just never seemed to end. *Did the interns make it out?* She would never know. Jax's rollercoaster of emotions had been spent. At this point, all she had was her stark resolve to keep on surviving. The floor started bucking harder.

"EVE, are there any lifepods left?"

"Yes, Captain, ten individual lifepods are still available on deck three."

"Stairs," they both said and were off.

"Did you see the other ship?" she asked as they ran.

"After the bridge exploded, I got rocked pretty hard; I just saw you falling back. You actually laid eyes on them?"

They entered the stairwell, and both were breathing hard. All the emotions and physical threats were taking their toll. Adrenaline pushed them onward.

"Yes, but there was also a different ship, it—"

The stairwell lurched. Henry and Jax were thrown against the wall. Jax's stomach somersaulted. As the gravity went out, she found herself rebounding in the air. Twisting, she caught the guardrail with one hand and made a grab for Henry's arm with the other.

"I hate weightlessness," Henry Rickson said with some malice in his voice. During his statement, the lights flickered and switched over to the dimmed backup lights.

"This can't be good. We need to get moving," she said.

"Next floor. Then down the hallway. The lifepods are halfway down on the right."

"Right," Jax said as her hands gripped handholds along the ceiling. Down and out into the walkway. She remembered thinking how worthless handgrips on the ceiling were. In modern starships, they just weren't used. In the last few minutes though, she had changed her mind; now she was nothing but thankful.

The Indiana continued to buck, screeching noises like fingernails on a chalk board getting louder and louder. As they reached the door, things warped. The ceiling spiraled down into them. Jax was batted through the slim opening of the Lifepod Bay. Henry was desperately trying to twist out of the way when the twisted serpentine metal caught his arm. He screamed. Instinctively, he tried to pull away. The whole outer corridor came alive like a vengeful creature and severed his arm.

More pain coursed through Jax's body as she scraped through the door and once again bounded off a wall. She heard Henry shriek. Before she could right herself to get back to him, she saw the blood floating around. The maelstrom of twisted metal continued to convulse. Jax launched herself at Henry, hooking him under his still remaining arm and around his neck, clasping her hands across his chest. Her legs hit and she shoved hard back into the room. She rotated to take the impact from the wall, bruise upon bruise screamed out in pain.

"Stay with me, Henry!"

"Captain... Jax... Leave... me... Get... out." He was passing out, the pain coursing through his body.

"I'm not leaving until you are safe, Mr. Rickson, so stay with me. Captain's order."

Jax spoke while she quickly surveyed the room. *Where was it? There!* First aid kit down the line of safety pods. The room continued to creak and moan, but the inward collapse seemed to have stopped.

Jax ripped off what was left of her left sleeve and tried to put a quick tourniquet on Henry's arm. She tied what extra she could to the hand railing for Pod #6. *Lucky #6*, she thought as she angled for the first aid

18

kit. As she grabbed the kit, she felt the wall shudder. *We have to go.* Pushing back to Henry, she allowed a quick survey of the lifepods. Those had better work or this is all for nothing. *Please work.* Back at Henry, she wrapped her legs around him to secure her position. He groaned and his breathing was very shallow.

"Hang in there, Henry. Come on, man, stay strong."

"Leave… me… huhh…"

She was saying it as much for herself as for him. She unzipped the kit and grabbed the medfoam. Used to treat small cuts, usually a small squirt was enough. She emptied the whole can onto Henry's arm. She then ripped Henry's shirt off and attached an AI Med Pack. Once attached, the AIMP lit red and ran a list of problems down its screen. Quickly, the word, "TREATING", began to flash across the AIMP's little screen. It addressed each issue as it formulated treatment. Jax heard the AIMP start to whirl as it administered the drugs and medical nanites it thought was necessary. Henry seemed to relax.

"You're going to make it, Henry, you're going to make it." She released Henry and twisted around, hitting the door release for lucky number six. Untying his arm, she maneuvered him into the pod. These lifepods were designed for a single person, used by stragglers who might have missed the regular evacuation vehicles. It was too tight of a fit for both of them to leave in one pod, but Jax had to cram in to get his safety straps on.

"Glad you're so skinny, Henry."

With the straps secured, she pushed back out of the pod.

"EVE, activate all auto controls for pod six and launch."

"…"

"EVE, activate all auto controls for pod six and launch."

"…"

Jax ground her teeth. Opening the side panel, she was relieved to see it was still functional. She keyed in her command codes and hit the check boxes for auto pilot and launch. Hitting the "Accept" button, she made sure she was clear of the portal before the pod closed and launched. She wanted to stay to rest, but the rumbling walls pushed her on.

She turned to pod five. Door open, she slid in and buckled up. Hitting the launch button, she was pushed back into the recumbent chair as the G-forces increased and shot her into space. Jax's eyes were closed as she finally felt the G-forces begin to subside.

Her bullet-like pod extended its small maneuvering thrusters. Still on manual control, Jax placed her hand over the flight knob and brought the tiny craft around. The display on the dash showed her the Indiana up ahead. Jax gasped. The Indiana was almost unrecognizable. The aft section was gone. Detritus spewed from the ship, plasma and explosions lighting it up like a perverse fireworks show. The middle of the ship was a twisted corkscrew of Escher-like proportions. She gazed in horrible fascination. One of the pursuer crafts had rammed into the Indiana, creating a bulge that threatened to tear the ship apart. The foredeck was littered with holes where the alien craft had decimated the ship.

She flipped a thumb switch and activated the check for safety transponders. A lighted list began to scroll down the side of her display. Some were found and turned green. Some turned red, which meant they were missing, or maybe they were already out of range? The sensors on the small craft were not good for much, but what else could Jax do?

What about the aliens? Five ships, she told herself. *One went kaboom. One stuck out like a sore thumb. That left two of those kind and the space shark.* The scanners showed nothing. She panned the craft, hoping beyond hope for a visual confirmation on their whereabouts. As her tiny craft swiveled about, it was right there. Once again, she was face to face with the shark. This time closer. A lot closer. She froze. She was out of options. Time seemed to stop. The silence was deafening.

"What now?" Jax whispered.

There was a flash of light and everything went black.

CHAPTER 3

BERT AND ERNIE

Jax opened her eyes wide with a gasp. She was seated at a table with a small light overhead. She tried to move and realized her hands were splayed out and stuck. Her feet were also immobile. She swiveled her head. At least something could move. A strange clicking noise kept echoing around. She focused her eyes. To the left and right, as far as she could see, was darkness. But there in front of her was something, a vague shape touched by the light. Jax squinted. There were two of them, each standing close to two meters tall. *Are those mandibles? Antennae?* Jax pulled her head back in fear. She couldn't see them clearly, these aliens. The thought rattled in her head. They moved slightly, a tilt of the head, chest expanding. The clicking noise, Jax realized, was jumping back and forth between them. *Are they talking?*

"Um… Hello?" Nothing but more clicking.

"Can you understand me?"

Clicking.

"Hello?"

More clicking.

"Anyone listening?"

Their conversation continued.

"Girl stuck to the table here."

Was the clicking getting louder?

"Take me to your leader."

Click. Click. Click.

Jax kept talking, but nothing changed. The clicking, or talking, was starting to annoy her.

"So, are you trying to torture me?"

Click. Click. Click.

She sat there in silence with an occasional burst of talking to break the monotony. She had no sense of time; it could have been hours. Her inability to move added to her frustration.

In front of her, a door popped open. The bright light caused her to close her eyes, to turn her head away. To Jax, it was a shadow that walked in and sat before her. The lady was talking before Jax could clarify what she was looking at. Who she was talking to.

"Captain Brandt, please listen carefully. We have limited time and you have a particularly important decision to make."

"Who are you? You look familiar. What is going on?"

"Please Captain, depending on your choice, there will be time for all that. Right now, please listen."

"All right."

"First, the passengers and crew that survived the attack on your ship are well and being maintained in their lifepods. We will monitor them and ensure their continued safety until they can be picked up by a United Earth vessel. That would also be your first option. We can arrange to have you among the survivors and returned to Earth. But know that if you choose this option, the powers that be will not allow you to tell your story. They will silence you. If you choose to speak out without their authorization, they will discredit you. If you do not abide by their wishes, your career as a captain will be over.

"Option two. We could use someone like you. The ingenuity you showed during the attack on your ship was impressive, Captain. We can give you the tools to fight against those that attacked you. You can strike back and help keep others from suffering the same fate. However, if you choose option two, you will be listed among the dead. Your life on Earth will be over.

"We have only a couple minutes. I can try to answer your questions, but I will need your answer."

"Are you kidding me? What is all this? Are you going to let me up?"

"Captain, please, our time is limited. I suggest you try and focus on something to make your decision. Go back to Earth or stay and fight. Our time is almost up."

Jax's mind raced. She needed more information. Why would Earth silence her? How is it these people can fight back? She had nothing on Earth, only her career. Fight or go back to Earth. She needed more time. That was when the old saying her father had been fond of rang in her head: "Those who don't prepare to fight simply prepare to be conquered."

The muscular dark-skinned woman across from Jax gave her a smile.

"I'll stay." *What did I just do?*

"Excellent. Lights please."

The lady stood and Jax could finally focus on her a little more. Her tailored blue uniform had what was obviously a rank bar across her heart. She was about half a head shorter than Jax, with curly dark brown hair.

"Can I get up now, and can you please explain just what in abyss is going on?" Now that the rapid-fire session was over, Jax needed answers.

"Of course," the lady responded as she worked some unseen controls on her side of the table. Jax's hands and feet jerked free and she began to stand. She jumped sideways as someone walked past her from behind.

"I'll get the MedBay ready for her, Commander, since I'm assuming I can treat her now." His voice had a bit of facetiousness thrown in. He twirled an injector in his hand that he stashed in his lab coat pocket as Jax glanced his way.

"Thank you, Doc. We will be there shortly," the commander said with sincerity.

"Great, now that you're done planning my immediate future, how about you tell me what the abyss is going on? Who are you people? What was that that attacked my ship? Why was I sitting here for so long? And what are those things?" Her finger shot out to point at the two creatures by the door.

"We call those 'things' Bert and Ernie. You were kept waiting because we were deciding what to do with you. The ships that attacked you, we call them the Screech. I'm the XO, Commanding Officer, on this ship. Commander Lewis. The rest can wait. Dr. Charles is correct that we should get you to MedBay for treatment."

Jax could feel her temper rising. Too many things were happening too fast, and all of them were out of her control. She needed more. Planting her feet and standing as tall as her one-and-three-quarter meters would allow, she crossed her arms.

"Listen, Commander Lewis, my whole life just got turned upside down; I've lost my ship, people I care about, people I was supposed to take care of, and now, according to you, I can't go back to Earth either. So, I need—by the abyss, I deserve—a little better explanation to what is going on."

The Jax and the commander stared at each other. To Jax, it seemed like a battle of wills. She was not sure how long she could last. Thankfully, the commander's face softened.

"Very well. Can we at least walk to the MedBay while I explain?"

"Fine."

As they walked out the door, a heavy plate slid down to seal what actually looked more like a hatch. She was struck by how cramped the outer hall was. On the Indiana you could walk four or five people abreast and all the ceilings were at least ten feet high. Here, none of that existed.

As she and Commander Lewis strode down the hall, they could barely stand side by side. The ceilings were about eight feet high. It was all gray metal and some kind of rubberized flooring. Nothing had been done for aesthetics. As they passed others in the hall, people would make room by pressing to the sides or standing in open hatchways. Jax felt like she was pressed into a can.

"En masse, we are The Humanistic Commonwealth, or the High C for short. Don't tell anyone from Earth that because we are operating in secret. The Screech are an intelligent alien species with very militant, possibly xenophobic, tendencies. Earth government is aware of them but keeps the information secret. Currently, the Screech mostly turn a blind eye to Earth ships since they pose no threat. Earth also believes they can make peace no matter the situation.

"Those of us in the High C believe different. We must arm ourselves and be prepared to defend ourselves from any hostile invader. I believe you can see why we have that opinion."

Jax nodded her head as they slowly walked the corridor. For a moment, she was at a loss for words. Listen. Walk. Listen. There was nothing else she could do.

"You are aboard the High C's first warship, the Ares. The Ares is the namesake of her class. She has been designed from the ground up to take the fight to the Screech. Advanced Particle Beam Weapons, High Energy Lasers, Railguns, variable yield Torpedoes, the works. A testament to her name."

A smile came back to the commander's face as they stopped in front of a portal where the word, "MedBay", was displayed on a small plaque. The door was open and Jax was waved through first.

"About time." Dr. Charles came over to greet them.

Jax realized how tall the older looking doctor was, his head reaching towards the ceiling, he was easily two meters tall. His wild mess of gray hair adding to his height. His long white lab coat billowed around him.

"I'll leave you in the doc's capable hands. He'll get you fixed up and then take you to your quarters. After some rest, I'll take you to the Captain for a more formal welcome and debriefing."

25

"One more question before you go, Commander."

"As long as it's quick."

"Bert and Ernie? What's up with the insects?"

"We don't want Earth or the Screech to know that humans are out here with gunships. In fact, we want the Screech to think we're another alien race encroaching on them so hopefully they look for us and leave Earth alone. We occasionally use Bert and Ernie to send messages and images out into space, or when we help Earth ships, so that we can get the rumor mill going about armed aliens.

"Good enough, Captain Brandt?"

"For now, Commander Lewis. And thank you."

"Take care of her, Doc. She has grit. Captain says to place her in the Admiral's quarters when you're done. That's also the guest suite when we don't have an admiral on board." The last part more for Jax as she nodded at her.

"Understood, Commander. If you would step this way, Captain Brandt."

Commander Lewis made her exit while Jax laid down on the medical table. She could hear the doc grumbling something about having to wait so long to treat her. Mostly, she tuned it out. The medical force field held her gently in place while it ran its scans. The pokes and prods of Dr. Charles caused her skin to prickle as he worked to heal her arm, her leg, and administering treatment to all her cuts and scrapes. She took it all as a moment of peace.

Sooner than she thought, he was sitting her up. A pleasant look crossed his face.

"You are in remarkably good condition considering what you have been through. Your arm was the worst of it. I'm surprised you could still use it."

"I don't feel a thing," she said, stretching the arm. It was a little stiff.

"That's because, before you woke up for your interrogation, I was able to at least give you a pain suppressant. You're welcome."

"Doc, what about the other people from the Indiana? My second in command, his arm was cut off." The words were muted as she said them. It was hard to talk about it. Hard to ask.

"Most of your lifepods are fine. I'm sorry to say the Screech targeted some of them before we could intervene. Your Mr. Rickson will live, though. We made sure he was stable before all the pods were maneuvered to a safe place. They will wait, perfectly secured, until they can be picked up by a passing UE ship. Many of them, including your Mr. Rickson, will have tales to tell of Bert and Ernie for days to come." He gave a small smile.

"How is it they won't know about all the humans running around?"

"The same way as if you had said no to staying." He flipped a small injector out of his pocket and spun it around, sliding it back in like a gunslinger of old.

"The medication makes short term memory a problem, but it has no other effects, so anyone that it was administered to will be fine."

"Thank you. So, they think I'm dead then?"

"Yes, I believe that is how it works."

He helped her to her feet as a young man in dark green jumper suit came in. He was on the short side, had boyish good looks and a shaved head, which seemed to be the norm for men on this ship. He snapped to attention and offered a salute that left Jax staring. Dr. Charles waved a salute back at him half-heartedly.

"Captain Brandt, this is Fleetwalker Percy. He will show you to your quarters so you may get some much-needed rest."

"Fleetwalker?"

"We call all new recruits Fleetwalkers, they're kind of like privates from the old Earth military. Sometimes, however, people choose to also use Fleetwalker to address anyone who is in the Gaia Fleet. You'll get used to it soon enough, Captain." He shook his head slightly as if he found the whole thing ridiculous.

"Thanks, doc. Please call me Jax. I'm not sure I'm a captain of anything right now."

"Don't sell yourself short, Jax." He gave her a paternalistic smile. "You did an amazing job with what you had. Please get some rest."

"Sounds good to me. Thanks again."

"Ma'am, Captain Jack, ma'am, if you would please follow me." The eager young man said. Jax looked at—what was he called?—Fleetwalker Percy and opened her mouth to correct him. As she saw the seriousness in his eyes, the sincerity, she stopped. She caught Dr. Charles chuckling as he turned away, back to whatever awaited him.

"Lead the way, Fleetwalker Percy."

The walk was short, or maybe it wasn't; Jax's mind had shut down. How could she process it all? It was all so surreal.

"Can I get you anything else, ma'am, Captain Jack, ma'am?"

"No, Fleetwalker Percy, that will be all."

He snapped a sharp salute and was gone before Jax could raise her hand. She entered the Admiral's quarters and let a smirk cross her face.

On the Indiana, she had a walk-in closet bigger than this. Admiral's quarters indeed. This was not what she had expected. *But things are not as they were*, she told herself. There was a bed, a desk with a main chair and two tiny sitting stools, an instant food maker called a foodfab, and a change of clothes. Past the bed, she found the head and a slim stand up shower. A shower. She stripped off her tattered UES uniform and stuffed it into the waste disposal.

Activating the shower, it rained down on her like a waterfall. The blood and grime was washed from her. Finally, her emotions were washed from her too. She cried and didn't care for how long.

Stepping from the shower, she hit the service button on the foodfab. "Chai tea latte." It hummed for a moment and then dinged. She pulled the small door open and grabbed her prize. It tasted like home. A home now lost to her. As she drank the wonderful tea, she found some basic underwear and a t-shirt. She slipped on the non-descript blue jump suit that was left on the bed. They fit well and were comfortable. She glared into the small mirror by the door to the head. Oh, she looked like someone had beat her with a stick. Her auburn hair, hanging to her shoulders, was clean but a mess. Small cuts and bruises were scattered everywhere. And her eyes... Everyone always said she had her Dad's eyes. She'd always thought they were more the phoenix-shaped eyes that her mother had, but now she saw it; her dad's eyes stared back at her out of the reflective glass. The hazel color seemed deeper somehow.

"Is this where that depth comes from, Dad? From seeing things no one ever should?" She closed her eyes. Sat down on the bed. Jax was asleep before her head hit the pillow.

Chapter 4

Welcome

Jax woke to the sounds of bongs going off in her head. Well, not in her head, it was some kind of announcement. She was groggy. She missed it the first time.

Bong. Bong. Bong.

"Battle stations. Running silent."

Bong. Bong. Bong.

Jax heart raced. *Battle stations. We're under attack. Where should she go? What should she do?* The message repeated one last time. A knock at the door. Jax almost jumped out of her skin. She shook her head and mentally chided herself. "Enter."

Commander Lewis, the XO, stepped in with a cat-like grace. "Sleep well, Captain Brandt?"

"Not sure yet. Are we under attack?"

"No. Standard operating procedure. For any call to action, we go to battle stations. Anything out here could be deadly; we aim to be ready. One of the reasons I'm here is to help you transition. The other is that the Captain would like to see you in Command. He wants to welcome you, debrief you, and there is something he wishes to show you."

"Okay. Do we have a moment? I could use some caffeine."

"A few. I expected to find you either still sleeping or in night dress. The doctor assured me you would be out. Finding you up and ready to go is a surprise."

Jax gave a chuckle as she ordered her chai tea latte from the foodfab. "Don't be. I slept like this. I didn't find or even look for pjs. Can I get you anything?"

"I'm fine, thank you. How are you? The doctor wanted to let you rest longer, but like I said, the Captain has other plans."

"I feel better, emotional wreck, but better. How long was I out?"

"Around fourteen hours. You should eat too, if you can. Doc's orders. The ship's foodfabs make a great blueberry muffin." The XO gave a slight nod of her head.

Jax nodded as she studied the commander's face before turning to order a muffin. Once again, she was struck by the feeling that she knew her. She turned again to stare. The commander met her analyzing gaze and tilted her head slightly.

"Question?"

"I—" She started to say, and then paused. Then the memory that was scratching at the back of her mind came flooding in. "You're Gemma Lewis. You won a Judo gold medal when I was, like, thirteen years old. I thought you were dead."

"As the saying goes, news of my death has been greatly exaggerated. Much like yours will be, I imagine. Mine was more on purpose. A transport ship reported missing and then some well-placed wreckage. I was recruited on Earth to join the High C and then we had an arranged transport plan."

"I knew you seemed familiar yesterday."

"You had some other things distracting you."

"A few." Jax pushed down some of the raw memories and shuddered a little. She took some tentative bites of the muffin and then set it aside.

"I think that is about all I can handle right now."

"We should go then. The Captain awaits."

"After you, Commander Lewis. Or should I say XO?"

"Whichever works best for you. I prefer Commander, but the Captain insists on XO. He likes his formalities. Before we go, we are running silent, which means we are in full stealth. Our energy output is being masked, including engines and scanning. Flying like this with our adaptive hull coloring, we could pass within fifteen meters of a UE ship. Conceivably, they wouldn't detect us."

"That's impressive."

"Yes, and very handy too. However, you should know that, aboard ship, there is a superstition when running silent that you shouldn't talk unless entirely necessary."

"Really?"

"Really. I guess it goes back to old Earth submarines during war time. Back then, any noise you make could get you killed. In space, it doesn't make much sense, but what superstition does? I suggest that unless you want the whole crew mad at you, you avoid talking."

"Okay. Thanks for the heads up."

"My pleasure. Shall we go?"

Jax waved her hand and tilted her head slightly in a grandeur gesture. Gemma Lewis suppressed a smile and headed off to Command.

Once again, Jax's expectations were shattered. *I need to adjust to my new reality,* she thought. The Indiana had this wide-open bridge with a grand ballroom kind of feel, the Ares was tight and efficient. The low ceilings that were a staple across the Ares were marginally domed here in Command. Along the sides of the room were four pods, each one with seated personnel. Commander Lewis whispered in Jax's ear as she gestured to each one.

"Navigation, Engineering, Weapons, and Operations."

There was a fifth pod that the Commander passed over, tucked in the back. They had passed it when coming in, but Jax barely registered it as she took in the rest of the bridge. Some of the station pods had two people seated in them while others only one. Navigation looked to have two, along with Weapons, while Operations and Engineering only had one a piece. In the middle of the room was a large oval table with a holographic display. The table had a rail running around it, which some of the people were holding onto or learning on. Currently it showed her "space shark", the Ares, and what looked to Jax like flight telemetry. There were four people around the table. One of them was constantly moving between the Weapons station and Operations. Two of them had small holoscreens open displaying information Jax couldn't make out.

The fourth person was hunched over the table, staring intently. When he noticed Commander Lewis and Jax enter he straightened his back and turned to them. He was a big man with dark skin, cropped white hair, and short white beard. As he moved towards them, Jax was amazed at how gracefully he navigated the small space with his bulk. It wasn't fat, she realized, just years and layers on a weathered frame.

"Captain Brandt, this is Captain Ichabod Moss." Commander Lewis made the introduction.

"Captain Moss, I know I'm a little late, but permission to come aboard?" Jax said as Captain Moss grinned a little when they shook hands.

"Permission granted, Captain Brandt."

"Please, just call me Jax. With the Indiana destroyed, I don't think I really have a job anymore."

Captain Moss stared at her for a moment like she had spit on his shoes. Once he started talking again, she was happy to hear a lighter tone than she saw.

"Sorry to interrupt your rest, Jax…" The Captain paused for moment as if making a decision. "But I thought you would like to see this. Engage Observation Deck."

"Captain, we are running silent."

"I know that, XO, but we are in no danger, and I doubt a little energy expenditure would reveal us in this case."

"On your orders, Captain. Engaging Observation Deck." The XO, Commander Lewis, gave in easily. There was slight smile on her face like this was a common occurrence.

Jax gaped in wide wonder as the domed roof and walls of the command center melted away. She was staring off into space. She was standing in space. Feeling squeamish, she planted her feet and forced some deep breaths into her lungs.

"Spectacular, isn't it? And if you look off to the starboard side, you'll see what you are here for."

Jax turned and followed the Captain's gaze. Unbelievable to Jax, Highguard Station came coursing into view. It hung there like a bright little moon. In the background, was a small, almost habitable planet. It was jokingly called Lowguard. Jax's mind was euphoric, a dream realized.

"Magnificent. But how? We were close to a year away."

"The Ares is a lot faster than the UE ships. A lot of it is thanks to your mother, actually."

Jax's head snapped around. Her mother had died on Earth. Had a heart attack at her workstation. Never could take a break. But with what Commander Lewis has said, could her mother be here?

"Wait, what? My mother is ..."

"Her research, I should say. Earth didn't seem too interested in her advanced engine designs. The High C, on the other hand, were. We secured her work and brought much of it from theory into reality."

"For a second, I thought... Never mind. Mom would have loved this. She was always complaining about how our ships weren't fast enough."

Jax returned her gaze to Highguard Station as it glided past. The Captain was giving orders about speed and distance, but lost in the moment, Jax didn't pay attention. The walls and ceiling melted upward as the observation deck was disengaged. The tight campiness of the bridge returned.

"Jax, if you and the XO would please follow me. Commander Moro, you have the Conn."

"Aye, Captain, I have the Conn," Jax heard from over her shoulder.

Jax turned to follow the Captain and found herself bumping into Commander Moro. He was a head taller than her, deeply tanned, and he stood stiffly. "Oh, sorry, Commander," Jax said as she tried to navigate around him. He seemed unmoving to Jax. She heard him grunt and, from the corner of her eye, caught his penetrating stare. It reminded her of the look Jennifer Hale gave her in their freshman year of college, just before they got into a fight. She didn't have time to consider it, though the Captain and XO Commander Lewis weren't waiting.

Off the bridge, Jax found herself in what was marked as Briefing Room One. The tight space was big enough for a table, and if Jax was right, enough chairs for the officers and plus a few extra. The Captain was already seated at the head of the table, the Commander at his right. Jax was waved to the left.

"I realize you've had little time to heal or process it all. I'm sorry for that, but we need a better understanding of what happened to you and your ship. The logs we were able to retrieve are a bit fragmented," the Captain said.

Jax locked eyes with the Captain. Even thinking about what happened to the Indiana made her stomach crawl. Much to Jax's relief, the Captain and Commander waited patiently. She steeled herself, and slowly, carefully, she began to tell her tale.

It took a while to break it all down. Jax had to pause often. Daniel Trucker, Jonathan Camp, Reason O'Connor—*oh, Reason, so new to space.* There were questions and clarifications. Mr. Rickson. She finished with her memory of seeing the Ares, her space shark, waiting for her.

The Captain and Commander were still smiling at her space shark description. The Captain continued, "I know it doesn't feel like it, but you did a remarkable job. Unprecedented, in fact. Usually, if we come on a

UE ship that the Screech have already engaged, it's a cleanup operation, saving any lifepods they missed, and then hunting them down."

Jax voice was choked up. All she could do was listen.

"Let me show you something," the Captain said, working some controls Jax couldn't see, and the table lit up like the one in the Command Center. A bright blue and green orb appeared.

"This is Earth." The image zoomed away as thousands of stars and planets joined the image. "This is the space, give or take a few light years, that Earth currently claims as their own."

In the area around Earth, and stretching way out into the galaxy, a huge block was highlighted green. Jax knew that Earth had embraced space exploration, but seeing it like this was phenomenal.

"… And this crowning achievement is Highguard Station."

A small line shot out of the regular green orb. It continued on and on and on until, finally, it stopped with less than a pin prick. The line it left behind was almost as long as the orb was.

"In our rush, we passed by so much." The Captain waved his hand across the expanse. "This is what we are now close to running into." He spoke as he tapped the table again.

The holo zoomed out more. A red wall that resembled the green one of the Earth territories appeared. It kept growing. More. Larger.

"That's all the area we know about so far, at minimum ten times what humans occupy. Probably a lot more. The Screech—" The Captain paused, working the controls until the images switched again. A humanoid appeared. Thinner and a little hunched. Beak where a nose and mouth should be. Some feathers. Jax's eyes were wide with a kind of disbelief. "—Are prolific in numbers. When they find an area to expand to, they move in and destroy whatever is in their way. They take no prisoners, and from what we can tell, don't even examine the technology they destroy. We have evidence of other alien races. The evidence suggests that the

Screech found these races and completely destroyed them. Many think this means they are highly xenophobic."

"I never knew …" Her words trailed off.

"Yet you had to go up against them all the same. I show you this so you can truly understand the choice you have to make now."

"I thought I already made a choice to be here."

"Life is a series of choices. You have another one to make."

The holo flew off in another direction. Faster, it seemed this time. Jax's mind scrambled to take it all in. It threatened to overwhelm her.

"This is Gaia, the planet established as the home of the Humanistic Commonwealth. As you can see, we are considerably smaller than the other factions."

The Gaia area was highlighted in orange and looked to consist of one planetary system, with four planets. A smaller sun a few light years away was also highlighted. Considerably smaller was an understatement.

"So, you're basically letting me know that I've joined a group that is hopelessly outnumbered? Not giving me a lot of confidence in my decisions."

"I know, but it's necessary for you to understand. They have the numbers, but our tech is better. The Ares proves that at every encounter."

"Great, so, quantity versus quality. What's this decision you need me to make?"

"We need people that can captain ships in both our private sector and our military. If you go private sector, I can pretty much guarantee you will be given a ship to captain. You will work running supplies, equipment, and personnel, much the same as what you were doing with the Indiana."

"And option two?"

"You join the military and we put you to work. However, you won't be captaining a ship anytime soon. You will need training on technology, weapons, tactics, and the workings of the Gaia Fleet. We do not hire people for jobs, here they earn them."

"So, option one, I get a nice job doing what I was, even though I know what's out there. Option two, I lose all I've worked for. Eventually I can earn a ship like the Ares to one day help take the fight to these Screech." She raised an eyebrow as she made her simplified assessment.

"That's the short of it."

"Not really much of a choice."

"No, it's not, but the XO and I both agree it's one you need to make before we continue on. We can give you time if you need it."

"No. I already said I'm in. My first instinct is usually the best. Now I just know the depth of it."

"I told you," Commander Lewis finally chimed in, smiling at the Captain.

"We had to be sure."

"So, where do we begin?"

"I can't give you official rank, that will have to wait until after we have completed our current mission and returned to Gaia. Fleet Command wants to evaluate you before deciding on a course of action. I can give you a field promotion."

He took a small box from his side and slid it over to Jax. Jax opened the box and saw a small blue bar with a single yellow stripe. Jax noted that the Captain had four on his and two stars. The Commander had three and one star. She smiled as if laughing to herself. From a small part of her memory she recalled what she was looking at. This wasn't army like her dad, but something from the navy. The lowest officer rank, what was it called?

"For now, you are assigned to Commander Lewis. You will be her shadow as she oversees your training. You will help out where needed and be given different tasks as we figure out where you can be most useful."

She nodded her head. All she had done to get to Captain and now it looked like she would have to do it again. *Fine. Another problem to work. But I've done it once and I can do it again. I will be Captain again, that's the plan.*

"When do we start?"

"First thing tomorrow," Commander Lewis said as they rose and shook hands. The Captain also rose but instead of extending his hand he offered his most formal salute. Jax stiffened and returned the gesture.

"Welcome to the Ares, Ensign Brandt."

CHAPTER 5

ATTACKING

Jax was flying.

Over the last few weeks, her life had regained some of its previous routine, if not its normalcy. Currently she was in her favorite room on the Ares, the Fitness Room. With its high ceilings and open spaces for workout equipment, it was the most spacious room on the ship. It had training areas for boxing, Judo, and MMA. There were even side rooms for high or low gravity training and lap pools.

Jax learned that all crew members must spend at least one hour three days a week in some form of physical training. Commander Lewis offered a Judo class twice a week for those that wanted it, which was where Jax found herself now.

Jax came down hard. The sprung floor took some of the blow, but the air still rushed from her lungs.

"Nice combo, but your timing could use some work, and you need to be a little closer to hit that Tai Otoshi. You left yourself open to my counterattack."

"Just trying to lull you into a false sense of security before I unleash my full brown belt skills on you."

Gemma barked a laugh that startled Jax. "Seriously, though, you're rusty. Let me guess, the last time you practiced with intent was in your first year of Earth Space Training. Just enough to get your physical credit."

Jax nodded as she picked herself up off the ground. It wasn't just the throw; she was aching all over from the training. Not that she would admit it.

"You have good instincts. Keep your training regular and we'll get you back up to speed, then we can work the long road to black belt."

"Might just do that. I guess back in school I never saw the need or had a real desire for it. Earth kind of frowned on combat training, but my dad always said that those in charge of hiring for Captain's positions liked to see it on a resume. I enjoyed it, but only worked for what I needed so I could advance."

"Well, you have the need now. Part of fleet training is zero G combat. We've learned the hard way you can't always count on artificial gravity. You have to know how to move and fight in any kind of spatial orientation. Nothing better than good old fashion Judo for that. And on Gaia we hold combat training in much higher regard." Gemma flashed her best smile.

Jax could believe it as she surveyed the room. Both officers and some high-ranking noncommissioned officers filled the mats. There were even some members of the Terrain Corps, the other half of the Gaia military, present. Gunnery Sergeant Locklear, a corporal and a private whose names Jax had forgotten. *What were they called, Viks? Newman?*

Jax tried to recall her introduction to the Gaia Military. The Terrain Corps handled any situation that required "boots in the mud", planet based operations, some positions on space stations, boarding ships, and so on. Jax wondered about boarding ships. *Had they actually done that? How was that possible?* Jax could believe it watching them train; they were intense.

Returning her focus to Gemma, Jax stretched her back, ready to go again, only to have her preparations interrupted by the announcement system a mere second later.

Bong. Bong. Bong.

"Battle Stations. Enemy ships detected."

Bong. Bong. Bong.

"Playtime is over. Get changed and double time it to the bridge. Duty calls."

Jax hustled off to her locker. She knew the Commander would head the other way, all the bridge officers had a private locker room. They would meet up again on the bridge. There was no time to have a shower; she just wiped off the sweat and put on her Ensign uniform. As the battle klaxons rang again, she wondered if she would ever get used to the ringing it left in her ears.

Bong. Bong. Bong.

"Battle Stations. Enemy ships detected."

Bong. Bong. Bong.

She was in the corridor and pushing to the bridge. She wanted to get there before Gemma could. Jax was getting the layout of the Ares down. When she started the shadowing of Commander Lewis, one of the first things she had to do was "know the ship." There were lifts but it was only a couple decks to the bridge. The stairwells were faster. At least, what was considered to be a stairwell here on the Ares. To her, they seemed much more like ladders, you could climb up or slide down them, depending on your need. Jax kept to the right as she headed up.

Her trepidations grew as she ran. During her introduction, she had learned that a call to Action Stations or Battle Stations were almost the same, anything can trigger the sensors, but if you hear Battle Stations, you know it's something malevolent. Coming near Earth craft like Highguard, or something unknown, could trigger Action Stations. Calling Battle Stations over the ship meant something dangerous was happening now. The enemy had come again. The Screech. Those things that had changed her life so much. She was not sure she wanted to face them again. *Enough*, Jax told herself sternly. *Focus on the job.*

The second thing Commander Lewis drilled her on was military operation. Rank. Chain of Command. Decorum. Her father was the, "Last Great General of Earth", but that was an army rank. This was more like the navy. There were some differences, though: the Ares had Fleetwalkers, not Seamen, for a start; and there were four-star levels to captain. *Was a four-star captain equal to an admiral?* That thought boggled her mind. She needed to study more. *Later.* She reached the bridge.

As she entered the Command Center, Jax glanced at the Stoplight. It had a military name but Jax couldn't remember what it was. Everyone just called it the Stoplight. The reference was also lost on her since it never really said to stop anything. They could be found all over the ship, the one on the bridge was nestled in the corner. A basic rectangle with rounded corners, it would flash or show different colors depending on current ship operations. Currently it showed a red light for battle stations and a blue light for running silent. It was capable of showing much more, green for all's well, yellow for alerts. *Maybe it has another use I haven't learned yet? Maybe it stops us from getting killed?*

Jax's hands relaxed. She hadn't realized they were clenched so tight. She wiped the sweat from her forehead.

Commander Lewis was already positioned next to the Captain. Her uniform looked impeccable. She looked like she had been on station for hours instead of rushing in from a workout. *How had she done that?* Taking her shadow position up behind Commander Lewis, Jax fell into the rhythm of the Command Center.

"Ops, any indication we've been spotted?"

"Negative, Captain. Targets are in orbit pattern around planet designated P4. No change since coming in range."

Jax focused on the holotable before her. It was so different from the chaos during her final minutes on the Indiana. Enemies highlighted in red, planet shown in its natural brown state. Commands were issued, repeated, and executed. *If only the Indiana had had this, maybe my crew wouldn't be dead now.* She shook herself. *Don't let your mind wander down that road. Stay focused.* The more she watched, the more her stomach started to feel queasy.

"Commander Moro, I want firing solutions for both targets. Termination. Navigation track targets on standard attack path bravo."

"Firing solution incoming. Termination. Targets designated T1 and T2."

"Tracking targets, attack path bravo."

Jax drifted forward, shutting out everything except the holo before her. *We are attacking. We are going to kill them. They don't even know we're here. Is this right? They attacked the Indiana. Guns on ships. Is this what I really want? Maybe we should try talking?* Her palms were sweating as the operations continued.

"Firing solution ready, Captain."

"Firing solution accepted. On my command."

"Awaiting command."

The avatar of the Ares drifted closer, small range numbers counting down as she came into distance. The firing solution listed beside it, a sequence of weapons waiting for the Captain's command.

"Fire," the Captain said, his voice like iron.

Jax's eyes went wide as she watched the Ares's avatar unload its Tactical Beam Weapons (TBWs) on T1 and T2. T1 shivered as its shields deflected the initial strike and then failed to handle the continued barrage. They launched the torpedoes. A spread of six decimated T1. It disappeared from the holo in a cascade of light. Target T2 moved.

"Glancing blow on T2. It has initiated evasive maneuvers. Incoming torpedoes!" The Ares shook as two torpedoes hit its shields. Lasers fractured into a prism of light. The Ares shook the attack off like a cool breeze.

"Track target. Match speed. Bring all forward TBWs to bear. Fire at will," the Captain said.

On the holo, both ships danced across the table deck. Jax was entranced by the show. Her heart was racing. Sweat was falling from her

44

forehead. *We can't take them. They'll destroy us just like the Indiana. Everyone I know died and now it's happening again. I can't do anything. I can't do anything!*

"Ensign Brandt, you are out of position. Remove yourself to the observation seating." Jax turned to see Commander Moro moving toward her. Venom in his eyes was unmistakable. Jax couldn't release the handrail that ran around the holotable. She couldn't move. Her knuckles were white as her grip locked beyond her control. *I need to do something.* The thought jarred her brain. *I can't go through this again. Someone stop them.*

"Ensign Harumi Brandt, Jax, please take up the correct position. Commander Moro is correct, you need to move." A hand fell on Jax's shoulder. She turned to face Commander Lewis. She expected to see a harsh, judgmental face, like when her mother had used her whole name. At least no one on the Ares knew her middle name. They never would, if she had her say. Instead, she saw a look of concern and sympathy. Her sweaty palms eased off and she repositioned herself. The Ares shook again. The commands continued, but she no longer registered where they were coming from.

"Our shields are holding 85%. Enemy shields are down."

"Fire torpedoes one to four."

"Firing torpedoes one to four."

All four hit home. A miniature sun appeared in the middle of the deck and then was gone. A slight tremor rumbled through the Ares. A quick cheer arose from the bridge but was cut short as the work continued.

"All targets down. Area is secure. Area is secure."

"Stand down from Battle Stations but maintain alert status. I want a review from all stations. That did not go the way it should have."

"Sounding stand down to Alert status."

Bong. Bong. Bong.

"Alert Status. All stations stand down to Alert status."

Bong. Bong. Bong.

As the announcement went off, Jax closed her eyes. Her teeth clenched. *What came over me? I've never felt like that. Is it always going to be like this? You can do better. You let the problem work you.*

Bong. Bong. Bong.

"Alert Status. All stations stand down to Alert status."

Bong. Bong. Bong.

I messed up. I'm better than that. I won't be afraid. I will not.

Bong. Bong. Bong.

"Alert Status. All stations stand down to Alert status."

Bong. Bong. Bong.

"All senior officers to the briefing room. Let's figure out what the abyss just happened," the Captain said with barely contained fury in his voice.

CHAPTER 6

MEETINGS

The senior staff poured into the briefing room. Jax followed. She wasn't sure if she was supposed to, but nobody stopped her. *I'm supposed to be Commander Lewis' shadow, so here I am.* She folded out an extra seat built into the wall, positioning herself behind the Navigation and Weapons officers, Commander Lilly Bard and Commander Isaac Haddock.

Still feeling a bit ashamed after her performance on the bridge, she sunk down in the chair, hoping to be able to hide behind Commander Haddock's muscular frame. Small and unnoticeable. She ground her teeth. *You will not ever let that happen again. I am better than that.* The chastisement of herself quickly came to an end as the Captain entered.

Like a stormfront washing over everyone, the Captain took his seat. A few punches at his consul command and a replay of their attack activated in the middle of the table. One hand slammed the table as the other pointed.

"How did this turn into a dog fight? We had them dead to rights. Yet, as we open fire, they are on the move. What did we miss? Give me some answers."

Jax knew the Captain often shouted angry statements at his displeasure. Afterward, he would settle in to a more even and understanding mood. Knowing it was coming didn't make it any less jarring.

"They didn't detect us and there was no indication they were powered up." Commander Haddock was the first to jump in.

"Yet they had shields and were moving the moment we opened fire."

"It was a trap. How long have we been hitting their ships? Around six months. They're tired of chasing us." Commander Moro had hate almost dripping from him.

"Poorly planned then. No backup. Just two ships out in the open."

"They're aliens, who knows how they think."

"They were waiting for a convoy." It squeaked out of Jax before she realized she had even spoken. A timid voice that in better times would have been her impression of Reason O'Connor. She bit her lip. Maybe nobody heard.

"Ensign Brandt, do not interrupt this meeting. You may be shadowing the XO, but other than that, you have no reason to be here," Commander Moro said, his eyes stabbing at her. She readied herself to stand and be dismissed. If only there was more room for her to sneak out.

"Commander Moro, any officer is free to have an opinion on this ship."

"Apologies, Captain."

Jax felt Commander Moro was anything but apologetic. With the Captain weighing in, she eased slightly back into her chair.

"Ensign Brandt, what were you saying?"

Jax tilted her body out to see the table around the frame of Commander Haddock. She forced all her will into her voice to assert: "They were waiting for a convoy."

"Why would you say that?"

"Earth ships run a lot of convoys and we often pick up ships from multiple systems along the way. Standard procedure is that ships waiting to join have engines powered but in standby. That way, when the convoy comes, the ship is already moving and can join in with no downtime." Jax swallowed as she noted all the Commanders' eyes were on her. "This would also explain why you wouldn't detect them powered up. Standby modes, at least on Earth ships, have little energy output. Almost the same as being shut down."

"Can anyone confirm this?" Captain Moss asked, eyes moving past each Commander in turn.

Jax thought Commander Lilly Bard looked too skinny for her own good, but her voice rang out like she was someone who was used to public speaking. Her voice projected more than even Mr. Camp had done. "Early in my career on Earth, I was a part of several convoys. This was SOP. Not something we do in the High C. We don't have the ships for it."

The Captain leaned way back into his chair and furrowed his eyes. Before he could delineate his thoughts, Commander Moro wrestled his way back into the conversation. "It's all just speculation. I still say they were setting an ambush, maybe we just caught them before they were ready. We should go on the offensive and hit the Screech hard instead of playing hit and run like we have been."

The Captain leaned back into the table, his hands pressing firm. "Whichever option it is, I feel as if something is building. Just a feeling at this point. This attack, the one on the Indiana, they are getting deeper, closer, into Earth space than ever before."

That last part seemed to be for Jax. His glare grazed past her.

"I might be wrong, but we need to be sure. We are out here to be prepared." He scanned the room and met the eyes of everyone there, herself included. Jax could practically feel the weight of his thoughts.

"Commander Bard and Commander Haddock, I want an immediate search pattern. Start with this last attack and expand outward into Screech space. I'll notify Fleet Command and see if they have anything to add. All departments double check your stations and stay sharp. Meeting dismissed."

The Captain stood and walked out. The Commanders waited a moment and then stood and filed out in his wake. Commander Bard gave

Jax a, "Good work, Ensign," while Commander Haddock also nodded his approval.

Jax held back while the others left. She would need to catch up to Commander Lewis. She needed to have her speech ready so she could apologize for her conduct on the bridge. She was pretty sure she had messed up the briefing too. Military decorum. She needed to study more.

She stepped out through the hatch, ready to run. She almost blundered into Commander Lewis and Commander Le Urud. Commander Urud was head of Engineering, he never talked much in meeting and seemed to avoid the bridge except when necessary. Jax tried her best to stand at attention as she overheard their dry talk. The finer details of sensor mapping and the affective use of sensors for the search pattern were being discussed. She absently started shaking her head.

"Question, Ensign?" Jax snapped back to focus as Commander Urud looked up at her. Jax had a good fifteen centimeters on him.

"Uh, yes, Commander."

"Well, go ahead."

"Why aren't we using pathfinder probes to do this search? Wouldn't that be faster?"

"The Ares' speed almost makes the pathfinders obsolete. Plus, shooting a hundred probes out will draw a lot of attention. The Screech will come looking in numbers to match. We don't want them coming down on us that hard."

"Oh, I guess that makes sense. I just figured with all the stealth tech the Ares had, you would have some kind of an invisible drone."

Commander Urud's mouth dropped open. His eyes grew wide. He turned and stared at Commander Lewis, who's own astonishment was clear on her face.

"What do you think, Le? Can we do it?"

"Oh, yeah. We have plenty of pathfinders we never use. The adaptive plating can be replicated to size. We can easily adapt the masking

50

components for its propulsion. It's so simple, we just never considered it."

They were both as giddy as children in a candy shop.

"Go ahead and get to work. I'll notify the Captain. He might actually laugh out loud at this one. Send an estimate to the Captain for when you think it can be up and running."

"Shouldn't take long; get a few Walkers to put in double shifts, and it'll be a couple days if that."

He turned and grabbed Jax by the shoulders. For a moment she got the feeling he was going to kiss her.

"Great work, Ensign, don't let Commander Moro knock you down." Then, dropping his voice, he said, "He's kind of a pain in the ass to everyone." He was practically skipping as he took his leave. Jax heart floated a bit at the sheer joy of it all. She was instantly grounded when Commander Lewis rounded back on her.

"You keep jumping from bad to good like this and you're going to hurt yourself, Ensign Brandt"

"I know, Commander, what happened on the bridge, it will never—"

"—You're suspended from active duty."

"I know I was in the way, but—what?"

"Sorry, but I don't like to draw these things out. You went right from a major tragedy into work. The Captain and I take the blame. We thought it would be more constructive for you. Dr. Charles disagreed. Seems he was right. You need time to heal. Three days leave, minimum. Spend it in the Rec room. Get in a VR Pod and get away. The Doctor has a great recovery from trauma VR program. After that, you will need the doctor's approval to return to duty."

"I don't want or need a vacation, Commander Lewis. Gemma, please don't."

"We all go through it in this job, Jax. There is nothing to be ashamed of. If you're going to be a part of this crew, you need your head on right.

51

Take the time. Get strong. Don't burn out your potential. That's an order."

Jax's temper flared and she snapped to attention, her salute as mean as she could make it. "Aye aye, ma'am. Permission to begin leave, ma'am."

"You'll see I'm right. Permission granted."

Jax stomped off like a little kid being sent to her room. With no real direction in mind, she ended up in the wardroom. She realized her stomach must had taken over since it growled as the aroma of hot food touched her nose.

Jax had discovered the wardroom, the officers mess, during her first week on the Ares. The foodfabs made a good chai tea latte, the cooks in the wardroom did it better. Mess Specialist 1st Class (MS1) Jeff Zakar was Jax's favorite person to see. He was so used to Jax's ordering habits that he had a hot mug waiting when she brought her tray forward.

"Thank you, MS1 Zakar, I really needed this."

"From the look on your face, you need more than that. Here."

He handed her a plate of ginger pot roast, stewed vegetables, and garlic mashed potatoes. A smaller plate came with MS1 Zakar's specialty cherry pie. Jax breathed it in as deeply as she could before saying "You're going to spoil me, Mr. Zakar. Huh, MS1."

"Nonsense. You work too hard. Enjoy."

"I will."

He was already off helping the next officer before the words left Jax's mouth. She turned to find a seat and saw Rosita Koike waving her over.

Lieutenant Junior Grade (LTJG) Koike, Jax reminded herself. She had already slipped with MS1 Zakar. She still fought not calling everyone Mr. or Ms.; like translating a new language, she had to keep her focus.

LTJG Koike was sitting with Ensigns Ambrose and Sales. These three Engineering Specialists were affectionately called the Rat Pack. They spent a lot of time crawling through the bowels of the ship to keep it running. They did it together and they did it the best.

In her initial days on the Ares, Jax followed Commander Lewis around as she was assigned different positions to learn and be tested. Her first shift was with the pilots had been a disaster. She could fly fine, but had trouble adapting to the firing controls the combat ships had. The only thing she hadn't done wrong was make the ship shoot itself. Her time with the weapons crew had just left her scratching her head. Then had come engineering and a couple shifts with the Rat Pack. Jax didn't think she had ever made friends so fast.

When they had found out her mother was the esteemed Nayomi Brandt, they were ecstatic and had started to hammer her for insights into her mother's work. Once it became clear they knew more about it than she ever did, they had relaxed and treated Jax like one of their own. LTJG Koike and Jax looked so similar and hit it off so well, people thought Rosita was Jax's little sister. Jax was actually the younger, but she had a good ten centimeters on the LTJG.

"Ensign Jax, you're too late to join us. We have to get back on station in a minute." Ensign Sales made a mock sad face.

"Sorry. I've been a little busy being relieved of duty."

"What's up with that?" Ensign Ambrose joined in.

"Great, now I won't have someone to rewire the communication relay wrong again," LTJG Koike joked with Jax, every word laced with sympathy.

"Yeah, they think I need a break. And I only wired it wrong because some Lieutenant gave me the directions backward."

They all laughed and consoled her the best they could. Jax's heart grew lighter and her sour mood began to fade.

"Sorry we can't hang some more Jax, but we do have to get back on duty. It's not that long and then we'll get you back working with the cool kids."

"Thanks, Lieutenant Junior Grade and Ensigns." Jax gave a slight smile and waved a salute toward them all.

"Heads up, Ensign Brandt."

"Enjoy the downtime, Jax."

"You can switch with me if you want?" Ensign Sales gave her a toothy grin.

Then they were gone. Jax found herself alone, her thoughts a jumble of her new friends, her trouble on the bridge, and Commander Lewis. Happiness, anger, and shame all rolled up into one. Hungry, but with no real desire to eat, she only picked at her food. She finished her chai and decided maybe she would go spend some time in the Rec Room. She got up and slammed her tray right into Commander Moro. He didn't move. He simply stared as the contents of the tray flowed down his well pressed uniform.

"I'm so sorry, Commander, I didn't see you." Jax tried to clear the debris of food from his attire.

"I see that we can add uniforms to the list of things you are good at destroying."

"Excuse me, Commander? I don't understand."

"Of course not, Ensign Brandt. Why would you seek to understand when you can keep bungling your way through?"

"What? I don't— Do you have a problem with me, Commander?"

"I most definitely have a problem with you, Ensign."

"Why? I'd never even met you before I came onto the Ares. What have I ever done to you?"

"You don't belong here. We should have left you in your lifepod and shipped you back to Earth. You were a Captain in name only. Only through sheer luck did you manage to survive."

"I worked hard to be a Captain. I did everything I could to save my crew."

"Worked hard? Worked hard where, at your cushy little Captain's college on Earth? On top of all your ignorance, you're arrogant too." He

54

had stopped wiping down his uniform now. He was standing tall, looking down his nose at her.

"I was born and raised on Gaia. I was one of the first graduates of the Gaia Fleet Academy. I've fought my whole life to be this. While we have been out here risking our lives for Earth, for you, you've had your nice soft existence, your college. I've seen plenty of Earthers like you come here and break."

"That's not fair, most of the Ares crew is from Earth like me."

"No. They choose to be here. They came here looking to fight, to have the ability to protect themselves. Your existence here is a random act. You didn't earn it and you don't deserve it."

"Captain Moss and Commander Lewis gave me a choice. I chose to be here!"

"A choice made out of fear. Fear that runs your life. I saw it on the bridge. I see it in you now. That fear is going to get us killed the same way you killed your crew on the Indiana."

Jax was stunned. His words hit a little too close to the mark, but that's not what stunned her. His finger coming up to point at her, to touch her shoulder, wasn't it either. She was stunned that she hit him a second time.

Her rollercoaster of emotion came exploding out. She had tried to control it, had desired to, but that was gone now. Jax found a focus for everything she wanted to purge from her system. Its name was Commander Terrance Moro.

They tangled with each other as they hit the floor. Jax tried to control it like a throw, but she was seeing nothing but red. Commander Moro recovered. Jax could feel him starting to move his hips away and bring his legs in-between them. He was not without skills. She swung her fists at him again. It was stupid from this position and she knew it. Everything in her body ached to hit him again.

Before the blow could land, her arm was locked back. Like an octopus pulling her away, four pairs of hands engulfed her, keeping her from her target.

With Jax restrained, Commander Moro pulled himself up from the floor. He stood arrogantly before her. His face was calm, but his eyes were a hurricane of anger.

"You are done. You will never be a part of the Fleet. Never. Take her to the brig."

"Screw you!"

Jax tried to launch herself at Commander Moro again, but the fingers holding her dug in deeper in order to keep her back. Jax felt her heels dragging as they pulled her away.

Through the halls and all way to her cell, two thoughts rang in her head: *that was so worth it*, and, *what the abyss did I do?*

CHAPTER 7

CHANCES

She breathed deep and took in a great lungful of the pine scented air. Opening her eyes, Jax marveled at the sunrise breaking over the Issaquah Valley. She sat at the top of Rattlesnake Ledge. She had the whole rock top all to herself. She had been here twice when she was eight years old. Coming up the trail early to avoid the crowd, Jax and her parents had always made it to the peak in time to see the sunrise. She had always wanted to go back.

As she felt her shoulders relax, her mind ease, Jax heard the little beep that signaled the end was near. She wanted a little longer, but she knew she wasn't going to get it. A small, glowing, green number ten appeared and started its countdown.

9... 8... 7...6... 5... 4... 3... 2... 1... Session over.

Jax slipped the VR helmet off and picked off the gloves. Not as nice as the full VR Pods, but still a nice getaway. Placing them both into the wall receptacle, she thumbed the button. The VR set slid away till her next session. Jax sighed. One hour a day was all she got.

Not all that time was her own, however. It started with forty minutes of a therapy session recommended by Dr. Charles, which she was starting to get used to. He had tailored it to her and a lot of it was talking and hanging out with AI versions of old friends. At least she didn't have to do the full criminal reclamation package. *Yuck.*

The last twenty minutes she could choose her own VR to escape into. Every day, she had spent that time outdoors. It had taken a few days, but she could feel her mind finding its center again. The tightness of her thoughts relaxed. It was as close to a vacation as she was going to get.

Now Jax was back in the general population area of the brig. She had it all to herself. *Guess I'm the only one who gets in trouble on this ship. Wonderful.*

The call to attention barked into the cell. Chief Petty Officer Cambridge's voice was as husky as ever. Jax's muscles snapped into place. *Studying pays off,* she joked in her head. She started a mental checklist: Arms straight but not stiff, palms in (*don't clench*), head erect but slightly down. Happy that her week in the brig had forced her to up her learning. She heard the cell unlock and Chief Petty Officer Cambridge's heavy boots moved away. Commander Lewis stepped in.

"At ease, Ensign."

Jax let her body relax but kept her eyes forward. *I can't meet her eyes yet. Please don't make me look.*

"How are you doing, Ensign Brandt?"

"Ma'am. Feeling good, ma'am, Commander Lewis, ma'am." Jax winced a little. *That wasn't quite right, so much for my studying.*

Commander Lewis gave a slight smirk and was shaking her head. "I don't think this is going to work this way with you. Let's try this. Sit down, Jax, let's talk, without ranks, so you can speak freely."

Jax's mind fell at ease. She sat on the rough bunk and hugged her legs up close. Maybe a little too informal but it felt right at the moment.

"Now, let's try that again. How are you doing?" Gemma said.

"I'm okay. At least, I'm as okay as I can be, confined to the brig. I don't like the tightness of this place, but I'm starting to accept it. The doc has been helping." Jax studied her toes. *I need to focus on something.*

"I want... I need to do better. If I get the chance, that is. I know I messed up pretty bad." Jax kept her eyes downcast; she knew eye contact was too much for her right now.

"We'll get to that issue in a bit. I just need to hear from you, see from you that you are mentally healthy. The doc thinks you're making the right steps, finally, but I need to be sure. I think you tend to live up to your fiery name, a creature of instinct."

"At least I don't live up to my middle name," Jax mumbled out. *Why did I say that?*

"Middle name? The records we got from the Indiana don't show a middle name. I assumed you used Jax in that capacity or as an honor to your father?"

Jax leaned back and stared at the ceiling. A smile crept to the left of her face. "Well, since I'm in for one crime, I might as well confess my other. Before entering Earth's International Space Agency's training academy, I used my parents' high-level clearance to hack the admissions database and delete my middle name from the record."

"That bad?"

"That bad."

"I don't suppose you'd care to share …?" Gemma let the question trail off.

"Not if you left me here forever."

Out of the corner of her eye, Jax was glad to see Gemma smiling at the whole thing. *Maybe purging myself of all my misdeeds will be good for me.*

"So, Jax is an ode to your father, then?"

"Kind of. Well, it is now, but not at first, originally it was more of a tease."

Gemma sat on the bunk across from Jax. Elbows on her knees, she laced her fingers together. Gemma's eyes creased as a smile grew. It was a motherly kind of smile. Jax glanced and then turned away.

"If you won't tell me your middle name then I demand you share this one."

"Fine." Jax couldn't help but smile as she finally made eye contact.

"I never knew the last Great General Jack Brandt, to me he was just dad. The whole Keres Incident that made him that legend happened just before I was born. What I remember most about both my parents is traveling the world. Living a few months or maybe a year on different military bases. I was too young to realize my dad was shutting them down. Transferring personnel to the First Responders Brigade, Peacesmith Co-Ops, the ISA and so on."

Gemma straightened up and tilted her head. Jax could almost see the memories scrolling in the Commander's head. Gemma shook her head as if she remembered those times too.

"Anyways, my dad was busy with that and my mom was always working on her engines. The bases were perfectly safe, and I had the run of them. They were also boring, and I hate boring."

"Oh no."

"Oh yes." Jax found herself standing and pacing as the memories flowed.

"I got into a lot of trouble. I once broke into a flight simulator so I could pretend I was a space pilot. I was always caught and taken back to my dad." Jax was looking down, shaking her head. She heard Gemma stifling her laughter.

"After a short time, they knew me. It was, 'That's General Brandt's daughter', 'Jack Brandt's daughter again', 'What did Jack's girl do this time?', and so on." Jax tried her best to sound like those officers from her memory.

"You must have been really bored." Gemma laughed it out.

"Yup. Dad would just ask what I learned from it and then let me go. If Mom was around, I got grounded. I think I preferred getting grounded. The other way, I spent too much time obsessed with it all." Jax smiled to herself. It was a crazy memory to make her happy, but it did. She missed her parents.

"Anyways. After a while, some of my friends picked up on the whole 'Jack's girl' thing and started calling me 'Jax'. I hated it at first, but I realized they weren't picking on me for my middle name anymore, so, that was a win right there."

"That's when Jax stuck?"

"It came and went a bit right up until my Dad died. Then I started to prefer it. Now only some of my cousins call me Harumi. To everyone else, I'm Jax."

"And how does Jax feel about who she is now?"

It was a change of subject, a not too subtle shift to get back on track. Jax wasn't sure if Gemma could be subtle. Just like her Judo, when she wants to throw you, she throws you. Get to the point.

"I'm getting there. Good. Wrapping my head around it all. The Screech and the fact there are other aliens out there they have wiped out. Armed spaceships, that still seems just as alien to me. And war. Losing people that I know and care— cared about." Jax felt the deep breath fill her lungs as she eased herself back down on onto the bunk. "I'm walking my way through it, not just jumping from one shock to the next. I'm good. I'll get there."

Gemma was sitting up straight, her eyes piercing into Jax's core. Gemma was thinking deep and the time between them stretched. The Commander decided whatever she was contemplating. Gemma said, "So now let's deal with the elephant in the room."

Jax thought she was ready for this. She had played it out in her head over and over. Planned what she would say. She had a plan. *Work the plan.* In an instant, it was all gone. She sat in silence.

"If you had been a fully commissioned officer, right now you would be up for a dishonorable discharge. Possibly jail time."

Jax closed her eyes. *Here it comes.*

"Thankfully, you're not."

Jax's eyes opened, a glimmer of hope shining inside her.

"Captain Moss, Commander Moro and I had some extensive meetings with Admiral Koonce. Well, we had meetings after spending a couple days getting Commander Moro to stop wanting your head on a pike."

Jax felt herself wince at the thought.

"Dr. Charles also came in to testify on your state of mind. He justified much of what was going on with you, but your actions put everything in chaos."

"So how far down the hole am I?"

"After an in-depth review of your Earth service record, including training and postings, and a complete review of your situation with the Indiana and all trauma and actions from there, it has been decided to officially induct you into the Gaia Fleet at the rank of Lieutenant."

"Huh? I'm being promoted? Rewarded? I'm so confused."

"Don't be. All militaries past and present have a long history of promoting their problems." The look on Commander Lewis's face, not Gemma at this point, was all business.

"You have the training. You have a natural talent. If you had not assaulted Commander Moro, you would have probably been tested and placed at Lieutenant Commander or even Commander."

"I still don't understand what this is accomplishing?"

"It's simple. First, according to upper command, it looks better to have a Lieutenant break down and strike a Commander then a new Ensign. Not sure I understand that myself, but when Admirals talk, I listen."

"And second?" There had to be more a lot more. Jax's glimmer of hope was shivering.

"Second, from now on you are responsible for your actions. Whether you know the rules or not, a breach like this will bring the full weight of consequences down on you. Do you understand?"

Jax froze for a time as she worked it through her head. *No safety net.* "I guess I'd better force myself to study those Fleet Procedure manuals."

"That would be a good start. With this promotion, you will be assigned to Engineering under Command Urud. I know you'd be more comfortable as a pilot, but you need more combat flight training. That's not training we can offer on ship." She paused for a second as if something was bothering her, then continued on. "Plus, the Captain still wants you on the bridge. We will carefully schedule bridge time for you to limit your contact with Commander Moro."

"That was probably his idea, huh?"

Commander Lewis shook her head, the graveness in her voice clear. "He wanted a lot more. A lot. Make no mistake, Jax, you may think Commander Moro is an ass, but he has respect on this ship. For everyone that despises him, there are those that adore him. Even those that despise him respect his skills. He is a product of Gaia, and a proud one at that."

"Yeah, you're telling me." Jax tried to make it light, but Commander Lewis wasn't having it.

"There's a political movement on Gaia, Jax. One that wants to leave Earth to its fate and focus on Gaia alone. Terrance Moro is a front runner on that platform. You may have just become the poster candidate for the opposition. Whether you want it or not."

"I don't want it."

"No one ever does. There are others, even on the Ares, that won't like you just because of what happened. Keep your guard up."

"I guess I'm living in interesting times."

Commander Lewis stern face broke into a smile. "At least you won't get bored and cause more problems."

Jax and Gemma shared the laughter.

"So, what now? Can I get out of here?"

"Yes. First, put on your service uniform. You'll get your new rank bar later. Before that, we have to go to the bridge to see off your little project, if we haven't talked too much that is."

"My project?"

"They're launching the modified pathfinder probes that you suggested. Took them longer than they thought to make it work. Some of your friends think you got thrown in the brig to avoid the triple shifts they've been pulling."

"Oh, that's not good."

"Consider it recompense for the trouble you've caused."

"Wonderful."

"That it is. Let's get moving."

Commander Lewis and Jax hurried into the Commander Center. Jax noted that Commander Moro was uncharacteristically out of place at the far end of the holotable. Jax averted her eyes and focused on the other officers moving about. Captain Moss had the appearance of being lost in a technical display with Commander Urud. Once Commander Lewis and Jax were situated, he broke off and assumed his usual spot.

"Commander Urud, I believe the honor is yours."

"Thank you, Captain. Preparing the Pathjackers for launch."

"Pathjackers?"

"They needed a different designation than the regular Pathfinder. Pathjacker seemed to be the right name for the job. Fleet Command can come up with an official designation later."

Commander Urud's face turned to her slightly and Jax could have sworn he gave her a wink. At the same time, from the corner of her eye, Jax saw Commander Moro's face scowl.

"Very well. When ready, Commander."

"All is ready, Captain. Launching Pathjackers."

On the holotable, Jax's space shark shot out a hundred tiny beams of light. They sped off and disappeared, a hundred tiny stealth probes to light the way into the unknown. Jax's chest swelled with pride.

Tomorrow was a new day for her. A second or maybe third chance, she wasn't sure, and right now she didn't care. She could see what lay ahead.

She would be a Captain again. Lieutenant Harumi 'Jax' Brandt was just getting started.

You'll probably think this story is about me, but you'll be wrong.
This story is about fighting.

Chapter 8

Surprise

"Ouch." The shock hit her again, even through the protective gloves.

"Four." Jax could hear the smile in Ensign Sales' voice through the communication clip on her right ear.

"Oh, great, we're keeping track of my pain now?"

"Of course. We always do when someone checks the Spine for the first time. Current record is eight. I got fifty credits saying you break it."

"Wonderful. Remind me again why I, as the Lieutenant, am not ordering you to crawl in here and do this for me?"

"Protocol. All engineering personnel must know and have hands-on experience in calibrating and maintaining the Spine. Since you're the only one in engineering to have never done it, this shift is yours."

The joy in his voice told Jax that Ensign Sales was probably up for this job in the rotation. Jax being assigned to the crew meant he could wait to take his turn. No one wanted to climb into the Spine. Jax knew protocol also said that these checks were supposed to happen every six months. Out in deep space, Commander Urud insisted they happen every three. Still, three months was a nice break from anything you wanted to avoid.

Just like it was in the human body, the Spine was the central part of the Ares' nervous system; a massive cord of wires, energy buffers, and power relays. The Spine allowed direct power flows from the qave drives to the rest of the ship. Communications lines also intertwined down its structure. Buried deep within the ship, heavily shielded with both plating and energy barriers, the only thing more guarded were probably the qave engines themselves. It was a technical marvel that Jax was sure her mother would have loved.

Along its expanse were small junctions, or hubs. Twelve in all. Each hub acted as a mini brain or conductor, making sure energy flowed in the right direction, transferring messages to the correct location, and so on. Buried deep in its infrastructure, each hub had to be checked and calibrated by hand. No robots allowed. The Gaia Fleet thought allowing robots to do the work made people complacent. Of course, there was no easy access to these points. For each check, someone had to crawl into the Spine and work their way down the length of the ship. It was an uncomfortable job, long and grueling, that could take most of the day. *Tight spaces are my favorite*, Jax joked with herself. Her shoulders and breathing were relaxed. *Doing fine. I got this.*

Jax brought up the schematic in her heads-up display (HUD). She focused her right eye and made the correct ocular contact, this time, to bring up the testing sequence. The contacts she was wearing worked flawlessly, but still made her eyes itch.

She started the test sequence again. The HUD showed the sequence, but she had that part memorized. What she needed was to know which line went with which number. That was where she kept getting lost. It had a peculiar order. Once you'd started, you had to keep the calibration device just ahead as the sequence fired. Link the device with each line in the Spine, clamp it down, keep it steady, let it test and calibrate the energy flow. It was explained to Jax that it worked much like a tuning fork. The calibration device issued a quantum wave into the line, and if the waves matched, all was good. If they didn't, it adjusted the harmonics of the line to bring it in tune. She had kind of glossed over the explanation. *I don't need to know how it works to make it work. Good enough for me.*

Once you got the green light, you moved to the next line. The wave had to be maintained across the entire field of lines. If you moved too much or got the wrong line, you got zapped. Jax gripped the handle. The tool reminded her of the hairbrush she used each morning, its oval scanner sticking up over her hand, the line hook protruding from its bottom. Follow the numbers and keep a steady hand. *Go.* The sequence began.

3, 1, 4, 1, 5, 9, 2, 6 …

Twenty numbers were needed to complete the sequence. Jax made sixteen this time.

"Ouch."

"Five."

Jax growled, but it was all in fun. "I'm so assigning you to KP duty."

"Then who will help you get all your work done?"

"Rose will."

"Ha. Lieutenant Junior Grade Koike is way too important to be helping a full Lieutenant, that's what us mighty Ensigns are for."

"You think you're mighty?"

"That's what my wife says."

Jax rolled her eyes. "Your wife must know something we don't."

"Of course," Ensign Sales chirped with pride.

Jax could feel him beaming. "So, how many did it take you?"

"I did it in five. Rose got it in three. Commander Urud got it done on the first try."

"Of course he did." *Commander Urud could probably start the engines just by looking at them.*

"The Captain even came down and worked the Spine once. He was an engineer on one of the earlier Fleet battle ships, but their design was based on Earth vessels. He wanted some hands-on experience. It only took him two."

"Wonderful." *Guess I have some work to do to be Captain material again. Best get to it.*

"All right, 'Mighty Ensign', keep it down so I can get through this. That's an order."

"Aye aye, Lieutenant Brandt, ma'am. This will be try number six, just for your information." He said, Jax could feel the grin on his face.

The banter was what she needed. It distracted her for a moment, let her refocus before she got back to the job at hand. Clear the distractions, work the plan. She found her pace and kept the numbers rolling in her head. A rhythm took over and everything fell into place.

"Done." Jax was amused. *Lucky number six.*

"No way. Damn, my wife keeps telling me not to gamble."

"Well ..." Jax was going to start in again when Commander Urud's voice interrupted over the comms channel.

"Lieutenant Brandt, please report to main engineering machine shop. I have a new task for you."

"On my way, Commander." She replied to the Commander and then switched over to her line with Ensign Sales.

"Sorry for your loss, but next time bet on me to win." This time she was beaming, and she could hear him groan.

Jax pocketed the scanner and started the crawl back. *No rest for the successful,* Jax mused. Hope the Commander is not in too big a hurry, it took time to crawl this far. With thirty-three decks to work with, you'd think they would make space for maintenance to work, at the very least. It was still hard for her to grasp, even crawling through it like this. Triple reinforced hull, every space inside optimized for arms and armament. Everything had at least one backup. The Ares even had two qave drives. *Crazy.* This ship still felt alien to her.

No space was wasted on personal comforts. *Now, on the Indiana...* She let the thought trail off. *Focus on the now.* The long crawl was good for her. While other engineers might not like working on the Spine, she had enjoyed the solitude of it. Walking the halls of the Ares, there were too many whispers following her around. Some whispered how they wish they had punched Terrance Moro. Some whispered how much they hated her for it. Some just whispered that she was crazy. If it hadn't been for her friends in the Rat Pack, it might have been too much to handle.

The machine shop was a place to get things made. It was still a strange place to Jax. On Earth ships, they relied strictly on construction fabricators, confabs, for parts. The Ares was much more hands-on; the crew fixed things on the go and everything had a manual, human, back up.

Jax surveyed the room as she entered. It was like a warehouse of tools. There were industrial sized fabricators, welding stations, electronic stations, cutting machines of all kinds, drills, screwdrivers, hammers, and more. In short, it contained everything a ship's engineer could ever want or need.

Off to the left, at one of the worktables, were Commander Urud and Commander Moro. Jax felt ice shoot through her veins. She did not want to approach unless she had to. Staying inside the entrance portal, she held herself in an "at ease" position, trying hard to keep her face as expressionless as possible.

The Commanders were in the middle of what seemed to be a heated discussion. She couldn't catch the words, but their posture and pinched faces made it clear. Commander Urud's usually happy face was stone cold. Commander Moro was pointing and moving his arms in a way Jax was all too familiar with.

Whatever it was about was not for Jax to know. The Commanders seemed to notice her at the same time, and it brought their argument to an abrupt halt. A few quick words and Commander Moro turned to stomp off.

Jax snapped to attention and displayed her absolute best salute. Commander Moro didn't even acknowledge her existence as he stalked past. Commander Urud caught her eye and flicked her a salute, a wisp of a smile returning to his troubled face. He waved her over.

"You called for me, Commander?" Jax bit her tongue. She wanted to know the details of what she just witnessed, but she knew it wasn't her place to ask.

"Got a project for you." He was back to his beaming self as they walked over to a worktable. He waved his hand and holo controls sprang to life. Jax couldn't remember if Commander Urud ever smiled while on the bridge. Here in Engineering, though he was in his element. *Happy as can be.* He was like a kid opening a gift right now.

Blueprints emerged in the holo field. They mapped themselves out before Jax's eyes and started rotating. *It looks like a backpack of some sort, but designed to house something? Was that a computer?*

"What is tha—"

"—Holy crap, that's Screech tech!" LTJG Koike shouted from nowhere, causing Jax to almost jump out of her skin. Her little sis, and newest best friend, Rose Koike appeared at the table. Jax quickly collected herself just in time to see Ensigns Sales and Ambrose also come crowding in.

"Wow. This is like Gaia tech and Screech tech combined. Look at that weave mesh of circuits at the bottom that leads to that cable connector. That plug cable is weird. The top must be our CPU, I wonder what the software to run –" Ensign Ambrose said but was stopped cold by the Commander. These might have been the most words Jax had heard from Ensign Ambrose. Ever. He was usually so efficient with his words. Even the Commander seemed stunned he had to interrupt him.

"—I don't recall asking for such a gathering," Commander Urud said.

LTJG Koike was still wide-eyed as she answered. "Sorry, Commander, I was on station when these plans got downloaded from Gaia Command. I had to see them."

"And the rest of the Rat Pack had to follow. Very well, look while you can. Lieutenant Brandt, this is your task. You are to follow the plans and construct the Adaptive Interface Device, A.I.D." He paused for a moment before continuing. "Yes, it is a hybrid of Gaia and Screech technologies."

"Wow. Ok, but why don't we just use the fabricator? Looks like all the info is there," the Lieutenant said.

Commander Urud waved his hand, zooming in on some technical specs. "Because of this."

For Field Use. Single Tech.

Shown in bright letters. Jax racked her brain for a moment until she found the right memory. 'For Field Use,' meant that the tech had to be serviceable away from the ship using only standard kit tools by human hands. No fabricators.

Single Tech. That one meant all repairs and maintenance must be able to be completed by one person.

The Rat Pack was already speculating.

"Could it be a spy tool of some kind?" asked Ensign Ambrose.

"The software must be to copy Screech databases," LTJG Koike mumbled.

"Or a virus," Ensign Sales chipped in.

"It's not a virus."

"It could be a virus."

"Enough." Commander Urud was still smiling but he made it clear who was in charge here.

"Koike, Sales, and Ambrose, get back to work. That's enough for now."

All three reluctantly saluted and sloped off as slowly as possible, their eyes not leaving the A.I.D. until they absolutely had to.

"So, you want me to build this?"

"That's the job."

"Why me? Surely one of those guys would be more qualified." Jax chucked a thumb over her shoulder, but her eyes were still glued to the plans.

"Those other highly qualified people have assignments you are not qualified to do. Which means until you are qualified, you get the extra jobs I can't spare personnel for."

"Can't or won't?"

"Don't have to, thanks to you." His smile got bigger.

"Okay then, guess I'll get at it."

"I have every bit of confidence in you. Oh, and one more thing, it must be done by tomorrow morning."

"Oh, come on. I only have a few hours left on shift."

"Sorry, orders are orders. I have mine and now you have yours."

Jax grimaced as she started to flip through the holo plans and organize her thoughts on attacking this assignment. Commander Urud slipped away without so much as a whisper.

Jax worked long into a double, triple shift? She had lost track of time. What started out as a fascinating project (Screech tech!) soon turned frustrating. She realized the blueprints were not as good as they first seemed. In the end she had started doing it "Jax's Way". *Does Gaia have trademarks? I need to trademark that. I must remember to check on that.*

She had swapped basic wires for tachyonic relays, added a bigger cooling unit, and completely dumped the proposed CPU. She used one from a stripped-down pathfinder left over from the retro fit to pathjackers. The straps to wear the thing were ridiculous. She stripped down an old spacesuit that had been damaged and left lying around, took the straps for the oxygen tank from that, and repurposed them on the

A.I.D. She even used a hammer to smash some things into place. *Whoever designed this has no idea about practical use of tech,* Jax grumbled. Her mom would have been throwing a fit.

Her mom had pushed her towards engineering when she was younger but Jax just never cared for it. Right now, she was happy with her work. *This one is for you Mom. You would be so proud of me, but I bet the critique of my work would be harsh. Though not as harsh as of those that designed it.* Jax chuckled to herself.

She loaded the software, thankful that had come to her fully finished. I can make the mechanics work, but I don't think I can beat code with a hammer. She made sure it ran but didn't pay attention to what it was for, just slipped the A.I.D. pack on, checking that all straps provided a secure fit.

With the machine room empty, she started striking some poses. *Must make sure it moves well*, she smirked. She whipped out the connection cord and pretended to plug it into the wall. She had lengthened it from the specs, so it should reach anywhere now. She examined the strange tip that must plug into a Screech computer and shrugged.

She was done. She slipped the pack off and placed it on the table, made sure her notes on the changes were entered in. Her eyes were drooping, she was crashing. Her fingers and shoulders ached as she walked back to her quarters.

No longer in the Admiral's Quarters, she had a proper officer's berth now. Still had her own head and shower, but no foodfab or desk. She missed the foodfab. *Have to go all the way to the wardroom for my tea.* A standard issue chest for all her stuff, not that she had any, was under the bed.

The bed. She couldn't wait to get to bed. So tired. She reached her room, and the door, recognizing her coming, slid open.

"Surprise!" The chorus that erupted out of her quarters shocked Jax. She fell backward and slammed into the far hall wall.

Rubbing her head, Jax peered back through the door to see three heads staring out in shock.

"You okay, Jax?" LTJG Rosita Koike's worried voice rang out.

"No, Rose, I'm not. What are you doing in my room?"

"We're here to celebrate your promotion to Lieutenant."

"A little late for that, isn't it? And how did you get in my room?"

"Commander Urud implied we should wait before any unsanctioned celebrations, so nobody would think we were celebrating your attack on Commander Moro. So, we had to wait for the right time. We couldn't find a right time, figured you had tomorrow off, so we chose now. And we take care of all shipboard electronics and machinery. Getting in a room is nothing."

"Besides, it's tradition, we must celebrate!" Ensign Coleman Sales slurred out. It seemed he hadn't waited to get started.

"Yeah, celebrate," echoed Ensign Ambrose.

"Come on, big sis." Rose held up a bottle. "It's tradition."

"Oh no. I thought alcohol wasn't allowed on board."

"This isn't alcohol, this is prime, 14-year old scotch, straight from the highlands of Scotland." Frederick Ambrose had a look of pride on his flushed face. "Besides, no one knows." He brought a finger to his lips and blew, spit, heavily across it, trying desperately to make a "shh" sound.

"I don't do well with hard liquor," Jax tried to protest.

"Too bad. We're celebrating!" the Rat Pack said in unison.

The bottle was mostly empty, so hopefully it would be quick. "Well, since there's not much left, I guess it won't hurt."

"We have more." Fredrick Ambrose was elated at his announcement, holding up a second bottle.

"We have more!" copied Coleman Sales.

"Give in, sister, you have no choice," Rose said grinning.

They ushered her into the room while Jax feigned resistance. *I should really stop this.* Deep down inside, however, she knew this felt right.

Her door closed. To those inside, the rest of the night was legend.

CHAPTER 5
MISSION

"Lieutenant Brandt, report to Briefing Room One. Immediately!"

"Why is that so loud?" Jax shoved her head back under her pillow. *Who could possibly want me in Briefing Room One? Maybe the Captain. The Captain!*

"Oh, crap." *How long had it been? Had she gone back to sleep? What time was it? No, forget that. Forget all that.*

"Go, Jax, go." She put on her fatigues and checked herself in the mirror. The face that stared back was miserable. Eyes sunken and red. Hair a mess.

"Not good." She splashed water on her face and dried it off. Grabbing her comb, she went running into the hall.

It was so bright. *I could really use sunglasses. No, focus. Comb your hair. Run.* Jax made the best time she could. Arriving at Briefing Room One, she stopped and composed herself for a moment. As together as she could be, sticking her comb into her pocket, she pressed the door pad to enter. She heard the chirp and waited. It was so long. Or was that the pounding in her head?

"Enter," boomed a voice from inside the room right as the door opened. Jax entered, keeping her eyes fixed straight ahead; looking around would make her too dizzy.

"Lieutenant Brandt reporting as ordered, sir."

Jax could feel the Captain's eyes studying her. It felt like when her father caught her coming home late. She steeled herself. *You're a little old for those emotions*, she reminded herself.

"Are you okay, Lieutenant?"

"Fine, Captain. Just a late night, uh, working on a project for Commander Urud."

"I see. That Project is why you are here. Have a seat, Lieutenant."

Jax finally allowed herself a glance around the room. Captain Moss was at the head of the table. Commanders Lewis, Moro, and Urud were all seated in their normal positions. The surprise in the room was Gunnery Sergeant Locklear. His lined face was deeply tanned and he sat stiffly. Despite being a noncommissioned rank, he looked like he belonged here. More so than Jax felt, anyway. Jax took her seat next to the Gunnery Sergeant as the Captain began.

"Since launching the pathjacker probes we've been cruising along the edges of Screech space, allowing them to gather intel. Our sister ships, the Agrona and the Kaua, have also deployed the pathjackers. A few days ago, Gaia Command started to assemble that information." The Captain took in a deep breath and let it out. "What it has revealed is that we don't know anywhere near as much as we thought we did."

The holotable lit up with Screech occupied space. Small points of lights began to appear. Thousands, tens of thousands, multiplied across the image and began to move. It was beautiful. Jax was in awe. If only each point wasn't another Screech ship.

"There is far more movement than we ever realized. Also, Gaia Command believes there is a pattern. A pattern that indicates a buildup of forces. This buildup might indicate an invasion of Earth space."

The holotable was turned off. The dance of light faded. The tension in the air was thick as the Captain continued.

"The truth is, we just don't know. Because of that, Gaia Command has decided we need more intel, and they've assigned that task to us. XO if you would." He nodded and Commander Lewis took over.

"The probes have identified what we believe to be a communication relay of some sort located near our position." Commander Lewis took control as the holotable came to life again. A swirl of planets formed, seven in total. "This collection of planets is now designated the Roost system. Most of the planets are little more than flying rocks averaging around seventy-nine thousand kilometers in size. The first planet out from the sun the only exception. Designated Roost I, it is a class one inhabitable planet." The holo flew through the outer planets and came to rest on small blue-green world. The Lieutenant could have sworn she saw some purple dancing in the clouds as the image shifted again. *So like Earth, yet still so different.*

Dropping past the atmosphere, a large spire blossomed up from the ground. The weave pattern that was typical of all Screech tech dominated the building. It seemed to sit in a crater with jagged mountains surrounding it. The ground around the spire was encircled by mounds of dirt. Each ring a little larger and further apart as it moved away from the spire, as if the building were just a drop into water. *Is that a decorative thing or some kind of defense?*

Commander Lewis paused as the technical specs outlined the image. Widest at its base and tapering on its way to the top, it was estimated at eighty meters tall. The base was around sixty-eight meters per side, but as was normal for Screech architecture, all the corners were rounded. On one side was what looked like the only opening, a garage style door that was listed as twenty-five meters high and about fifty meters across.

"The mission is simple in theory. We will do a stealth approach from the far side of the planet. The ground team, led by Gunnery Sergeant Locklear and I, will deploy to these points." The holotable moved as she talked, highlighting two point a grassy plain. "We will make our way on foot to the structure that we have designated the Nest. The team will breach the structure, locate an appropriate data port, and use the A.I.D. to recover what information we can. Then we will backtrack along our route for pickup. Any questions?"

Jax's eyes were wide. She was so focused on the mission plans before her that the pounding in her head seemed to have passed. The holotable was still a bit bright, though.

Commander Moro was the first to speak. "Your squad is only listed as two four-man fire teams. With a structure of that size, it would seem the possibility of opposition is high. Wouldn't a larger force be more advisable?"

"If possible, we want to get in and out before the Screech know we are there. Continued surveillance of the Nest has identified only a skeleton style crew. Gunnery Sergeant Locklear is confident his Terrain Corps can handle the situation."

"Correct, Commander." The Gunnery's voice sounded like gravel to Jax. "We've staged infiltration ops like this before. The Corps can handle it."

The Captain and Commanders all nodded as if the Gunnery Sergeant saying it made it fact. Jax wished she had that ability. She couldn't believe she was witness to all this, which prompted a question of her own. "Excuse me, Captain, or Commander Lewis, why am I here?"

"First, we need your report on the A.I.D.. Is it ready for field use?" The Captain's stark tone was a bit jarring.

"Yes, Captain. The A.I.D. is pretty solid. I did have to deviate a lot from the blueprints since some of it was just not practical from a user standpoint; some of it was over complicated, some of it just wouldn't hold up under sustained use, I don't think the people that designed the A.I.D. have ever been in an actual work environment before, it seems as if …" Jax was going to continue but saw Commander Urud waving her off. *Oh no, my mother used to do that, go on and on about her engines. I've become my mother.* Jax cut herself off. "It's ready to go, Captain."

"You were also able to review the software?"

"It's installed and running, but I don't really know what it's for or have any way to check it. The specs said something about Screech computer code?"

"That's correct. While we are still having troubles translating their spoken language, the technicians at Gaia Command believe they have a handle on the written and computer code."

Slowly, Jax nodded. *Don't let the room spin.*

"Well done, Lieutenant. The next reason you are here is because you will be joining the ground mission."

"Yes, Captain. I just wanted— Wait. What?" Before Jax could get the clarification she desired, Commander Moro disrupted her thoughts.

"Captain, at this time, I need to voice my formal disapproval of Lieutenant Brandt's inclusion on this mission. She has zero field experience and is recently coming off a pretty serious offense. An offense which included time in the brig. We would be better served with a replacement."

Jax's anger started to boil at him coming out against her like that. Her eyes pinched. *Wait. What am I thinking? He's right. Do I even want to go on a ground mission?*

"It's my understanding that Lieutenant Brandt is the only Engineering Specialist with working knowledge of the A.I.D.. Is that correct, Commander Urud?"

"Correct, Captain. As Lieutenant Brandt explained, she has made a lot of deviations from the initial plans. It would take some time to get someone else trained on how to maintain it. Even then they may not be familiar enough with any specialized work Lieutenant Brandt has put in."

"Very well. Commander Moro, if you wish, you may log a formal complaint to be filed with the mission logs."

"I do."

"So be it. The assignment, however, will proceed as described. Gunnery Sergeant, assemble your team and stand by. Current estimate for drop is approximately twelve hours. Any further questions?"

The silence in the Briefing Room stretched out. Jax avoided eye contact but could feel Commander Moro's eyes burning her core.

"Briefing dismissed," the Captain said.

Jax waited for the Commanders to file out. The Captain had remained seated, which was unlike him. Gunnery Sergeant Locklear and Jax rose to leave together.

"Lieutenant Brandt, if you would wait a moment more?"

"Of course, Captain." Jax allowed the Gunnery Sergeant by and resumed her seat. The Gunnery Sergeant made a sharp exit. The Captain waited for the portal to close. He leveled his gaze at Jax.

"You cannot afford to make mistakes right now, Lieutenant Brandt. No matter what traditions—" The Captain made little air quotes with his hands around 'traditions'. It might have been comical coming from him, but he was so serious. "—Might say. Do you understand me?"

He knew about last night. *How could he not?* Jax could feel her headache returning. Her head slumped. "Yes, Captain."

"No matter your current situation, you are a Captain, and I expect you to behave as one. Captains are always held to a higher standard of behavior. Do you understand?"

That was a surprise. She had expected a much harsher dressing down for her behavior. Jax's eyes rose to meet with the Captain's. "Yes, Captain."

"Two more words of advice for you." The Captain raised his finger. "Your mind is more important than your tools. Make sure to keep yours safe and clear at all times."

"Yes, Captain. Uh, thank you, Captain."

The Captain held up his second finger. "You have around twelve hours before the mission is due to start. Get eight hours of sleep and use the rest to prepare. Ground missions are dangerous, and I want you back safe. That's an order."

"Aye aye, Captain." Jax nodded her head.

"Dismissed."

Jax stood, saluted, and left. He seemed so harsh but somehow it soothed her. *There's another skill I could use.* She made her way back to her berth. *Bed sounded so good.* She needed sleep before the ground mission. She stopped in her tracks.

"Oh my. I'm going on a ground mission."

Even Jax could hear the mix of excitement and fear that echoed in her voice.

Chapter 10

Drop

Jax walked from the Armory to the Hanger Deck. Her strides were powerful, augmented by the exo-armor she had been issued. She kept wanting to call it, "The Bert and Ernie Armor", but its official designation was Klick-Klick Battle Armor. Her mind was wandering. Six and a half hours sleep was all she had. She should have slept more, but she was too excited.

Upon waking, Jax had waved her hand at the wall and activated her holoscreen. The rectangular screen blossomed out in front of her. A mission packet greeted her, containing the mission briefing for all team members. First up, the briefing covered individual assignments. Jax was the Engineering Specialist, no surprise there. Mission parameters, general intel, she already knew that, boring. The last thing on the list was what she was most excited about, the equipment. *New toys to play with.*

First among the equipment was the classification of Klick-Klick supplies. The whole concept of the Klick-Klick amazed her. The length they had gone to for a made-up alien species. Gaia Military Command had outdone themselves with their creation, inventing biology, language, culture, technology, and more. It all had two goals in mind. First, to convince the Screech that this was a threat big enough to keep their attention off Earth. Second, to create an 'alien' they could project at Earth. Messages in space, flybys of Earth ships, anything to create a buzz that couldn't be silenced.

Part two had been partially successful. The rumor mill on Earth was working, but it was suppressed. Jax remembered that even Mr. Rickson had mentioned strange things happening. *I wonder how he's doing? I wish I could find out. Maybe when this mission is over, I'll ask Commander Lewis.*

Earth Government was the problem. They had too much control over what information got out. They countered rumors with disinformation. Video evidence disappeared, news authorities ignored vital leads, and so on. The rumors were growing, but it was slow. Thinking about it made Jax sick. *Could I have saved the Indiana if I had known?* Better not to think about it.

They had no real way to measure the success of the first goal. It wasn't like they could poll the Screech. The information they currently had would say it was a complete failure. The Screech didn't care about the Klick-Klick. They continued to move and spread how they wanted. Gaia's small armada of ships was like an ant trying to move an elephant.

The Screech and the Klick-Klick. Jax almost laughed as she made the last turn to the Hanger Bay. She stopped; she needed a moment. The Screech had been named for their shrilling verbal language. So, when the GMC created their own alien race, they copied what they knew, hence, the Klick-Klick. An annoying race that made an annoying sound that Jax recalled only too well from her first day on the Ares. Bert and Ernie.

At least, that's what the Ares crew called the two robot stand-ins. They were just the faces of the Klick-Klick, used to record messages to beam into space; designed to have specific alien movements; and to speak the made-up language. The amount of detail that went into them was staggering. The Ares crew called them Bert and Ernie because they worked like part of the crew. They had to have a name. Klick-Klick was merely the official name. *They will always be Bert and Ernie to me.* Jax smiled at herself.

Stepping through the portal onto the deck of the Hanger Bay, Jax checked out her amazing armor one more time. She had expected battle armor to be bulky, but this thing felt no different than a light winter coat. It fit her form perfectly from her toes all the way up to her neck. The bug-faced helmet was currently tucked under her right arm. The whole thing had a chitin-like texture with small overlapping plates. They were generally black in color, but with shades and highlights mixed in throughout. *Someone had actually thought of the aesthetics. They could use more of that on this ship.*

Enhanced strength, protective shell, enclosed filter and oxygen systems, this thing had it all. The only thing that bothered her was the weight on her back-right hip. Seventy centimeters of standard issue military firearm. Thinking about carrying that thing made her twitch and grimace. *Keep moving.* She pushed herself on.

Stepping onto the flight deck, Jax wrinkled her nose. The smell of oil and ozone assaulted her. She had only been here once before, on a brief tour of the ship when she first arrived, and she was as in awe now as she was then.

The Hanger Bay was easily the largest open space on the Ares, but it was hard to tell. Packed from floor to the top of its three-story ceiling were flight craft of all kinds. *Fighters, dropships, and shuttles, oh my.* She stifled her own laugh.

She looked around. A short distance off, she saw the staging area she needed. As she strolled over, the noise of the Hanger Bay taxed her ears. Jax knew they didn't use these crafts often, but they all had to be constantly maintained and tested. The Hanger Bay was like its own little city.

As she approached it, she slowed her pace and her shoulders dropped. She had hoped to arrive early, but looking ahead, she could see that the rest of the team was already assembled. *Denied again. How does everyone always show up before me?* Commander Lewis and Gunnery Sergeant Locklear were off to one side, deep in conversation. The rest of the mission team were spread around the staging area, some perched on supply crates, some others lounging around what must be their dropship. Bold letters on the side marked it out as the Reckless.

Let's hope it lives up to its name, Jax thought grimly as she studied the ship. It looks like a fat vulture. *Sharks, bugs, vultures, someone needs to pick a theme. Or maybe I just watched too many nature holovids as a kid.*

"Lieutenant Brandt." The voice was loud like crushing gravel as Gunnery Sergeant Locklear approached. He gave a sharp salute, which Jax did her best to return before he continued.

"There is someone I would like you to meet. Corporal Chambers!" The Corporal appeared at her side before Jax even realized he was coming. He stood at about one point eight meters and had brown, badly chopped hair that was short and stuck out at all angles. He didn't salute or stand at attention, he just relaxed there and waited.

"Corporal Chambers, this is Lieutenant Brandt." The Gunnery Sergeant's voiced dropped low before he continued. *What was that about?* "This is her first ground mission and she is carrying the only piece of mission critical gear we have. You will ensure her safety."

"Yes, Gunny."

"Ma'am." With that, the Gunnery Sergeant turned and left. "Five minutes to dust off, tender foots, final checks." Everyone in the Docking Bay probably heard that announcement roar out of the Gunny.

"Corporal Chambers." Jax offered a salute.

The Corporal didn't miss a beat and snapped one back. "Chambers is fine, ma'am. We tend to be a little less formal on ground missions. Last names mostly. If you don't mind, that is?"

"Fine by me, though I would prefer Jax over Brandt. Brandt was my father." Jax gave a slight smile.

"So he was, ma'am." Chambers gave a thoughtful grin. "Jax it is then. Now technically, Jax, you out rank me. But seeing as you are new to ground missions, I would like to recommend that you let me run the team. You make the big calls; I'll handle the details. Basically, same way the Gunny and your Commander operate. Is that acceptable?"

"I'll make it an order if I have to." Jax smiled. She was happy to see one in return. *Glad he had brought that up, not sure what I would have done.*

"Now, quick final check, that's our fire team over there. Rallic and Nelson. The Gunny's team is your Commander Lewis, Thirgood, and Saville. Would you like an equipment check?"

"Please."

Jax tilted her head as Chambers checked her Klick-Klick armor. She glanced at what she could see of his and then at the others standing nearby. She felt underdressed. Everyone else had belts, straps, and even painted designs that filled out their armor. Jax's armor looked so new when she compared it next to theirs. *I didn't know you could do that. I just followed the list they gave me; engineering tools, survival pack, and everything else that came ready equipped. I'm not sure what else I would add anyway.*

Jax jolted a bit as Chambers pulled something across her lower back.

"Overall, it's an excellent fit. I just tightened the lower back support, because when we get moving, it will loosen and shift. Tender foots always miss that."

"Tender foots?"

"People new to the Corps or those that have never been on mission."

"Didn't the Gunnery Sergeant just call everyone a tender foot?"

"We're all tender foots to the Gunny."

"Ah, I see, it's a Terrainwalker thing," Jax said and Chambers' faced pinched.

"Only upper brass and the uninformed call us Terrainwalkers, Jax. To us, we're the Corps. If you want to be part of the team and keep 'em happy, you'll use that."

"A Corps thing, then?"

"Yes, ma'am." This time Chambers wore a devilish grin. "Weapons check?"

86

Jax nodded her head as she shifted uneasily. Passing her helmet from her right hand to her left, she swiped her thumb control and her weapon swung up from her back hip and placed itself firmly in her hands. Both hands on, she presented the weapon as best she could remember how.

"Just the one?" Chambers lifted an eyebrow.

"Only one I'm qualified to use. Shooter rating." Jax grimaced. Shooter was the lowest rating to qualify to use the weapon. Shooter, sharpshooter, and expert. Her lease favorite class when going through the Ares Basics Induction. Everyone on board had to have basic personal weapon proficiency. Jax had just barely passed, but she wasn't going to tell him that.

"Well, it's a fine weapon to have. The workhorse of the Terrain Corps. One we all carry."

Jax glanced around and sure enough they all had the same weapon on their back hips. Along with many other weapons, she noted. That feeling of being underprepared crept up her throat one more time. Corporal Chambers continued.

"The Nath Industries Energy Weapon 24. NEW24. Adjustable energy output. Capable of beam, three shot burst, and full auto. Almost impossible to run out of energy with its qave fuel cell batteries. Collapsible stock for when needed and sights that hook directly into your armor's HUD. A Corps member's best friend."

Jax had heard all this before. It didn't feel right to mention it, though, so she focused on watching. The Corporal ran through the weapon, sighting with it, opening compartments to check the inside, reading screens on its side. The ease he had with it was impressive. *Don't think I will ever be that comfortable with it.*

"If you have no objections, I'll set you to 'three shot burst' as default. You Fleet types tend to like the beam setting, but the Corps finds you don't keep your head exposed as long with burst. Safety first. Plus, the bursts hit with a small explosion on the end. Gives you some stopping power for when the beam doesn't cut."

"Sounds good to me. I agree with safety first." *I never would have thought of that. I don't know why I would need stopping power; I'm just along for the ride. Let the Corps do the work, that was the plan.*

The Corporal handed the weapon back. Jax reattached it to the energy straps that kept it in place, thumbed her finger controls, and moved it back to its hip standby position.

"You have a knife?" His eyes were darting around her body.

"No, do I need a knife?" she asked, shaking her head.

"You always need a knife. Here, you can take this one, it's my second backup."

He pulled a twenty-two-centimeter sheath from his back and handed it to her. She pulled it out and examined the dull black blade. Looking more closely, she could see multicolored swirls dancing along its length. It looked more like a small sword than a knife.

"Second backup? How many do you have?" Jax raised an eyebrow as she secured it to her left hip tool kit.

"As many as it takes to get the job done." That devilish grin again. *He sure is having fun.*

"Helmets on and all aboard, tender foots. Time to show some birds what apes can do." Jax couldn't help but laugh at the Gunny's proclamation. The other Corps members seemed to enjoy it too, as whoops and cheers rang out.

When she donned her helmet, it came alive. Jax had thought it would be awkward to wear, but it just felt like a full head baseball cap. To her surprise, it melted away in front of her eyes. *Nice.*

The big surprise was watching the seven Klick-Klick warriors before her also melt away. Each one was replaced by a Corps member and one Commander. Everyone was standing around in grey fatigues, battle helmets, various gear, and weapons.

"Wow," she gasped.

"Must be your first time with live image overlays." Chambers voice echoed in Jax's ear.

"Yup." Jax turned her head, checking out each team member in turn.

"Keeps things personal, looking at humans rather than aliens. Less likely to shoot the wrong target that way too. At least, that's the theory. You'll get tactical overlays and mission updates once we're on the ground."

"Nice." As Jax walked into the dropship, the rest of her heads-up display began to list the Fireteams. Two text columns appeared and then floated to the left of her eyes. Each name was highlighted in green as the person it belonged to spoke on the open channel.

"Let's go, sweethearts, we've got work to do." The Gunnery Sergeant's voice echoed in her ear, followed by complaints and some of the most colorful language Jax had ever heard. All the Corps members seemed to have an opinion to share.

There was no waiting; the gang plank came up, everyone entered their seating pods, and strapped themselves in. The Gunny made a quick run down the aisle, making sure everyone was in place. Once he was satisfied, he took his seat, and from the corner of her eye, Jax saw him hit a big red button near his pod. Her stomach lurched. She knew there was a large gantry arm grabbing the ship and moving it to a launch tube. She had expected a warning. *I'll remember that next time.* Her stomach swayed. *Like a roller coaster. Just like a roller coaster. Focus on what you know.*

The pilot's voice came over the comms. "Welcome to the Reckless, I'm your pilot, Hat Trick. We have pleasant weather and a smooth flight planned for you today. Hold on to your breakfast because here we go. Launching in 5… 4… 3… 2… and… Launch."

Jax's body was pressed hard to her left as she bumped the side of her pod. The pressure was momentary as the Reckless exited the Ares. Once away, the ship levelled out and everyone relaxed. Conversations broke out almost immediately amongst the Corps. She ignored most of it.

Instead, Jax took a moment and examined her pod. Actually, it was more like a tube than a pod. There was a basic seat, some seatbelt straps, and a gravchute attached to the back. It seemed simple enough but the idea of it made her shudder. A question sprang to mind.

"Hey, Chambers, anything I should know about the drop?"

"You ever drop before?"

"Nope."

"Simulated?"

"Nope. I skydived once. I checked the procedure last night but wanted to double check. It seems easy enough but safety first and all."

"It's not really like skydiving, unless you're skydiving and your chute doesn't open, then it's a lot like skydiving." Jax startled at that as his head came around from his seat to look at her. "I guess they figure you're fine since were dropping in a safe zone and then running in. We'll be moving fast, though, so be ready. We drop from five point eight kilometers. Arch position only for about the first kilometer to orientate. Then arms to your sides and feet first. This is a combat drop insertion. At seven hundred and fifty meters, hit your activation bar." He made a pulling motion at his chest. "You'll feel a lurch, but you'll ease nicely to the ground. Hit it too early and you'll gain speed, too late and you won't slow enough. Keep your knees bent and let the exo-armor do the work."

Jax shook her head. *Easy enough, a lot like parachuting, except for the drop position, I guess. What does he mean it's like skydiving if my chute doesn't open? You're over thinking it. I'll be fine.* She was about to relax when the conversation exploded.

"Hey, its Lieutenant Brandt's first combat drop! I got fifteen that says she bites it on the landing." Rallic's name popped green on her heads up. After that, the switching was too fast for her to keep up with.

"No way, she already blew up a bunch of birdies. Thirty-five says she sticks it."

"I'll take fifty-five she bites it."

The betting and joking continued at her expense. A private comm came in from Commander Lewis.

"Lieutenant Brandt, Jax, I'm sorry we completely missed that you didn't have basic drop training. Usually that happens in basic training before you get on ship. We never thought to put you through it when we went through the basics with you. You going to be okay?"

"I'll adapt. I've skydived before. Same thing, right?" She hoped the Commander's answer would be different.

"Not really. We can scrub the mission. It's not too late."

She could feel her shoulders dropping, but pushed them straight, sitting stiffly. "Don't. This is important. I read the briefing, I studied the procedure, and Chambers gave me the run down. It's simple. I'll be fine; I adapt well. I think the betting is harsher." Jax tried to layer confidence and humor into her voice. *I can't afford mistakes right now; I've got to make it this work.*

Commander Lewis sighed. Jax glanced at her and could see the calculating stare ripping through her. Jax tried to keep her face impassive. The Commander finally broke. "Fine. Mission is a go. Listen to Chambers, he knows what he's doing. Don't take the betting too personal, its tradition to bet on the newbie landing. I got it too on my first drop."

"I'm okay. I'm getting used to people betting on my pain. Though I'm starting to hate the word tradition. Seems like it always involves bad things coming my way."

"Ha. Welcome to a warship. Make sure you stick the landing. I'm betting eighty you make it." Jax saw the Commander smile, but the look of worry persisted.

A general call came from the pilot. "Entering atmosphere of planet designated Roost I. Drop in ten minutes. Repeat, drop in ten minutes."

"All right, tender foots, you heard the pilot, time to earn your keep. Drop positions. Fireteam Two, you are go for the first drop, and then Fireteam One. Drop zones have been uploaded to your HUDs."

Jax was out of step while everyone else stood. She scrambled to her feet as her seat dropped away. Taking a step back, she felt the click of the gravchute attaching to her back. The straps wrapped around her legs and body. She looked down to the see the activation handle sticking out of her chest on the right side. Easy to find. *I got this.*

"We are green for drop run," the pilot said.

Below her, the floor slipped away, and she was suspended there. Jax's stomach rose. *Don't look down. Don't look down.* She looked down.

Greens and browns blurred together until she could barely separate the colors from one another. This seems a lot higher than I thought. Clouds whipped into view and were gone just as fast. *How fast are we moving? Are we supposed to be going this fast? This is not like parachuting! Maybe we should scrub this mission. I can call the Commander. I think I'm better on the Ares.* The minutes were gone before she could act on her doubts.

The pilot announced, "Dropping in 3... 2... and... drop."

The skin on Jax's face pulled up, her heart gagged her throat. She exploded out of the bottom of the Reckless, her arms and feet flailing.

Get it together, Jax. Her heads-up display showed her altitude countdown. She focused on it. It was going remarkably fast. She tried to stabilize herself. Ease into the arch position, no this is a combat drop, not the same.

19 km... 18.5...

Get in the correct position. She forced her hands and arms back into the drop position. Her body righted itself in the air. Plummeting feet first, she dropped faster.

16.5...14... 12.5...

I must pull the release. When was that? The readout in front of her switched from kilometers to meters, the numbers running down from a thousand now. *I'm getting close. I need to pull the lever. When was that? Oh crap.* The numbers seemed to jump in front of her.

950... 900... 880... 870... 840... 790... 780...

That's it! She yanked the handle. The gravchute energy bubble expanded around her, negating her weight. Tiny jets on her back canceled her downward motion. Even with the Klick-Klick armor on, she felt the straps pulling at her armpits. She slowed. The ground was still so far away. She was almost stopped and then she was falling.

She was five stories up and Jax's eyes opened wide. Her mind raced. *What do I do? Bend your knees. No something else. Yank the handle again.* She pulled and pulled again. The gravchute was spent. *No! No! No!*

She hit the ground and her ears rang as her exo-armor squealed, tightening to protect her from the impact. Her left leg collapsed. She was rolling. The alien grass and foliage flattened under her. Small trees were crushed as she rolled through them. The large tree, however, was not.

Jax clutched her stomach as her body wrapped itself around the tree. She bounced off it, rolled over again, and came to an awkward rest on her side with the A.I.D. backpack propping her up. She closed her eyes and let the pain wash over her.

CHAPTER 11

BACON

Jax was laughing. It was a deep laugh all the way from her stomach. That made it hurt. She opened her eyes to find Corporal Chambers standing over her. The confusion—or was that concern?— etched deep into the crease of his brow.

"You okay, Jax?"

"I think so, help me up." She had got it down to a chuckle as Chambers took her hand. Her bio chart lit up her HUD. The minor injuries it showed were already being treated by the medical nanites built into the battle suit. "Suit says I'm fine, but I could use some more painkillers."

"Medical AI only gives painkillers if it's really needed. Pain keeps you sharp when your life is on the line. At least, that's the theory. Care to share what was so funny?"

Jax was bent over, with her hand on her stomach. She wished she could get the armor off. It hurt to talk. It hurt to laugh too, but she didn't seem to be able to stop doing that.

"Pretty sure with that landing I was the first person to ever set foot on Roost I. First human on an alien world. Lifelong dream achieved."

She was laughing, but the pain was fading.

"Great, she's looney." Private First-Class Nelson came trotting up, PFC Rallic right at his heels.

"Check that talk, Nelson."

"Yes, sir." Nelson turned his head like a scorned puppy.

"Fireteam Two, what's going on over there?" Gunnery Sergeant Locklear's voice boomed over the squad comm channel.

"Lieutenant Brandt had a rough landing, sir. Just making sure she is good to go."

"Roger that, Corporal. Fireteam One is all present and accounted for. We are beginning our run on path alpha one. When you tender foots are ready, your path is beta two. Rendezvous is at delta in fourteen hours."

"Roger that. Request to have the mission logs show that Lieutenant Brandt was first to touch down on Roost I."

There was a pause before the Gunnery Sergeant replied, with a hint of humor in his voice, "Roger that. Get your asses moving."

Jax was standing straight, making sure she could move everything. She tilted her head. "What was that about?"

"Makes it official." Chambers gave a wink.

"Great, Chambers is in love. You two want some alone time?" Rallic said as he and Nelson bumped fists.

Jax was sure she was blushing. *Does that show through the VR overlay?* Chambers didn't seem phased, he just turned, his voice sounding more like the Gunnery Sergeant.

"Let's get moving. Rallic, you're on point, Jax and myself next, Nelson you have the tail."

"Great, I'm stuck eating everyone's dust. Again."

"That's because you're too fat to stay out in the lead." Rallic was starting his jog to the front.

"This is muscle. Real men aren't the size of a twelve-year-old."

"Less talking, more running. Twenty meters spacing. Let's go, Jax."

They were running. Well, everyone else in Fireteam Two was running; she was stumbling and flailing. With the extra power the exo-armor gave to her steps at a run, it took a while to find the correct rhythm.

She found her stride and her team cruised along at about fifty-five kph. Every so often, her HUD would show the medical nanites going to work, working her muscles, keeping the fatigue at bay. *They want you to feel the pain but not hinder your ability to fight,* Jax determined. They got into a pattern of a half hour run and then a five to ten-minute break. Run. Break. Run. Monotony set in.

Each break, she had nothing but time to check out the rest of her team. Her HUD showed Rallic as a scanner technician and long-range weapons specialist. Jax wasn't sure what that latter part was for, but he worked the scanner. With each stop, he popped out his tripod, screen, and disc setup to take some readings. Scanned the area for possible threats. He was slim and on the shorter side. His face was kind of rough. His Klick-Klick armor had a circle and cross hairs painted on the helmet. The VR overlay showed it like a tattoo on his face. Besides some other red slashes here and there, the only other standout was a G1 on his shoulder. *Must be another Corps thing.* He always seemed too busy to look at anyone, just had his nose in the scanner.

Chambers and Nelson would separate, pretending to rest, but they were obviously keeping a lookout. Their Klick-Klick armor was decorated similarly; each had some red stripes circling their arms. Chambers had three and Nelson had two. Nelson also had some kind of shark sketched on his shoulder. *I like him already.* Everyone had a job. Everyone but Jax. She felt like a fifth wheel in the four-person fireteam.

The unchanging scenery, tall brown grass with touches of green, didn't help her souring mood. Shrubs and the occasional tree would pass but nothing interesting to occupy her mind. The air had a purple, smoke-like tinge to it that just added to her growing gloom. Jax kept track of their progress on her HUD. It felt like watching water boil. The miles wore on. With only about two hours to go till they met with Fireteam One, Chambers called for a stop.

"Break here for chow. Long break, we want to be well rested and ready once we're at delta. Rallic, run your scans. I'll take watch while you do, then you take over. Nelson, you'll take last watch before we head out again."

"What about me, Corporal?" Jax's lips were pressed tight together as she waited for a reply.

"What about you, Lieutenant?"

"I'm a part of this team. I can do my part. Stop sidelining me."

"Uh oh, lovers quarrel," Nelson whispered.

"Better watch it, Chambers; she likes to hit native Gaiaians." Rallic was grinning.

She ignored Nelson and Rallic. Her eyes stayed square on the Corporal, hands crossed, feet planted firmly on the ground.

"We're supposed to keep you safe. You're mission critical." .

"All the more reason you three should be well rested. Let me help the team or do I have to make it an order?" That last part jumped suddenly into her head. *I forgot I outrank these guys. I could have done this a while ago. Another thing to remember.* Nelson and Rallic were chuckling in the background. Chambers' creased brow stared down at her. Their gazes locked, it didn't seem as if either would budge, but then that devilish grin crossed his face again.

"Very well, Lieutenant, you take second watch. That good?"

"It's a start." Her shoulders relaxed as she shook her head.

Chambers made his patrol while Nelson, Rallic, and Jax ate. For a while, Jax turned off the VR overlay. Watching Nelson and Rallic with their helmets open, eating, was strange. The bug bodies with human faces were too odd for her to handle. She turned the overlay back on, and the two Corps fighters returned to their fatigues, now brown and green to match their surroundings.

Nelson was listed as a Heavy Gunner and he sat with his Nath Industries Heavy Machine Gun 42. To her, it was just a big scary gun. She brought up the specs on her HUD. *When in fear, learn more.* Technically, it was designated the NHMG 42, but everyone called it the Meg42. It was a rail gun that accelerated its ammo to near light speed, but condensed to the size of a machine gun. Its Gatling-style rotating barrel could fire at rate of up to ten thousand rounds a minute.

Not sure that information makes me feel better about it. Hopefully I'll never see it in use. Jax studied Nelson with the heavy weapon. On their run, Nelson often complained about carrying the thing. It had a physical gantry arm to store on his back, swing down and help stabilize it for use. The more elegant energy straps that the NEW24s used just weren't practical for it. That, plus the physical ammo he had to carry, added weight and looked awkward to run with.

Despite all the complaining, Jax noticed that, every time they rested, Nelson would swing the gun down and carefully check the Meg. At first, she had thought it was protocol, until she noticed him whispering to it. It sounded like he was talking to an old lover. Sounded like he called the Meg42 Sally. It was cute, but also kind of creepy.

Rallic was also obsessed with his equipment. She was pretty sure his was about protocol, though. At every stop, he would set up his scanner with great efficiency. His nose would be pushed into the scanner and often wouldn't leave until they started running again.

Their Klick-Klick suits had their own scanners, but they were limited to a couple hundred meters. Rallic's scanner could cover hundreds of kilometers. It allowed them to get a picture of the lay of the land ahead and to keep track of Fireteam One.

While he seemed absorbed in his work, she kept getting the feeling Rallic was watching her. Every time she looked, his nose was buried in the scanner, but then she would feel his eyes again. *They're all watching me, I bet. Tender foot. Weak link. Stay focused; thinking like that will not help.*

Chambers ambled up from being on watch. He casually took a seat with his fellow Corps. "Pretty quiet. I just did a short circuit. Mostly just grass and trees. Some wildlife, birds, and some kind of coyote or something, too far off to make out, so shouldn't be a problem."

"Roger that," she said, standing and adjusting her gear. She headed back along the path Chambers had come in on.

"Weapons at the ready while on watch, Jax."

"Roger that." She tried to keep her voice neutral, but she was grinding her teeth. *Of course you need the weapon out, Jax,* she berated herself. She hesitated slightly before bringing the weapon to bear. *Get used to it. How does someone get used to carrying a gun?*

She walked and scanned the horizon. It was so drab, Jax longed for those beautiful hikes back in Issaquah, Washington. *When I get back on the Ares, I really need some VR time.* She shook her head. *No daydreaming.* It had been a while since she had allowed herself that luxury. Jax snapped her focus back and that's when she saw it.

Only about twelve meters out, its eyes like burning charcoal, it stared at her. Standing chest height, a hairy mohawk, two large tusks, small horns, it snorted and stomped.

Some kind of boar? Not like any she had ever seen. Its skin was dry and cracked with browns and greens to blend in with its surroundings. *You are an ugly thing.*

"What do you want?" She stared back while it snorted and tossed its head. "Go on, get out of…"

Jax was flying, her HUD warning her of heavy contact on her left side. Her armor stiffened to absorb the impact. She was flipping head over heels. Jax instinctively angled herself to land on her back instead of her head.

Rolling up to her feet, she saw a second boar creature starting its turn back toward her. Her NEW24 was still in her hand thanks to the energy straps. She brought it up to fire. She remembered the first boar. *Oh crap.* She could see it coming from the corner of her eye. She dove, intending to roll away, but her feet got clipped by the charging creature. She went spinning, tumbling out of control across the hard-grassy ground.

She scrambled to her feet. Sinking into a low crouch, she made eye contact with the first boar (or was it the second?), barreling down on her. No time for a shot. *No time.* Jax fell backwards. Her left hand reached out as she rolled onto her back, grasping one of the boar's tusks before it drove into her. Her feet came up, connecting with the creature's underbelly. She kicked, the enhanced strength of the Klick-Klick armor sending the boar flying.

Tomoe Nage! Jax would have to remember to thank Commander Lewis for drilling that throw with her. *That might be my new favorite throw.*

Wait. Where is the other one? Jax turned to the rushing boar. This time, there was time. She brought the NEW24 up and squeezed the trigger. Three shots automatically beamed off. Miss. Jax squeezed again. Miss. *Oh, come on.* Again. She pulled the trigger as fast as she could. Again. This time she clipped its side. Again. Finally, the boar creature fell.

The terror fled from Jax's mind as the bile built up in her stomach. *I killed it. What have I done?* Her throat was seizing. *Don't throw up. Hold it together.*

"Jax, get your head in the game!" Chambers yelled. *Damn.* The one she tossed. She turned to see it roaring at her. *No time. This is going to hurt.* She gritted her teeth.

It fell. There was a burning spot in the side of its head. It happened so suddenly that Jax could only stare. They were still yelling at her, but the words weren't registering. When she turned to look, they were waving. Jax waved back. *Just worried, I guess.*

"Thanks, guys. I'm o—"

Jax's eyes grew wide as Nelson took aim at her. *Why is he aiming at me? Firing? What!?*

Nelson's barrel spun and the muzzle flashed. Jax screamed. To her right, she heard a popping like wet bubbles in a bath. Turning, saw another boar creature, its flesh shredded, disintegrated, by the Meg42. *Where did that come from? How did I miss it?* Jax whipped her head around. *Were there more?*

"Jax, are you all right?" Chambers called.

She was startled that they were so close. Chambers and Nelson came up beside her. Things move so fast on the ground.

"I'm fine. Didn't know there were three. I only saw two."

"Yeah. Always check your six." Chambers sounded relieved.

"Hey, bacon for dinner!" Rallic exclaimed, running up, completing their group.

"We are not eating local species," Chambers deadpanned.

"I could use some bacon." Nelson licked his lips. A huge smile crossed his face.

"You can stow your weapon, Jax. Area is secure," Chambers said.

"I've never killed anything before. It's so- so final." Her weapon swung back to her hip.

Chambers came up beside her and slowly swung his head around, checking each target and preforming some kind of mental evaluation. "Not bad for your first firefight. I've seen worse." He eyed Rallic and Nelson, but just for a moment. Nelson turned away. Rallic stared on as if he was chewing on something sour.

"Next time, try not to approach head on. You're better off to come from the side or behind. If you have to switch targets, don't rush, be smooth. Trust the weapon."

At first, Jax thought he was going to tease her about the mess she had made of the situation, but the tone of his voice was sincere. It was just another day on the job for him. He wanted the same for her. *Thank you.*

"Roger that, Corporal." Jax nodded her head as she met his eyes.

"We should get moving. Ninety minutes till we have to be at our rally point."

"Right, let's get moving. And Chambers?"

"Yes?"

"Next time I want to do something I'm not ready for, you have my permission to knock some sense into me."

"I'll leave hitting superior officers to you, ma'am." Chambers winked. "But I will let you know."

They were all laughing but Jax was okay with it. She deserved it and she was laughing with them.

CHAPTER 12

ENTER

They ran. Checking the telemetry Rallic had picked up during chow, Jax was sure they would make the rally point ahead of Fireteam One. She was wrong. They were moving into more rocky ground. The long grass and occasional trees were broken up by small outcroppings of rock, and scattered around were larger buttes that looked like small buildings.

Around ten minutes out from the rendezvous, Chambers called for a halt.

"What's up, Chambers? Some kind of trouble?" Nelson had Sally out and was scanning the area.

"No, we're good." His head was on a swivel. "This could be a good place for our evac. That high ridge would provide good cover, clear space for pickup, and it looks like anything coming from that way—" He hiked his thumb towards their destination. "—Would be funneled into a kill zone. Rallic, lay down a marker."

She looked around. They were in a small crevice between two buttes. The one on the right was around eight meters tall, the other was almost triple that. With the image of the Reckless in her mind, she could see it landing easily between the two.

"Roger that." Rallic pulled a small tube from his side belt, while eyeing the ground. Finding a spot he was satisfied with, he placed the tube on the ground and thumbed a button. They heard a small pop and, then Rallic looked up, smiling.

"Marker in."

"So, with that we can find our way back?" She glanced at the small disc.

"That's the theory. Your HUD can lock on and give you directions back."

"You don't seem so sure."

The Corporal just shrugged and gave her a slight grin. "Time's a-wasting. Let's finish our run."

Up to speed and moving fast, it couldn't have taken them more than a few minutes. As they came over a ridge, they saw Fireteam One about a kilometer off, nestled into a rocky embankment.

Jax's squad slowed to a jog. *How does Commander Lewis do that? She's always first. What's worse is, it looks like they've been there for a while.* Chambers put out a call over the all squad comm and established their link for the entire mission team. Jax's HUD ran a list of all eight team members now. As they moved closer, their jog became a walk. Jax scanned the horizon. The sun was finally dropping. The purple haze hung low. Browns turned into deeper browns; greens started to turn black. What would have been an orange sunset on Earth was shifted red. Jax shivered at the eeriness of it all.

As she finished her walk into camp, a private comm popped up in front of her. "Commander."

"How you doing, Lieutenant?'

"Oh, you know, Commander, just another great day in the Corps."

"Ha, you have any problems with the Screech?"

"The Screech? Nope. Had a run in with some local animals, but I'd rather forget about that."

"Nothing serious I take it?"

"Nope."

"Okay, we'll talk about that later. But no Screech?"

"No Screech. Your team have something happen?"

"No. Nothing. I don't like it. This is not what we expected. Way too easy."

"Easy is bad?"

"Easy is scary. Easy when you expect hard is bad. It means we're missing something. Keep your guard up, Jax."

"Roger that." She tried to make it light, but when Commander Lewis had said, "Jax", instead of, "Lieutenant", a shiver had gone down her spine. *What has happened to my life that, "easy", is something to worry about?* She started to get that cold feeling again. *Come on Jax, you're a Captain, act like it. Well, at least like a really strong Lieutenant.*

Gunnery Sergeant Locklear's gravelly voice boomed into everyone's ears. "All right, tender foots, we are going to do this one by the numbers. Thirgood and Rallic, get your scanners running. I want to know if a flea farts anywhere within five kilometers of us."

"Roger that, Gunny," PFC Thirgood responded sharply. Her voice was a lot higher than Jax had expected. Jax hadn't really gotten a good look at her when they boarded the Reckless, but glancing at her now, she realized just how muscled she was. Even her VR overlay looked like it was going to burst out of the seams of her uniform. *Wow, I wonder how long I'd need to work out to get like that? Probably forever.*

Rallic also responded, "Roger that, Gunny." His voice rose in what seemed to be his impression of Thirgood. PFC Thirgood just rolled her eyes and moved on. Rallic followed her closely, a small smirk on his face. *Must be another Corps thing.*

The Gunnery continued, unfazed. "Chambers, you're on watch. Everyone else, sit tight and be ready. The Nest is only about two kilometers away. Sundown is in thirty-eight minutes. Then we are on the move to crack that thing open."

The sun fell way too fast for Jax's liking. Sundown and move again. They were in columns, moving at a steady jog. Her helmet went into night mode, so everything looked just like daylight. Fireteam One was out front.

PFC Thirgood was on point, followed by the Gunny and the Commander. Private Saville's big frame trailed them, his Meg42 out and ready.

Jax's team kept some distance in a covering position. Chambers out front, Rallic and Jax next, Nelson taking the flank once again. His Meg42, the love of his life, was also out and ready. As they neared their target, silent commands came from the Gunny over the HUD. Simple text messages flashed by. Move. Stop. Left flank. Cover. Fireteam One moved up, Fireteam Two covered. Fireteam Two moved up, Fireteam One covered. Simple. Efficient. Jax found a rhythm to it that was easy to follow.

The Nest was before them. They came up a ridge, crawling on their hands and feet like spiders up a wall. The Nest rested in a crater only a few hundred meters away.

Jax gasped, her eyes wide. The VR model from the briefing room was unequal to the reality. It looked like someone had dropped it in place. The earth rippled out away from its base. The spire weaved up out of the ground and shot for the sky. Blacks, reds, blues, yellows, the colors weaving together in a mesh pattern the Screech always used. It had seemed so small on the VR, here it seemed insurmountable.

"No guards. No patrolling ships. Where is all the activity we registered before?" The Commander's voice was no more than a whisper.

Everyone sat speechless for several moments till the Gunny broke in. His usually loud voice was a little more than a murmur. "All right. Sit tight, people. Chambers and Thirgood, you're on recon. Find us an entrance."

There was no reply as the two Corps members sneaked off. In a few steps, they disappeared like shadows in the night. Her HUD signaled where they were, but with no clear line of sight, they were just blips on the screen to follow. *Don't watch the kettle boil.*

Time stretched on interminably. Jax tried to copy everyone else and stay perfectly still, but she couldn't help but fidget. Rallic seemed to turn a sour eye towards her, but anytime she checked, he was looking away. *My imagination is working overtime again.* She glanced around at the other members of the squad. Commander Lewis nodded at her with a reassuring smile. Nelson and Saville were back to back, looking like each other's shadows, expecting an attack any minute. They both glanced back. *Great, everyone is watching me. Keep an eye on the tender foot.*

Hours passed. Except... they didn't. Jax checked the time; only fifteen minutes had passed. *I hate waiting.* Hours passed again. Except they didn't. Jax jumped as Chambers and Thirgood came sliding back into their hideaway.

"We found what looks like a possible back door. Far side." Chambers said as he pointed with two fingers. "Thirgood gets the credit. Sharp eyes, Private."

She was grinning as she chimed in with, "There might be more options higher up, but I don't think we want to do much climbing."

The Gunny nodded as he stood. "All right, butterflies, let's get moving. Staggered column. Chambers and Thirgood on point. Nelson and Saville, you guard our backs."

"Again?" Nelson snarled.

"Best for last," Saville said.

"Now, Corps, five-meter spacing. Stay low, stay quiet, move fast. Move out." The Gunny didn't wait to see who was following. When you're the Gunny, people keep up with you.

A zigzag run around the perimeter brought them in sight of their target. I'm really starting to hate running. Kneeling behind a small ridge, staring across the empty space to the Nest, she didn't see the 'back door'.

As if on cue, Chambers said, "Here's what we're looking at."

Thirgood had a slightly larger version of the NEW24 out. Jax used her HUD to double check herself. The NEW28 was a longer rifle version of the 24. It had greater power output, longer range, and a faster rate of fire. A small warning on the technical readout said it was prone to overheating. It looked heavy compared to what she had, but the Private held it with grace. Thirgood was sighting with it and relaying her target to the Squad.

A small rectangle appeared in Jax's view. She sighted it and zoomed in. Way in. *How did Thirgood ever spot that?* Inside all the hatch work, there was a slight deviation, a place where things didn't quite match up. It looks like they could slide away or maybe pull back from each other. A small etching inside one of the cross hatches, must be Screech writing, a control pad maybe?

"Wide open spaces, no scanner or guards to speak of. Anyone else catch anything?" The Gunny's voice was a harsh whisper through the comm channel.

"We couldn't detect anything on our initial scout," Chambers said as Thirgood nodded in agreement.

"These guys are so alpha they don't need it," Nelson said.

"Roger that," Thirgood and Saville said together.

"Yeah, we're like chicken's running into a fox's den," Rallic fired back.

"Enough, people, essential comms only." Chambers shut them all down. "I still got nothing. What's the call, Gunny?"

"We do the job. Fireteam One, move up. Team Two, cover. Go."

Fireteam One covered the ground smoothly. Focusing on Commander Lewis, she looked for inspiration. The Commander moved like she had been born into the Corps rather than the Fleet. *Is that training or a state of mind? Remember what the Captain said, you're a Captain. You can move like that too. This is not going to be a bad day.*

Fireteam One secured their perimeter at the entry point and called Team Two forward. Jax tried to fall right into the rhythm again. *That felt better. Maybe I can salvage this day yet. Be like the Commander. Be like a Captain. You are a Captain.*

"Rallic, do your thing," the Gunny ordered.

Rallic moved up to where the symbols showed on the wall. From his back pouch, he pulled out a hand-sized disk and slapped it down. He started fingering his wrist screen, gritting his teeth and squinting his eyes. They darted back and forth between his wrist and the disk. Tense seconds stretched out.

"Got it," he said, but nothing happened. He pulled the disk from the wall. Stepping back, he pointed. "Bang."

The door didn't open, it was more like it unraveled. The hatch patterns pulled away from each other. Toward the end, it looked like teeth opening to devour them. *Wonderful, here we go, into the belly of the beast.*

CHAPTER 13

CONNECTION

They stalked the hallways. Each step was placed with care, careful was smooth, smooth was life, rushing was death. Move and cover, move and cover. Like all things Screech, there were no sharp angles; the hallways were tubes that twisted and turned. They spiraled up, they spiraled down, the ever-present weave pattern and kaleidoscope of colors making it hard to see openings or branches. Closed doorways were easily missed with their hidden markings.

PFC Thirgood's sharp eyes caught openings the others couldn't see. There seemed be no rhyme or reason to the spacing of the doors. As they searched, both Thirgood and Rallic were laying down digital flares, small, thumb-sized discs that stuck to the walls, each one broadcasting its location. A map was being built step-by-step, but it seemed inadequate for the task at hand. On the road, Rallic always seemed to be watching her, now she was thankful for that attention to detail. His watchfulness was keeping them safe.

Jax liked to keep the map open on her HUD to track their progress. It was painfully slow. Each door had to be checked and secured. Sometimes they were led into a room, sometimes they found another tube to walk down. Empty rooms or what resembled storage seemed abundant. Still not what they needed. We just need a terminal to jack into and then we can get out of here. Room after room and still nothing.

At first, they didn't notice it, but there was a kind of humming in the air. If you listened closely, if you strained your ears to hear, it was always there. Nothing else stirred, it felt abandoned. She shivered. *Is it wrong to wish for something to happen? No, don't think that way. Find a terminal, and let's get back to the Ares. Stay focused on the task at hand.*

Thirgood raised a hand to bring them all to a stop. Jax wasn't watching, but inside her HUD, a small HALT appeared above her line of sight. Their squad comms didn't broadcast outside the suits, but still no one was talking unless they had to.

Thirgood pressed a spot on the wall. A door twice the size of all the ones they had encountered so far unraveled before them. Thirgood and Saville swept in, followed by Gunny and the Commander. Fireteam Two was quick to cover.

A collective gasp rang out over the comms. The room opened up like a large cavern in front of them. The far walls disappeared through a kaleidoscope of hourglass structures that went from floor to ceiling. In some areas, they would bubble out and stop part way, looking like odd, rounded mushrooms. They rose up from the floor in the same way they fell from the ceiling. It looked like some kind of strange, alien warehouse. A strangely empty warehouse. That humming sound echoed louder now.

The Gunny's voice broke through the amazement. "Fireteam Two, hold this position. Fireteam One, spread out, but stay in sight. Let's see if we can find our connection."

Jax's team fanned out across the opening. She faced back down the hall from which they had come. Once again, time seemed to stand still. Her body relaxed; already the waiting was becoming second nature. *I can be patient. A Captain is patient. I am a Captain. I wish they would hurry up.*

"I got something," the Commander said.

"Everyone to the Commander," Gunny responded.

A short jog and they all converged.

"Will this work, Lieutenant?" The Commander eyed Jax.

Jax started to analyze the bubble protruding from the wall. On her HUD, she brought up the plans from the AID to do a comparison. The virtual display of what the AID was supposed to plug into floated around and overlaid the wall unit. It was, at least, similar, if not exact.

"It should. We'll have to activate it and find the connection ports." She had already started scanning the wall for them.

"Good. Get on it, Lieutenant. How long do you need?" the Commander asked.

"Don't know. No one's done this before. Once I get it hooked up, it might be a minute, might be hours. The AID has a DNA memory core, it can pretty much store all human knowledge about a hundred times over. So, who knows?" she shrugged.

"Great." It wasn't sarcasm from the Commander as much as it was a statement of disappointment. "Gunny, let's get on the secondary objective, and since we don't know how long we have, we'll have to double time it."

"Roger that, Commander. Fireteam Two, guard the Lieutenant while she completes the operation. Fireteam One, we're moving out. Double time it, tender foots!"

Jax's eyes went wide as she watched Fireteam One file away.

"Something wrong, Jax?" Chambers asked.

"I didn't realize we had secondary objectives."

"Of course we have secondary objectives. You don't think they sent the Commander along to plug in a toaster?"

Her mouth started to gap, but she was sure she stopped it in time. *Of course they don't need the Commander to plug in a toaster. Well, I did think that, but I'm not going to admit it now.* "Any idea what that objective is?"

"Sorry, above my pay grade." He shook his head as he scanned their surroundings.

"Right." *You, Jax, are just a Lieutenant, not the Captain, you are not in the line of command. Above my pay grade too, I guess. Stay focused on your job. Work the plan you know.* She turned back to the bubble. *I really need to get back to being a Captain.*

After a few minutes of silence, Chambers' voice rang out again. "Rallic, you stay and watch Jax's back," he commanded. "Nelson and I will scout around and make sure any nearby portals are secure."

"Roger that." Rallic knuckled a lazy salute.

Chambers and Nelson jogged off. Jax turned her attention to the console. If the plans she had were accurate, there should be three small holes that, when pressed, would activate the interface. A little searching. A small press. The console came to life. Lights following the intricate weave patterns, and a disc-shaped holoscreen appeared. The screen split and moved off to the left and right of Jax's vision. Lines and pictograms danced across the screens. She didn't care about that; she needed a connection.

With the schematics floating in front of her, she began to probe the console. A spark caught her eye. After a little study, she found a spot that was more cable than woven metal and she was able to pack it aside. Three connectors stared up at her. She smiled until she checked a little closer. None of the connections matched what she had built into the AID. She tried all three anyways. Failure.

"Something wrong, Lieutenant?" She felt Rallic's hand on her back as he peered over her shoulder.

She waved her hand, brushing his off. "The connections don't match. I'll need to figure out how this is going to work." She pulled pliers and a laser torch out of her tool kit. *Maybe I can re-tool the end point?*

Rallic droned on behind her. "You know you should really treat those native to Gaia a little nicer. We're the ones out here risking our lives to keep the soft Earthers safe."

"I know that, Rallic. I really need to focus on this."

"Yeah, yeah. It's just that you should never have attacked Commander Moro the way you did. I've been wanting to talk to you about this. His weapons skills have kept us safe and killed more of the birdies than anyone on the Ares. You need to respect that."

The pliers slipped off the AID connections, bending the inner prongs to a funny angle. She clenched her teeth. "Okay, Rallic, I get it. I'll tell you what, when we get back, we can sit down over coffee or whatever and you can convince me all you want. But right now, I really need to focus."

"Sure. Sure. I'll just be here watching your back like we Gaiaians always do for the Earthers."

"That's great. Thanks." *Maybe I can pull that prong and reshape it? Weld it back in.* She leaned in closer to the console, eyes squinting at the shapes she saw. *Careful not to break it, steady hand. I wish someone could stop that humming sound.*

The comms beeped and Chambers' voice filled her ears. "First door was clear, but second one goes on a way, looks like it opens up. Going in to check it out. You still good?"

"Just trying to reconfigure the connections, need to focus."

"I got us covered, Chambers; we don't need you babysitting."

"Babysitting PFCs is what Corporals are for, Rallic. Don't forget it."

"Yeah, yeah."

Jax shook her head. She was never going to figure the Corps out. They watch each other's backs but argue like enemies. *Come on, no time for that now, what do I do with this connection? Maybe I can make a bridge somehow?*

"You need some help there, Lieutenant?"

"No, I don't, unless you're an engineer?"

"From what I've seen, it doesn't take much to be one. Maybe I should try."

"How about you let me do my job and you do yours?" She rolled her eyes, thankful that she didn't need to look at him.

"Just trying to help. You could be nicer about it." Rallic droned on, his words becoming more of a jumble.

114

"Right." She waved him off again. *Where was I? Oh, that's right, a bridge. Do I have anything that might work?* She poured through her tool kit looking for inspiration.

There was a beep on her HUD and a small screen appeared. *Great. Another interruption.* Commander Lewis's voice had an uncharacteristic quiver to it. "Everyone needs to see this."

She eyed the screen and it expanded around her. She now stood where the Commander stood, saw what the Commander could see. Jax's head pulled back for a second as she adjusted. She gasped. The Commander was panning her head. They were in a room that looked a lot like the warehouse, yet this one was triple the size. It was also occupied.

They sat, or rather, perched, everywhere, their feet clinging to the woven patterns like birds on a wire. Crouched down, knees to chest, arms wrapped around themselves like wings and with their heads nestled under their armpits, they would twitch, shake, stretch, and resettle at irregular intervals. There were thousands, maybe even tens of thousands, of them, packed in side by side, row by row, level by level. Whoever called this place the Nest didn't realize how right they were.

The hum that they had noticed before was emanating from them. It was clear now, more like a cooing sound, an orchestra of Screech sounding off together. She stood frozen even though the Commander continued to move.

"We are getting out of here. Lieutenant Brandt, finish up, we're coming back to you. Be ready to run."

"Roger that." Jax's response was little more than a whisper.

"Commander, something is happening over here." The Gunny's voice did not sound happy. She disconnected from Commander Lewis before she heard the rest. Need to hurry, need to get connected.

"We're all going to die."

"No, Rallic, we are not. Make sure Nelson and Chambers get back while I finish this."

"Right, I'll get on that." She felt Rallic slap her on the back again.

Why does he keep doing that? Annoying. Stay focused. Nothing in my tools to bridge it with. If the plugs weren't there, I could weld the wires. That's it!

I need a way to get the socket out. I need... Her hand dropped to her waist and squeezed, her fingers wrapping easily around the handle. Unsheathing the knife, she brought it up in front of her face. *You always need a knife. How about that?*

She jammed its tip into the console beside the top socket. Working it back and forth, it quickly came loose. Keeping the knife in her right hand, she grabbed the socket with her left and yanked. The wire came flying out, ripping a fissure deep up the wall. *Oops, forgot about the enhanced strength. Hope I didn't disconnect anything inside the wall.*

She laid the freed socket on the ground. She hacked at it with the knife, once, twice, three times, until the severed socket fell away, exposing the wires within. Grabbing the AID's wand, she worked that the same way.

Sheathing the knife, she grabbed both ends and eyed them. *Looks like the same kind of wire to me. This had better work. Everyone will be back soon. Faster. Faster.* Laser torch in hand, she butted the ends together and soldered a connection. *Please work. Please work. Please work.*

Fingering her wrist control screen, the AID came to life. A small holo clock popped up, showing it working. *Come on, go faster. We need to get out of here, where is everyone?* Her eyes stayed glued to her work. Within seconds, it had changed to an arrow pointing down, a green light cycling through it.

"Are you going to work or not?" It switched to a red circle with a green pie piece starting a rotation to fill it up. *Yes!* "Rallic, I got it. Is everyone almost back? Rallic? Rallic?" Her head swiveled frantically. *Where did he go?* Tapping her controls, she worked to open the comms channel. Bright red letters flashed across her HUD:

UNABLE TO CONNECT

She tried again. Same response.

She glanced at the loading circle. 21% and moving. *Come on, go faster. What is wrong with these comms? And where did Rallic go?* She flicked her eyes and started a suit diagnostic check. A small image of her armor appeared on her HUD, swiveling and zooming in on a small red spot behind her neck.

Her left hand reached back and pulled. A small disc lurched free. She exhaled sharply, her eyes going wide. Rallic. Like something was reading her mind, a vid screen appeared before her. It showed her Rallic's angular face, the dark stubble shadowing his jaw. His eyebrows furrowed as he began speaking.

"Hi, Jax." He spit her name from his mouth like a cuss word. "If you're seeing this, I guess you found my little surprise before the birdies got to you. Good. I want you to know. I'm not dying for you Earthers. You especially. I've seen enough friends, good Gaiaian friends, die for Earth."

"Rallic!"

"Coming from Earth and thinking you can lead us? We've bled for your soft bodies. Commander Moro has bled for you. You attack him, you spit on us. Well, no more. All you Earthers can die for what I care. You'll die alone when the birdies come for you, I made sure of that. Shame about Chambers. He's a native too, but he likes you Earthers a little too much, I think. Maybe I'll make up some good, heroic story about his death. The rest of you can rot. Bang bang." He made little gun fingers at the screen and then it was gone.

Her eyes narrowed at the point where the screen disappeared. *How could someone do that? He left us all here to die. When I get my hands on him...* She growled.

First things first, though. I need to get going. Find the others. She glanced at the loading icon. 82%. *Come on, hurry, before things get worse.*

Then she saw it. It had more of a hop than a walk. It stopped, hunched over and balanced high on its feet. Its full, blue-grey body suit, which ended at the forearms and the calves, looked just like the holo she had seen when she first arrived on the Ares. Three long claws and thumb-like appendages graced the ends of its limbs. Its face was almost human, except for the beak that looked smashed against its head, and its large disc-like eyes. Those eyes were set too far to the side of its head to be anything human

Don't move. Stay close to the wall. Her eyes glanced at the loading icon again. 92%. *Almost there. Don't notice me.*

Its head spun like a lighthouse scanning the coast. Its body, which was disproportionately wide, was oddly still. She was holding her breath. The head stopped. Her right thumb started twitching. The pupil of its left eye narrowed in on her. She tilted her head. The Screech yelled. Jax yelled right along with it.

The room exploded with sound. Thumbing her controls, the NEW24 sprang to life, firing as it came to bear.

The Screech's loud shrill was unending as it sprang into motion. Balls of energy left her gun and went flying past the creature. The single Screech burst forward, circled back, and returned down the path from which it had approached. A few shots hit the wall before she realized it was gone.

She checked the load screen one more time. 98%. She could still hear the shrilling noise, that distinctive screech sound that gave them their name. Thankfully, it was moving away, the sound echoing and fading.

Then it was getting closer again.

Then it was multiplying.

Louder.

Louder.

"Oh. That's not good."

Chapter 14

Gun

She glanced from the load screen to the entryway. It seemed stuck at 99%. She extended the NEW24's stock, eyes continuing to dart up and down again. The noise grew in her ears. Her heart was keeping a beat that felt as if it would rupture her chest.

"Come on." *If I see something, I'm running, 100% or not.* Check the screen. Check the noise. 99%. Back and forth, back and forth. Noise. Screen. 100%. She released the gun, energy straps swinging it around. Grabbing the fused wire connection, she pulled. The armor's enhanced strength tore the cords apart.

A wave of Screech flowed into the room.

Jax's gun was back up as she pushed off. Her mind didn't even register that she had squeezed the trigger. Three energy blasts erupted into the horde. Again. Again.

The Screech moved with eerie precision. Some were on the walls, their claws digging into the grooves. Those on the ground turned, parted, and came back together like a well-orchestrated show. Her shots were wild, and the creatures would scatter and reform, avoiding them easily.

Small flames of blue and green energy flew her way. *Where is that coming from?* She noticed that some of them had small, curved sticks in their hands. The sticks would flash, and the energy would blast her way. As they ran and openings became clear, they would raise and fire. Their precise run now included a deadly array of fireworks.

119

Her HUD showed around twenty Screech, but the number kept fluctuating. Their fast movement combined with near identical appearance made exact counts hard even for the suit's AI.

She had angled towards the door her squad had entered by. Too late, she realized it was now closed. *Had they done that or had Rallic? No time for that. Focus. You need a plan.*

Fire! Run! Fire! Run! It was all she had as she made her way down the cavern. The far side of the room was closing in. Shots burst around her. The Screech's formation was interrupted but never stopped. They parted, moved, circled back, came together, and fired deadly shots all as one.

She dove behind one of the mushroom-like structures. Shots missed her head and peppered where her feet had been.

She was out of room. What had once been the far wall now stared at her from only a few meters away.

"Can anyone hear me?" Her shout into the comms was met with silence. The Screech came. Louder. Seconds now till it was over. She was out of running room and she was out of options.

Screw it.

Her hand flipped the controls on the NEW24 from three shots to beam. She came out from hiding, the energy beam already lancing forth from the barrel of her gun. The Screech in front of her had not time to react; the red beam cut them down.

She hit five or six of them, she didn't know exactly how many. The rest scattered. Holes appeared in their ranks. *Oh, I like the beam setting. Not now. Run!* She drove forward, her head scanning left and right as she made the opening. She should have looked up.

A single Screech had swooped down from the wall and landed on her back. They tumbled forward. Jax tucked and twisted, trying to control the roll. The alien's claws held fast, scratching, slashing, trying to work their way into the seams of her armor. There was no room to bring the weapon to bear, but she tried anyways. The creature caught it and tore it from her grasp. The energy strap popped as the gun went hurtling away.

Their tumbling stopped. The Screech was on top of her. While her armor protected her, her instincts took over. Her hands shot up to shield her face. The creature's claws rained down slash after slash. She bridged her hips; the Screech planted its hands to stop itself from being thrown. She grabbed hold of its arm, bridging her hips again and rolling.

The creature's free hand continued to claw at her relentlessly. Its feet were also digging into her armor. She released the arm and smashed her Klick-Klick enhanced palm into its chest. Her other hand crushed into its leg and pried it away. Creating an opening, she slid her legs through and mounted the flailing beast. It kicked and squirmed but her base was too strong.

This was taking too long. She glanced around. The other Screech were starting to reform after her surprise beam attack. She tried punching the creature, bringing all her enhanced armor strength to bear. She missed. Her hand smashed into the ground, leaving large a dent in the finely woven floor.

Its frantic twisting and turning almost threw her off. She pushed her legs back and entangled its legs, limiting its movement, pinning it to the ground. She reached for her gun, but the gun was gone. She grabbed the knife. She angled the twenty-two centimeters of metal under the creature's jaw and pushed the knife deep into its head.

No time to think about what she had done. She rolled off the now silent beast and came to her feet. *The rest of the flock—was it called a flock?— no, that didn't seem right. It was a murder of crows. No, that didn't work either; this was more terrifying. That's it, a terror.* The terror had reformed and were moving again.

Run. I hate running. But where? I'm trapped in this cavern. Where can I go? I know where there is an opening. This is crazy. She angled to where the Screech had entered the room. *I need to find cover and find the team.*

121

More of the birdies dove from the walls. This time she was aware. Dodged when she could, dived and rolled if she had to. She zigzagged her way across the room again.

She made the door. Closed. "No." She punched it with her left hand, hoping beyond hope to break through. A loud thunk was the only response. She turned round, the knife in her right hand her only reassurance.

I need to get back to my gun. Where is it? Back on the far side of the room somewhere. I lost it and I let it slide away. I was near the wall when it was ripped free. Next time, hold onto your gun. If there is a next time.

She turned and looked out over the heads of the Screech. Twelve more encircled her. Only a couple of them had the stick guns. They raised to fire, while the other Screech danced around.

There was no plan. She launched herself at the closest stick gunner. "Noooo!" The Klick-Klick armor, amplifying, translating the roar that burst from her lungs. Clicks and screeches echoed in the hall.

Both she and the gunner slammed into the ground. The death grip on her knife held true as she pulled it from its chest.

"Come on!" The clicks rang out, the Screech answered. *I need to get back to my gun.* They circled her, answering her scream for scream. "Come and get me already!" A creature swooped in, her scanning eyes catching it just in time.

She caught it over her shoulder before its claws could lock in. Jax pushed the enhanced strength to its limits. Commander Lewis would never give her points for the throw, but the results were satisfying. The creature flew, hammering into a group of three. The crunching of bones when it hit added to the volume of noise.

Another opening appeared and she rushed for it. She tracked and circled. They darted in and she slashed out. The last stick gun circled outside, waiting for openings. *They won't fire on their own, that's good to know.* The stick fired. *Don't think about it, use it.* She dove on top of two of the birds. *Get in close. Don't tie up. Hit. Trip. Move. Can't keep this up.* She broke free, found herself standing alone.

Move your head! A shot clipped her left shoulder. She spun round, and her HUD exploded with warnings. She fell behind a column. The medical nanites went to work, but her bio display showed only minor damage. *At least the armor is doing its job. I really need that gun.* Jax pressed her back against the structure. *Come on, give me a break, where is it?*

Then a twinkle caught her eye.

The gun. Just a glint at the edge of her vision. *That must be it. Have I come that far? Who cares? Get to it now.*

She bolted. A creature stepped in front of her. Dropping her shoulder, she barreled through, sending it reeling back. They flanked her, left, right, and above. Even pushing the armor, she was barely keeping her distance. *Faster. Focus. Dive.*

The rough floor scratched her armor as she slid across it, the sound it made was like a death cry rising into the air. Her hand reached out and found the handle. *I'm never letting this go again.* She came up firing, but they were upon her.

Three tackled her as she swung the beam around. She squeezed harder and the beam continued to lash out. She tussled and fired and stabbed. If one was cut away, it was replaced by another. They were no longer content with pecking at her, there was no more swooping in to take shots; they swarmed her, claws scratching, beaks biting, tearing, grabbing. Chunks of armor, her shoulder, part of her helm, they were all torn away.

Her knife hand underhooked one birdie and brought it down over her shoulder, smashed it to the ground. When she turned the gun, the lethal beam cutting through the torsos of two more. She dropped to one knee, her breathing labored, her HUD showing multiple points of damage. Her eyes swept the room in front of her. She couldn't see anything, but her HUD registered one more. She wanted to relax, to give into the exhaustion. *Where is it? Check your six.* She turned. The creature with the stick gun was hunting her from a distance.

Her body was exhausted; it was never going to move in time, even with the help of the medical nanites. She had just enough energy to pull the trigger. She couldn't wait to get sights; the crimson beam ignited and slashed a path through the floor. The creature was already firing.

The blast hit her in the chest. She was flying back as alarms blanketed her HUD. Her trigger finger held tight as she crashed to the floor. The creature was slashed from toe to head, never to rise again.

Her ears were overtaken by the sound of her own screams. The fire in her chest echoed out to her whole body. Her HUD showed the medical AI kicking in. *I guess that was enough pain to warrant some help.*

"That better be the last one because I'm not sure I can get up." The clicks echoed out into the cavern as the armor translated and amplified her speech. The only answers were thankfully silence.

I survived. I made it. Maybe I can just rest here for a moment.

No, you can't afford to stop now, time to get up, time to push through. She dragged herself up off the floor. Bodies, dark alien blood, and burn marks littered her surroundings. Her HUD showed that the armor was highly badly damaged. There were deep gashes in her shoulder, on the helmet, and along her arms and legs. Her chest piece was a burned crater with smoke still swirling around it.

I love this armor even if it doesn't look so shiny and bright now. Maybe I'll paint a big red spot in the middle of the next one to remind me of this day. What am I thinking? I'm staying away from ground missions from now on.

Her injuries all registered as minor now. The medical nanites were doing their job; her chest still throbbed, but the pain was fading. *Need to focus on more important things. What to do now? Where's my entrance? Need to find the others, find a way out of here.*

She stumbled for the wall, the gun and the knife clasped firmly in her hands. *Always have a knife. I love this gun. Never dropping it again. Never.*

Her steps dragged as she made her way down the wall. She sheathed the knife and placed the stock of the gun deep into her shoulder. She had to grip the weapon with both hands to keep it from shaking.

Stay smooth and scan for targets. Check your six and check above. It was like a checklist that rolled constantly through her head. She pushed her way along. Nothing looked familiar, the face of the cavern transformed by the damage she had done. *I can't believe I caused all this.*

Leaning against the wall, she took a moment to orientate herself. *I'm on the far side of the room. This should be where the Commander and her team went. Up ahead, somewhere, is where Chambers and Nelson should be. How do I find them?*

Heat and light burst into her eyes, a thunderous pounding that caused her to step back as debris exploded into the room. Smoke drifted from the new opening only meters away.

The noise of the Screech once again filled her ears.

CHAPTER 15
SALLY

Debris flew into the room. The smoke hung heavily in the air. Chambers backed through the newly created opening, closely followed by Nelson. Chambers' gun was firing a nonstop burst of energy, and Nelson's Meg42 was whirling to match.

Their armor was caked with dust and stark, oily residue. Cuts and bruises littered both men. Momentarily, she considered turning off the VR overlay to get a better view of the damage, but before she could decide, a green light appeared in front of her.

Short Range Comms Activated. Connected to Fireteam Two.

Rallic either missed the short-range comms, or thought we'd never get close enough again to use them. She opened the channel and called out, "Chambers! Nelson!"

"Jax! You okay? We lost comms, everything locked down and then all the birdies went wild," Chambers said.

"I think it was Rallic. He left us all to die." She ran up beside them, the beam from her NEW24 adding to their assault.

"What? You sure?" Chambers never stopped firing. Every burst found its mark.

"Positive. He left me a message. Hates me. Earthers. Then he was gone."

They held the opening for a moment, but no matter how much they fired, the Screech advanced. Each time they fired, they gave way, and step by step they were pushed back.

126

"I'll kill that fripping hack," Nelson bellowed. Shots from the stick guns flashed around him. Chambers and Nelson targeted them with lethal efficiency.

As the enemy advanced, their numbers seemed to be growing, not shrinking. The trio that was Fireteam Two continued to lose ground.

"Head toward our entrance point," Chambers barked as he danced sideways to avoid the blasts from creatures' stick guns. Nelson swept the area with the whirl of his MEG42 and the creatures fell.

"The portal is closed," the Lieutenant shouted back.

"Don't worry." Chambers patted his belt pouch. "I've got the key."

They continued their retreat. Now that the fireteam was fully clear of the opening, the birdies were free to fly through it. They flowed through the portal like a wave hitting the beach. Scrambling up the walls, spreading left and right, they continued to swarm.

"Fire in the hole," Nelson said, smiling as a large tube swung up on his shoulder. Releasing the MEG42, it's gantry arm automatically swung to his hip. His hands gripped the tube. They heard a small pop.

The opening occupied by the Screech lit up like a noonday sun. The shock wave staggered the trio, sending Jax to her knees.

"That will wake you up," Nelson smiled, his face giddy like a child being given a gift.

"Let's get to the exit," Chambers said.

The trio turned to go. They started to jog back towards their original entry point. Halfway to their target, another section of the wall behind them started to unravel. A whipping noise echoed inside the cavern. Fireteam Two turned backwards slowing. The entire wall was exposed, a tube several stories tall lay open before them. The Screech terror counted in the hundreds, maybe the thousands. At the head of the terror horde was something different; five armored Screech led the way.

While the normal Screech would hop or run with long strides these five were walking with their heads held up high.

Their helmets rose up like feathered crests. The mirrored faceplates swept out with a menacing beak. The armor's metallic gloss shone bright with reds, blues, and golds. Each piece of the arms, legs, and torso were engraved with feathers that had sharp edges. The Screeches' normal aesthetics didn't apply here.

The other Screech gave them a wide berth, moving in and around them, but never getting too close. Each of the five carried longer, thicker versions of the stick guns, possibly their version of a rifle. *They're like us, the soldiers, the other Screech are just what? Support? Drones? We are in trouble.*

The lead Screech moved with a flash. He locked on her, his shrill cry amplified as he lifted and fired his rifle.

"Jax!" Chambers moved, his instincts and reflexes exploding. He tackled and turned himself into her. The concussion, fire, and light, rippled down his back. Jax and Chambers were sent spinning, flying to the ground.

"No!" Nelson was spraying fire as he back peddled to them.

"Come on, get up! Be alive!" He positioned himself over them, between them and the enemy.

Jax groaned. "I'm okay. Chambers, how are you?" She rolled up to her knees and looked down on him. "Oh no."

The Corporal was face down, the back of his armor flared at the hip like an erupting volcano. She patched into the suit's biometrics, his vital signs popping in front of her. Red glowed everywhere, radiating outward from the impact. Hip shattered, upper leg broken, ribs broken. Cuts, gashes, and shrapnel all littered his skin.

"Chambers!" His life signs were barely registering. She grabbed him, trying to get a better look at his face. He rumbled a groan that gave her hope.

"Nelson, he's alive. Hurt pretty badly, though."

"Help him up. We need to move." He swung his Meg42 to its stand-by position as he pulled another weapon from his side.

128

"I'm not sure I should move him; it might hurt him more."

"It will kill him if you don't. We're not lasting long here."

She looked up from the Corporal. The room was shredded by the Meg42, torn alien bodies adding to the chaos. More and more Screech advanced. The armored Screech moved with less fervor than their smaller, unprotected counterparts. Still they hung back, possibly wary of Nelson's onslaught. Each move they made was precisely calculated to keep them out of his firing path. The little birdies were acting as their shields.

"Get him up and move!"

The multiple tubes on his new weapon began to rotate.

Throom. Throom. Throom.

It sounded over and over again as the chamber began to rock with explosions.

The Lieutenant hoisted the Corporal up, her enhanced strength making it easy. He roared in pain as she cupped her hands around his waist.

"Pain means you're alive, right, Corporal?" She tried to sound confident, but she knew she was missing the mark. *Keep him focused and keep yourself moving.*

"Yeah… good… pain." His feet were moving like he was walking, but she was carrying him along.

"Nelson, come on. We're heading for the door." She couldn't spare a look. *Must keep moving.*

"I'm right behind you. Me and Sally are just going to keep our friends here busy for a moment."

Nelson sounded almost giddy as the throoming noise stopped and the whirl of Sally kicked in. She pushed them to make it to the door. Chambers continued to moan. Her HUD showed the painkillers flooding his system, but it just wasn't fast enough. Her heart sank at the realization that the portal before her was still closed.

"Nelson, its closed." Desperation crept into her voice.

"A little busy here. Chambers has the key." The sound of Screech and gun fire almost drowned out his response.

"Key." The Corporal squeaked out a response as he held up a sphere with a deep groove down the middle. She missed the word amongst the uproar around her but caught the meaning clear enough.

"Big… boom… clear…" He tilted his head and actually grinned at her. *I guess the painkillers are working.* Her HUD showed it as a frag grenade. She found the firing stud and ignored the rest of the technical input that scrolled past her eyes.

She pulled her arm back and threw. The armor's enhanced strength accelerated it like a rocket. A red light in the groove began to flow around the fist-sized ball. *Clear. Get clear. Move, Jax, move.* She grabbed the Corporal and pulled him around the nearest pillar. There was a flash, a piercing bang, and debris went flying.

She peered around. A rough opening had become visible among the settling dust and smoke.

"Let's go, Corporal." She lifted him from the pillar and hustled them both through the opening. He was groaning less now. His head was dropping and bopping as they went. On the other side, she went far enough to find a clear patch of floor to lie the Corporal down on.

"Rest here, I need to get Nelson." His hand raised as if to grab her, but it was too slow.

Back at the hole, she opened the comms and called out, "Nelson! Let's go." Sound crackled in her ear, a mix of shouts, and was that singing? Something about riding Sally? Horses? "Nelson!" she shouted again.

"Jax… Nelson… not coming," Chambers squeaked out.

"What? No. Nelson get over here!" She could feel her tension raising as she gripped the wall, wanting to run after him.

The comms crackled. "All I want…" Crackle. "…ride along…" Crackle. "…Sally…" Then there were screams and the cry of the Screech as the comms went silent.

"Nelson?" Her throat felt like it had been punched.

"Gave... us time... Need... to go."

She wanted to wait, to run in and save him, but she knew it was hopeless. She hurried back to the injured Corporal and squatted beside him. His breathing was rough, and he had one hand on his chest.

With his other hand, he was holding up another sphere. "We need... to close... pass..."

Jax grabbed the ball, her HUD automatically showing it as a Nova grenade. *Right, they'll be coming, close the hole.* She jogged back to the opening. She heard the creatures before she saw them. She backed away while flipping the arming button. Her throw was straight and true. As the orb passed the gateway, it burst bright white, and then shifted blue as it began to expand.

"Oh crap." She turned to run. The walls around the opening were melting and warping in. She didn't know what the walls were made of. In the end, it didn't matter.

She made it back to the Corporal, ready to grab him and run. A look over her shoulder showed her that the expansion had stopped and reversed faster than it had grown. What had once been a portal was now molten slag.

She took a knee. His breathing was deep and labored. When she checked his biometrics, it showed the painkillers in full effect. Medical nanites were working on the small cuts, bruises, and torn muscles. The broken hip and other bones would need more attention. For now, the parts of his armor that were still working had tightened up, working as a makeshift cast.

"Stay with me, Chambers."

"Hard... to breathe... Helmet..." he gasped.

She checked his armor status. A warning blossomed out from his hip impact, red marks pulsing as if they were angry. The repair nanites were trying to fix it, but the damage was too expansive. A red slash around the helmet showed a problem with the respiratory system. *No wonder he's having trouble.*

"Hold on." She reached in and released the helmet latches. Carefully, she pulled it from his head. His face contorted as he took a large breath.

"Is that better?"

"All I hear is click-click-click." He pointed at her helmet.

Oh, right. She placed his helmet down and removed her own. Her whole face pinched as she took her first breath. The thought of rotten eggs and spoiled milk clawed its way into her mind.

"This air is disgusting." She scraped her tongue with her teeth.

Chambers was laughing at her. "At least you know you're alive. You could have just turned off the translator."

"Now you tell me. How are you doing?"

"Been better. We safe?"

"For the moment. That Nova grenade did the trick. You have any more of those?"

"Nope, all out. Used most of them to get back to you."

"Great. So now what?"

"We should try and head out before the Screech find a way to us."

"What about the Commander? Fireteam One?"

"They'll be doing the same. We don't have the capabilities to search for them."

She nodded as she stood, grabbing her helmet and securing it to her hip. "I guess I'll need to carry you some more?"

He shrugged as he tried to flash her a grin. She underhooked his arm and brought him up.

"I thought you were supposed to protect me?" She situated a hand around his waist, careful to avoid his injury, while he grabbed her around the shoulders. The powered armor lifted him easily.

"I think I'm doing an excellent job of protecting you," he said on heavy breath.

She squinted one eye at him. "How do you figure that?"

"Are you injured?"

"Not really."

"See, perfect job."

She couldn't help but laugh and shake her head as they made their way down the hall.

Chapter 16

Exit

"Going to toss him on his head over and over and over," she grumbled as they stumbled along. It had only taken a few moments into their journey to realize Rallic had disabled all the markers. They were lost in the twisty corridors.

"That really sounds like it's going to hurt." Chambers' voice was raspy, but it was better than it had been.

"Still not good enough. Not even close." She had joined the Ares to fight the monsters. *I never thought the monsters would be human. Bad enough when it was the Screech. Why had Rallic done this? Was it all about what she had done to Moro? Gaia versus Earth? When the Commander told me I had stepped into the middle of something, I never thought it could be this drastic. It doesn't matter, once I find him, I'll show him drastic.*

They walked the corridor as it in fed into another tube. This tube was angling up and down, the intertwining of color and twisting of the walls gave no indication of which way to go. They rested their, bodies tired, their eyes sore from scanning for any clue to direct them onward. The silence was broken only by their own labored breathing.

Now which way do we go? Coming into the Nest, their path had seemed so straight forward. Leaving was like navigating a labyrinth. *Round and round we go.*

"Wait. Do you hear that?" She turned her head.

"Hear what?" Chambers lifted his chin off his chest to listen more closely. The painkillers were working, but he was going in and out. Awake for one moment and then exhaustion would take over. Even with the power armor, she had to be careful he didn't slip from her hands.

"Popping sounds." She strained to hear. She wanted to put her helmet back on; it's enhanced senses would help. To do that she would have to set the Corporal down, which just didn't seem like the right idea. *We need to keep moving, stay mobile.*

"There it is again." She tilted her head.

"Yeah, I heard it that time. There's a whistling sound. I think that's a Meg. It has to be Fireteam One."

"Right, let's go." They hurried up the tube, towards the discord. Not really a run, but Jax willed them on as fast as they could go.

As they ascended, the tube curved to the right. The noise of a firefight became more and more clear. The tube flattened out and ran straight. Twenty meters down stood Fireteam One, their backs to the Lieutenant and Corporal.

Saville was out front, his Meg42 singing as it hurdled lead down the corridor. The Commander, Gunny, and Thirgood added to the barrage, bursts of red light spraying out like never-ending fireworks. They had lost their helmets, their hair was matted with sweat. Their armor was torn and shredded, splattered with human and alien blood. The Gunny was firing one handed, his left arm clasped close to his side. That arm was completely bare, deep gashes running from his shoulder down past his elbows.

Past them advanced the Screech. They filled the tube. Moving in their strange dance, crisscrossing, some would fall, but more would take their place; they were always advancing.

"Commander!" Jax's beam shot over the XO's position. She didn't have to aim; there was no way to miss.

The Commander did a double take over her shoulder. "Jax. Chambers. About time you got here. Where's the rest of your team?"

"Nelson didn't make it, and Rallic—" She was interrupted. The Screech pushed forward as the two wayward fireteams formed up. The volume of noise rose with their advance.

"Fire in the hole!" Saville's call was barely audible above the noise. He launched a small globe from his hand. The now reunited squad retreated with haste.

The tunnel rocked with the explosion. The squad staggered as they backed away. Alien bodies were shredded and thrown from the epicenter of the grenade blast. The few live creatures that were thrown toward the ground team, were sliced down, energy weapons flaring. The rest of the bird-like creatures fled, retreating from the blast.

The commander turned, placing a hand on Jax's shoulder, sweat dripping down her dark face. She spoke quickly. "That will only give us a moment. Jax, how are you? Chambers looks like crap. Where's the rest of your team?"

Before she could answer, Saville called out, "Only got one grenade left and it's a nova. Meg's almost out too."

"I got one concussion grenade left. Weapons check, everyone; they'll be back soon," the Gunny replied, his voice strong despite his injuries.

Jax gulped, finding her voice. "Nelson is gone, he covered our escape. And Rallic." She stifled a growl. "Rallic, he did this to us, he left us, cut us off from each other."

Rage burned in the Commander's eyes, but it was Thirgood who lashed out first. "That little frip! I'll kill him. No wonder he kept so close when we were planting markers. Thought he was just being creepy. He must have masked the signal, no wonder we couldn't find our way out."

The Commander talked through clenched teeth. "Can you fix it?"

"Yeah, now that I know what's going on. Only a couple ways to do that kind of thing. Give me a moment." Thirgood let her NEW28 swing to stand by as she brought a holoscreen up on her wrist.

"We only have a moment. They'll be ready anytime now," Saville yelled back as he trotted forward to scout the hall.

The Gunny came up to her. "Let me help the Corporal, together our battered bodies can make a whole Terrainwalker," the Gunny said, smiling. He took the Corporal and shared a shoulder with him. The front of his injured arm was just as mangled as the back. For the first time, she noticed he had strapped a small ax to the injured limb. It was dark and covered with an oily substance that dripped as he moved. *That is one hard man; he fights on no matter what.*

"Thought I trained you better than this, Corporal?"

"Sorry, Gunny. Guess I still have more to learn."

They were smiling at each other. The Lieutenant could only shake her head.

"I've got our path," Thirgood said. "But, Commander, we've got another problem. Rallic has already called for pick up. The Reckless is incoming."

"How soon?"

"Don't know. They're meeting resistance up there. Ares is involved and they have launched fighters, they're working on clearing a path. And I can only see incoming data, outgoing is still blocked."

"We have to go! Here they come!" Saville's Meg42 started to whirl up.

"Damn. First, let's get out of here. Which way, Private?" The Commander glanced down the tube, then back at Thirgood. She had her arm stretched straight, pointing to where the Screech were beginning to advance once again.

"About twenty meters up, there is a 'Y' we missed that will circle down and out," Thirgood said above the noise of Saville's Meg, followed closely by sounds of NEW24s spitting light.

"Double damn. Gunny, we need to get twenty meters into the enemy line."

"Roger that, Commander. Everyone form-up behind Saville. Guns free. We push one step at a time. Move it, people."

The Screech danced down on them again. Saville was pushing forward as if to dare them all by himself. The rest of the squad advanced, firing around him. Thirgood, with her NEW28, screamed as she fired. The Corporal and Gunny were leaning on each other's shoulders. Their weapons sang from their free hands. The Commander fired off shot after shot and Jax swept her beam at anything that moved.

The tunnel filled with burnt flesh and alien blood. Slowly, they gave way to the squad's onslaught. With each round, they pushed forward. Each heavy step grained them ground.

"There it is." Thirgood waved her hand.

As one, they began to angle to the opening. The whirling sound of the Meg squealed and stopped.

"I'm out." In one fluid movement, Saville shed the large gun and backpack. His own NEW24 swung up to start firing with no interruption. Any other weapons he had, like Nelson, were long since used and gone.

"Jax, check the tunnel," the Gunny said.

She ran. It was smaller than the current one. They would have to move in twos. Jax hurried down and scanned it the best she could. Keeping an eye on her back, she ran down and made the call.

"I think we're clear!" With her call to the team, the return fire started. The green and blue of the creatures stick guns filled the corridor.

"Hit the deck!" cried the Commander.

The squad slammed themselves to the ground and to the walls. Everyone except Saville. He stood like a wall before the assault, his armor absorbing the blows. Shots hurtled off his shoulders, his legs, and they drove into his chest. Yet, he stood.

The squad had been targeting any alien with a gun, but the loss of the Meg42 had cut back their efficiency. The aliens adapted to the new weakness and exploited it. The creatures, now reinforced with more stick guns, advanced in force.

"Get down the hallway! Move! Move! Move!" The Gunny was dragging the Corporal, firing his gun while his gravelly voice served to push everyone else like a physical force. They ducked their heads and ran.

Jax pushed herself to the side of the hall, trying her best to shoot around and over the squad as they retreated past her. But it was Saville who held the line. Stopped in the middle of the tunnel, the heavy Corps refused to be moved.

"Saville!" she cried.

Too late, the Screech were upon him. He flung several off, like swatting flies. A shot clipped his leg, shattering the armor, and he fell onto his knee. He fired a few more rounds before they swarmed him. A vicious slash turned his head, blood flying. He was engulfed, by a mass of alien bodies.

"No!" The Lieutenant let loose several more beams. The shots cut all around him. A desperate last attempt. Among the tangle of limbs, she caught a glimpse of Saville's hand and a glowing orb.

"Nova!" She turned and launched herself down the tube. The light passed her as the heat pushed into the back of her head. The air in her lungs was punched out in a primal scream. The others moved past a curve in the hall and out of sight. She hit the wall, twisted, turned, and fell, eventually rolling to a stop.

"You okay, Jax?" The Commander's hand grasped hers and pulled her up.

"Yeah. Falling just lets me know I'm alive." It was her attempt at the kind of humor the Corps used. Her heart wasn't in it. She looked back up the tunnel. Saville was gone.

She didn't really know him, but it was a name to add to the list. A list that was growing way too long. *Daniel Trucker, Jonathan Camp, Thelma Ines, Reason O'Connor, so many more from the Indiana.* Names she didn't know or

139

couldn't remember. And now Nelson and Saville. She didn't even know their first names, just the initials that had been given on her heads-up-display: R and M. *I'll find out. I should know, they gave their lives for me. Names are important, I must remember.*

Her eyes were locked on the passageway, she just couldn't turn away.

"Jax!" The Commander—Gemma Lewis, she told herself—pulled her around.

"Mourn later, take care of the living now. We still have to get out of here. Gunny."

The Gunny nodded. "All right, let's file out. Thirgood and Commander Lewis, you are the lead. Chambers and me next. Jax, you cover the tail. Slow and steady, people, let's get out of this fripping hole."

Two by two by one, they pushed down the hall. Rounding the last curve, it flattened and ran straight. At the end of the hall were six Screech standing guard, each one armed with one of those deadly stick guns.

Thirgood and the Commander were laser focused; they had fired their rifles before the creatures could even aim. Despite their injuries, the Gunny and Corporal followed in smooth succession. Even Jax turned and lashed out, so the Screech were cut down in short order.

"It's not going to open for me," Thirgood said, working controls at her wrist.

"I got my final key." The Gunny held the grenade high. "Everyone get clear."

The Lieutenant shouldered the Corporal and fell back with the rest of the squad.

"Fire in the hole!" the Gunny shouted as he threw it and fell back in one fluid motion. The blast wave passed through them. As the smoke and debris cleared, a sense of relief passed over the battle-worn squad. The outside shone like a beacon through the newly-created hole.

They stepped through the portal and exited the Nest.

Chapter 17

Bang. Bang.

"Thirgood, can you get the Reckless on comms now?" The squad was already moving, a primal need to get some distance driving them on.

"Negative, Commander. Long range comms are still down. I can listen in, but I can't broadcast."

"Damn. How long until they can come in for pickup?"

"Probably not long, sounds like the fighters are almost done clearing the sky." As if to emphasize the point, lines streaked across the sky, loud booms following in their wake.

"Double damn. We need to find Rallic, and hurry."

"I think I know where he went, Commander. Jax, can you check our marker?" Chambers eyed her from the Gunny's shoulder.

"Right." She holstered her weapon on the run and recovered her helmet. Once it was securely on, she used the eye controls and to flip the screens. The homing beacon came to life on her HUD. Success.

"Got it. It's still active. He probably didn't think we'd get this far."

"Jax, turn off the Klick-Klick translator," the Commander said.

Oh, right. She eyed a few more controls. "I said, I got it. I guess he didn't see a need to turn it off."

They made it to the delta staging area where the group had first formed before their assault on the Nest. The night had passed, the sun was just rising over the rocky land. It seemed like so long ago that they all had gathered here.

"What do you think, Gunny?" the Commander said.

"Jax, feed the coordinates to everyone. Rallic doesn't think we're alive, so we have surprise on our side. We double time it to the pick-up zone. We overwhelm the little fripper, alive if we can, but dead is fine by me. Then we get our asses off this rock."

"Nice and straight forward, I like it. Any suggestions?" The Commander made eye contact with each person in the group. They were all of the same mind.

"Good. Form us up, Gunny."

"Roger that, Commander. Thirgood, you're eyes up front. Commander, you follow on, then me and the Corporal. Jax, you're tail gunner. We run a staggered column. The Screech will be coming, so stay sharp. Any questions?"

"No, Gunny," they responded in unison.

"All right then, Corps, let's move out!"

She was several meters into this run before it registered within her mind. The Gunny had said Corps and not tender foots. Something had been forged here, with this small group of people. She would know them, respect them forever. *Gemma Lewis, J. Locklear, T. Thirgood, V. Chambers, R. Nelson, M. Saville.* She would know their names and honor them all. All except for the one name she hadn't listed. *Rallic. One way or another, he would pay for his treachery. He won't be worth remembering.*

As they ran, the purple haze that colored the landscape rose up from the ground. Thirgood raised her hand, bringing the column to a halt.

"What you got, Private?" the Gunny said.

"Markers up ahead. No sign of Rallic, but it sounds like the flyers have cleared the sky."

"Got it. Proceed slowly then. Something's finally breaking our way." He turned back towards Jax. "Any pursuit, Lieutenant?" She turned and activated the optical zoom on her helmet.

"No clear view from here. Need to get a little higher."

"Roger that. Let's move up this ridge, that should give the elevation you need and provide cover till pick up arrives."

Heads shook all around and the squad started a slow jog up the slope. They zigzagged slightly as they made their way up on a natural path. They came to the crest. Thirgood's head exploded.

"Sniper!" The Gunny threw himself and the Corporal behind a rock formation. The Commander dived back down the hill, rolling to a halt over a dirt ridge. Jax was momentarily frozen. Thirgood's body fell. The Lieutenant recovered and threw in beside the Commander.

"Where is he?" the Commander snarled.

With a few blinks, Jax's HUD went to work. A video rolled before her eyes and replayed the gruesome scene. She tried to block it from her feelings. It tracked the shot and gave a telemetry across the short valley.

"Suit shows him on the far ridge, nestled into three splintered rocks."

"Can we get a shot on him?" barked the Commander.

"I see the spot." The Gunny was sneaking a peek and had to duck quickly as a shot passed over his head.

"Negative on hitting him. We can shoot that far, but he has the cover. That bloody sniper rifle of his will hit us before we can get lucky," the Gunny said.

"Can we get back down the hill?" the Commander asked.

"Negative. He could have hit us way before. Waited for the right spot to pin us down. Damn sloppy of me. Sorry, Commander, we're stuck." The Gunny's face contorted with rage.

The Commander growled. She was doing her best to scan the area. "Fine. We hold and let him keep us pinned. The Reckless should be incoming, he won't dare take a shot with them hanging over us." The squad grumbled, shook their heads, and muttered curses under their breath, but with no better options, they were forced to agree.

Except for Jax. The Lieutenant lay next to the Commander, sitting up just enough so she wouldn't break cover. Her iron gaze was focused over on the rocky terrain and rolling hills down toward the Nest. Her suit's telescopic abilities, pushed to their max, showed her the Screech.

An overwhelming number of them poured out of the structure. The rhythmic circular movements from the cavern were lost to the direct approach. It was a stampede and they were coming straight at them.

"Commander, we can't wait; the Screech are coming." Her voice was flat.

"How many? How soon?"

"All of them. Now."

"Fripping damn. Gunny, any of you, we need options."

The silence that followed sent a chill across the squad.

She was the only one with a helmet on. She scanned the area, looking for an opening, a place to cover, anything they could use. The Screech advanced and Rallic was high on his perch waiting for them to peek out.

"I need cover and something loud." *Time for a plan.*

"You got an idea, Jax?" The Commander eyed her.

"Yeah, but no time to explain."

She held up her NEW24 and double checked the beam setting. "I need something that makes a lot of noise and then some cover fire."

"Here." Chambers tossed his shotgun down to her. "Probably the loudest thing we have, but it's short range and you'll only get twelve shots."

"Range won't matter and twelve should be plenty." She sneaked her head up and got a read on Rallic again. "Okay, I'm ready, cover fire on my go."

"Jax, you can't rush Rallic, fighting him one on one would be suicide." The Commander put her hand on Jax's shoulder as if to stay her.

"Don't worry, I'm not rushing to fight Rallic," she said, letting out a deep breath.

The Commander's hand relaxed and she turned to ready her rifle.

"I'm rushing the Screech."

"Oh, well that's good. Wait. What?"

"Cover fire now!" She launched herself down the ridge before the Commander could voice her objection. To the credit of the squad, none of them missed a beat as they lit up the far ridge with everything they had.

Just give me time to get clear. She let the armor open up and run, crisscrossing her way down, changing angles as much as she could. A shot exploded off a rock next to her. A scream punched itself out of her chest. She danced from side to side to avoid the beams of light that Rallic rained down on her. She dropped below a small crest and the fire stopped.

On her HUD, she brought up the surrounding landscape and laid in the Screech, Rallic, and herself. Then, she overlaid an estimated shooting area for all three. *Thank you, Mr. Trucker.* For now, she ignored Rallic. The Screech's weapons were similar to her own. At least, the little stick guns were. *Who knows what those armored birds have? Don't over think it, just go. This is the plan.*

Her circle slid across the screen and the creatures pushed towards her.

"What're you doing, Jax?" Rallic's face popped into her HUD.

"Go away, Rallic." She dismissed the screen.

The screen came right back on. "Can't get rid of me that easily. Finally realized it's hopeless so you're throwing yourself at the birdies? I can make it faster for you. Quick shot to the head. Bang. Bang."

"The Reckless is coming and they'll see us and anything you try. You're screwed, Rallic."

His laughter was jarring. "They'll see what I want them to see, Earther. I'm in control here. With the signal I'm uploading, you just look like more Screech to them. They might even drop the ordnance that kills you." He laughed again. "You're already dead. You're nothing but bird food."

"Frip you!"

"Temper temper, Eart—" She ripped the long range comm device off her back and sent it flying off to the side.

"I told you to shut up."

She slid to a halt, the two circles in her HUD were almost touching. The little green one that represented her and the much larger red one showing the Screech. She didn't need enhanced optics to see them now. Or hear them. *Oh, there are so many, it is so loud.*

She ignored the numbers on her HUD as it tried to count them. The number just kept going. *Well, that's no help.* She dismissed all the tactical data from her screen. *None of that matters now. I just need me, the Screech, Rallic, and the ground we run on.*

She bolted sideways as the circles met. Blue and green sparks flew past her eyes. The fireworks had come alive and were attacking Jax. *Were any of them unarmed this time?* At least the armored versions are missing or hidden amongst the overwhelming numbers. *Forget it, stay on plan. Time to make some noise.* She eyed her controls, turning on the Klick-Klick translator and her external speakers and pushing the volume to max.

Her NEW24 swung into one hand while she held Chambers' shotgun in the other.

"Screw you, you dirty birds!" The suit let loose with the Klick-Klick language. The sound was still drowned out by the noise of the Screech. She didn't stop, she let loose with every curse, every insult she could imagine. Sometimes, she just screamed.

She ran and unleashed her NEW24. At this range, she would need extreme luck to hit anything. She didn't care and it didn't matter. The red beam slashed at them, curved wide, went over their heads. The creatures pushed on, not slowing a step. Her other hand pulled the shotgun and sent slugs into the air.

She yelled. She beamed. She shot. She ran. *Pay attention to me, you frippen birds.* The creatures started to tighten their shots. More blue and green energy exploding closer and closer. The terror turned toward her. She checked her map and decided it was far enough.

Even if it's not, I need to go before I get roasted. She made her turn away from the Screech. *Now that I have their attention, I need some distance.* She let the armor get into rhythm and hit its full stride. Her legs were sore as the muscles pushed to keep up. She screamed. *Come on, suit, this has to be enough for some painkillers.* The armor continued to go faster but ignored her silent plea.

The two little circles that showed firing distance parted, the little green circle on her HUD drifting away from the large red mass. It was met by a few more blue and green sparks dancing at her heels. She checked the rear-view screen on her HUD. They were still coming, but they knew they were just out of range. *Xenophobic and smart, what a great combination.*

She adjusted her speed to stay just ahead. *Don't lose me, I need the whole terror on me.* She came to the base of Rallic's ridge and started her staggered climb. The Screech dropped out of her rearview as she crested the first ridge and hit a straight run. *They better not lose interest, please keep coming for me.* She saw, from the corner of her eyes, flashes of red shoot towards Rallic. Her squad, her friends, could see her. It must had dawned on them what she was doing, and they wasted no time in helping. The distracting fire continued to rain on Rallic. *Thanks for the cover fire.*

Her short-range comms turned on and Rallic's face popped in again. "Got too scared to throw yourself to the birdies? Decided to let me pop you in the head instead?"

"Bite me, Rallic." He was too focused on her, too sure of his hiding spot. *Good, sit tight, I have a surprise for you.*

"Bite this, you fripping Earther." She cut hard left, almost losing her footing. A shot flew past her head. *Thanks for the warning.*

"You're a troll, a worthless piece of scum, a traitor. I'm more Gaia than you'll ever be." She hit the final climb to his location, a rocky open field. *The Screech will be coming, I have to get moving.*

More shots exploded around her. She dove and rolled, pushing past it. She came up running, never missing a step. Her pace had slowed, and the approaching Screech circle was fast closing. More red shots from her squad exploded ahead of her, pushing Rallick back into his hiding place.

"So, you coming for me then? Want to fight me face to face? I'll rip you apart, you stupid little Earther! I'm Corps trained! You don't stand a chance. Come get some!"

"Oh, I'm coming your way, Rallic, but not to face you. I'm just bringing some friends."

"What the frip are you talking about?"

He said some more but she wasn't listening. She was almost on him. He was so mad he wasn't even firing anymore. Now he was waiting for her, anticipating the moment. He wanted to face her one on one. *Too bad for him.*

She made the plateau. He was standing, meeting her eye to eye. Covered by the rocks, shielded from her squad. She, however, had a straight shot at him. She leaned into her run and angled ever so slightly right. The rock formation she wanted was about four meters high and had a slight incline.

In a few strides, she was up the natural ramp and launching herself with everything the armor had to offer. She was flying.

Rallic's face gasped in shock as Jax began to sail over him. He tried to bring his sniper rifle up and let loose one more attack. She was already twisting in the air keeping her eyes on him. The red flash from the rifle passed over her shoulder. Time seemed to freeze. She continued to fly, her eyes never once leaving Rallic's face. She was falling backwards.

"Hey, Rallic! Birdies are coming to meet you." She shot her arms straight out. Showing him the backs of her hands, splayed out, and pulling the middle finger down.

It was an obscene gesture. She had only done it once as a kid. Her mother had seen her and given her a tongue lashing so severe she had never dared do it again. Until now. It was childish, but it felt right.

"Bang. Bang." She said as she watched his face turn from anger to horror. He spun to see the terror coming.

148

As the Lieutenant fell, she saw him fire one shot and heard another as she dropped over the ridge.

As his screaming started, she turned off the short-range comms.

The fall was like her landing on Roost I, but this time there was no panic. Her concentration was on, her breathing regular. She hit and rolled. The armor, the fabulous piece of technology, once again did its job. As beat up as it was, it still did its job. *I love this thing.*

She came to a stop. The rest of the squad was there to meet her.

"Nice work, Lieutenant," the Gunny said.

"Frippen awesome, Jax!" the Corporal cheered.

"That was definitely not something I would have attempted." The Commander was smiling as she clasped her hand and pulled her up.

"If I had thought about it too much, me neither," she said as she removed her helmet and threw it aside.

"Any ideas on what to do now?" The Commander had spun and was returning fire up the ridge. The Screech packed it tight, it could barely hold them all.

The Commander, along with Gunny and the Corporal, was picking off targets. They began to fall off the ridge, crowding and pushing each other with no place to go. Some were climbing down, their claws making easy work of the steep surface.

Jax brought her NEW24 back into play. "Sorry, all out of ideas."

The Screech were yelling and firing down on them. The battered squad began to retreat, the green and blue lights shadowing their steps. The ridge top burst open in a wave of fire and heat, forcing the squad to turn away.

A high whirling sound pierced their ears, drowning out the Screech. The Reckless unleashed its duel chain guns, spraying metal death. The Screech on the ridge top were erased from existence. With the threat of return fire neutralized for the moment, it began its landing.

The squad pulled tighter together. The Reckless dropped its landing gear and settled gently on the ground. The gang plank dropped, and they needed no encouragement to run inside. They took their seats, the Gunny and Jax helping Chambers to buckle in.

The Commander hit the intercom to the pilot. "Good to see you, Hat Trick. It's about time you got your ass down here."

"Sorry, Commander, Screech flyers kept us busy. I only had one of you on screen until a minute ago. Heard the rest of you were dead."

"Greatly exaggerated. Dust off, and once we're in the air, get me Ares Actual."

"Roger that. Dusting off and bringing Ares Actual on comms."

"This is Ares Actual, what's the situation, Hat Trick?" The Captain's deep voice echoed in the crew hold of the Reckless.

"Ares Actual, this is Commander Lewis." The Commander didn't bother to put on a headset; she let the conversation carry across the cabin intercom.

"Fantastic, Commander. Last we heard the team was dead and only Private Rallic was alive."

"Long story, Ares, better left for debrief. Right now, I would like to request a tactical strike on target designated the Nest. We lost some good people down there. And those frippen birds don't deserve to be in the same universe as us." The Commander went quiet. That probably wasn't a 'by the book' way of asking for a strike. *I don't think she cares about the 'book' right now.* Commander Gemma Lewis was not known for her subtly. *When she wants to throw you, she throws you. When she wants you destroyed, she drops massive ordnance on you.*

The Reckless banked and turned as it entered space. The team braced themselves as they waited for a response.

"Request approved," cracked on the intercom as Ares Actual responded.

The Commander eyed each team member in turn as they all nodded agreement. The Commander took her seat and strapped in, but she left the channel open for them all to hear.

"Reckless, this is Ares Actual. Maintain heading. Be advised, we are firing a kinetic missile and you are between us and target. Again, kinetic missile strike, you are in fire zone, do not deviate course."

"Roger that, Ares. Holding course. Aim true." There was a slight quiver in Hat Trick's voice.

With her helmet gone, Jax pulled a holoscreen out from the side of her pod. As an officer, she had access to the tactical displays on the Reckless.

Ares position was quickly highlighted before her, then the Reckless, Roost I and the Nest. She wasn't familiar with kinetic missiles; her eyes scanned a small sub display with the details.

Jax knew the Ares had railguns similar to the Meg42. The Meg42 could only push ammo to the speed of light. The Ares could use a quantum field to push ammo past that mark. The ammo, gaining near infinite mass, plus velocity, could cut through almost anything. Shooting that at a planet could crack its crust and destroy it. *Not the plan for this one.*

So, a kinetic missile was called for. A kinetic missile worked different differently than a railgun; it was very slow by comparison. A 10-meter by 1-meter diameter poll would be shot from space at a planet-side target. Gravity did all the work, accelerating the missile to terminal velocity. The resulting explosion, over a hundred mega tons, would wipe away anything with in 50 km of the target.

The display before her showed a flash from the Ares as the missile was released. Directly in its path was the Reckless. She was holding her breath as the image passed by. *No wonder Hat Trick was worried. That was almost close enough for a haircut.*

As it entered Roost I's gravity well, its velocity increased. Live images of the target and from some of the attack ships still planet-side showed the Nest. Their optics zoomed in from outside the fire zone.

The cabin around her was quiet as the missile struck home. A blinding flash temporarily blocked the view. As it came back up, a giant mushroom cloud stood in its place, a bellowing dust cloud expanding outward from its center.

"We have a hit. Direct contact on target. Awaiting confirmation." The announcement rang from the intercom. The cabin remained quiet as they waited.

"We have confirmation. Target is destroyed. Repeat target is destroyed." They could hear a cheer erupt from the Ares.

As Jax looked around at her surviving squad mates, she didn't hear any cheers from them. She did however see a look of satisfaction. She saw relief pass over them. She saw tired bodies slump from exhaustion, a nightmare coming to an end.

Her own chest relaxed as she realized that she had been holding her breath the whole time. Her head slumped back, and her eyes closed.

"Ares Actual, this is Commander Lewis. Nice shooting. We're coming home."

Jax didn't recall if there was a response. She just liked what the Commander said. The feeling that went along with it. She was going home. Back to the Ares.

CHAPTER 18
NAMES

The Lieutenant sat up in bed. There were curtains drawn around her, giving the illusion of privacy. She had been confined to the MedBay for twenty-four hours by the Doc for observation. Ordered to rest. *I'm plenty rested, going stir crazy.*

The Gunny and Commander had been treated and released. At first, she'd thought rank had privileges, but she outranked the Gunnery Sergeant.

The Doc had gone on a long rant about the medical nanites used in the Klick-Klick suits. How whatever technician designed those things should be hanged for not knowing how the human body worked. He claimed no one should be tortured with as much 'help' from those machines as she had. While the armor hadn't given her much in the way of painkillers, she guessed they had been doing extensive repairs to her muscles.

She felt fine, but there was no arguing with the Doc. *So, I have to sit here and be bored.* Only the holoscreen in front of her kept her occupied. She had started by looking up some names. *I need to remember Ryan Nelson, Marton Saville, and Teagan Thirgood. More names to add to my growing list.* The others she would find out, those that were alive, more personally. From personal lists, she moved through ship status and accessed what screens she could. Since leaving Roost I, the Ares had been running silent. More and more Screech ships arrived by the minute.

153

Like kicking over a hornet's nest, we've got their attention now. Thanks to that, the Ares was playing hide and seek. Currently the Ares' scans registered twelve ships hunting them.

We can't take that many by ourselves. It turned out the Screech's scanning technology was a lot better than that used by Earth ships. She remembered the Commander once commenting on how close the Gaia-made warship could get to Earth ships without being detected. Not so with the Screech.

If they got close enough, they would detect them. So, a deadly game of move and counter move was ongoing. The Screech's search pattern was erratic, and the Captain was making constant adjustments, trying to stay outside the danger zone, while moving in and around multiple enemy ships. It was scary and fascinating all at once.

"You are supposed to be resting," the aged voice said as its owner pushed the curtain aside to enter. Dr. Charles, or just Doc, was easily the tallest person on the Ares. Jax was amazed he could squeeze his head through the entryways. His balding head with hair on the sides was as scraggily as ever.

"Sorry, Doc. Just itching to get back to work. I feel fine."

"I'll decide how you feel." He entered the room, twirling his ever-present injector. "Officers always think they are better than they really are. Checking themselves out on a whim, glad to see you have a little more sense." He was reviewing her medical screens as he talked.

I can check myself out? Is that how the Commander and Gunny got out of here so fast? Guess I'll have to remember that next time.

"It seems, however, you're doing well enough. I'll release you, but I want you to take another shift off before starting active duty. Relax, no exercise, sleep in your own berth, all of that. If you feel any discomfort or headaches, come back to me." His twirling stopped and he pointed the injector at her like some kind of gun. Even his eyes looked like he was focusing down sights.

154

"Roger that, Doc. Thanks."

"Yes, I suppose so. I believe Corporal Chambers is up and would like to see you before you go. Try not to disturb him too much, if you please." The Doc turned to leave, once again twirling the injector and holstering it in his pocket as he went.

"Oh, Doc, before you go, I was wondering, what's your first name?"

He stopped and cranked his neck around to look at her, pausing for a moment before saying, "Dutch." Then he turned and left. She hopped off the bed and slipped her shoes on. *Dr. Dutch Charles. I wonder if he goes by D.C. when he is not being all doctor like? Probably not.*

Thankfully, she was already in her sweatpants and t-shirt. Rose had brought them by almost as soon as she hit the MedBay. *Thank you, Rose. Didn't have to worry about hospital apparel. Wrapping myself in what basically amounts to a sheet is not my idea of fun.*

She caught a quick glimpse of herself in a small mirror. The fleet logo on her shirt a black circle on the gray background was a dominating presence. It showed a short sword with an eight-pointed star at the guard. Sharp metal wings spread out behind it. Around the circle in plain script was the Fleet motto in what she now knew to be old Earth Latin: "Nos ire tenebras. Sine timore. Sine pari." *We travel into darkness. Without fear. Without equal. I'm getting there. At least, I think I am.*

Her hair was a little messy, so she grabbed a tie from her pocket. *Always have one ready.* She pulled her shoulder length hair back into a neat ponytail. *Well, I might not be ready for a night on the town, but it's passable. I'm ready to tackle the world, or at least the ship.*

She went to see if she could find where Corporal Chambers was bunkered. Her eyes wandered around the MedBay as she walked, until a bump on the shoulder jarred her.

"Excuse me, ma'am." Fleetwalker Percy snapped to attention and did his best salute, forgetting that he had a small tablet in his hand. He grimaced as he hit his brow.

"At ease, Fleetwalker. It's Percy, right?" She gave him a salute and a smile. Fleetwalker was the lowest rank in the Gaia Fleet, but it didn't mean they weren't important. *Everyone's got a name, and everyone matters.*

"Correct, Lieutenant Brandt, ma'am." Even at ease, Fleetwalker Percy was as rigid as a board.

"Not injured, are you?"

"Huh, no, ma'am." He ruffled his brow.

"Not the brow, I mean you being here in MedBay."

"No, ma'am. I'm trying to track down some supplies, but I can't seem to find where they were delivered. They're supposed to be in MedBay 4 but have gone missing." He glanced at his tablet.

"I see. Well, good luck in your search. Before you go, Percy, what's your first name?"

"Tobias. Tobias Percy, ma'am." His eyes had gone wide with worry.

Probably thinks I'm going to put him on report for something. She smiled to relieve his tension. "Good to see you again, Fleetwalker Tobias Percy. You're one of the first people I met on this ship. I hope to see you accomplish great things."

"Ma'am, yes, ma'am." He snapped to attention, his chest almost bursting with pride.

"Dismissed, Fleetwalker." Jax gave him a salute.

"Yes, ma'am. Thank you, ma'am." He saluted and turned to go, hitting a side table and almost knocking off a tray of medical injectors on his way. As he fumbled to right it all, the Lieutenant turned back to her goal with a smirk. She peeked her head round a curtain and found Corporal Chambers sitting up in bed, downing some kind of drink. His face was pinched. As it went down, he shook his head and stuck his tongue out.

"Am I interrupting anything, Corporal Chambers? I can come back later."

156

"Lieutenant Brandt." He put the cup down and offered a salute. "No, please come and take my mind off that strange brew the Doc has me drinking."

She walked in and claimed a small stool beside his bed.

"Please, call me Jax. There's no one else around and I don't need the formalities right now."

"Jax it is." He gave his trademark grin.

"And what should I call you? Chambers seems a little formal."

"Varick."

She squinted an eye at him. "I don't know if you look like a Varick."

He barked out a laugh. "Take it up with my mom. Old family name from her side. Ancient name of kings." He puffed up his chest and raised his chin.

"Oh, I see that now," she mocked him.

"What about you? Jax have a story to it?"

"My actual name is Harumi, but only some of my family call me that. Jax works best. And yes, there is a story to it, but not one I want to get into right now."

"Is it based on your middle name? Seems there's some debate about that one. I got time for a story."

She leveled a stare at him. "I don't know what you're talking about."

"Come on, everyone wants to know. The betting pool is getting pretty high. We could make some credits if you let me in on it."

"A pool really? What have you got your credits on?"

"Bob."

"It's not Bob. What would make you think it's Bob?" She brought her hand to her head.

"It could be Bob. Has to be something. I figured the more unlikely the choice, the better the chance. The folks in Engineering are betting on something like Tesla, Einstein, Susskind, or maybe Nayomi, after your mother."

Well, those would all be an improvement, she thought as she gave him a small grin "Oh, and what are the Corps members betting on?"

"Carrie, Annabelle, and Morticia are running high. And, of course, Bob." He was chuckling as he spoke.

"I don't know any of those names. Where did those come from?"

"Old Earth flat movies. I guess you wouldn't realize, but Gaia loves old Earth stuff."

"Really? How come?"

"You have to remember Gaia is still a pretty new culture, they don't have a lot of history of their own. Still trying to figure stuff out, not just military stuff, but civilian stuff too. So, most people have started by adopting some old or forgotten things from Earth's history. Music, entertainment, even clothes."

"Clothes?" she said, happy for a change of subject.

"Yeah, I guess the 19th Century is really big right now. Top hats and formal wear for everything."

"What's a top hat?" She asked, shrugging.

"It has a brim and then goes up high." He waved his hands, making motions the best he could to shape it in the air.

"That will be interesting to see. So, everyone is into that on Gaia?"

"Not everyone, some have picked up on different things. Like the Doc really likes Spaghetti Westerns."

"What are Spaghetti Westerns?"

"Old Earth flat screen entertainment. Cowboys and gun fights."

"The Doc? Gunfights?" She tilted her head up and again imagined his injector being a pistol. *I guess I was right about that.*

"Yup. He's pretty good too. Bunch of Corps challenged him and some Fleet personal to a pistols-only VR game. The Corps made quick work of the rest of Doc's team. Left just him versus six of the Corps."

"That doesn't sound good for the Doc."

"You would think so, but nope. Doc wiped them all out."

"That's crazy. I never would have thought." Her grin stretched out from ear to ear. *I guess that was a lucky six for Doc. I knew I liked him.*

"Yup, we still call those guys Doc's Half Dozen. They'll never live it down." Varick started to laugh and then clenched his face as he grabbed his side.

"You okay?" She shifted forward on her stool.

"Yeah, laughing hurts, painkillers don't seem to work on laughter. Doc wants me to rest."

She nodded her head and sat back. "Well, with that I should go, but Doc said you wanted to see me?"

"Yes, I do." He turned and grabbed something from the far side table. "I have this for you."

He extended his hand and opened it palm down. A small rectangular metal piece, about the length of her finger, dropped down on a chain.

"Is that a dog tag? My father had a set of these, besides his wedding ring, that was only piece of jewelry he ever wore." She reached out and cupped the tag in her hand. She had a warm smile on her face as she looked it over.

On one side was the Terrain Corps Logo. The Terrain Corps Logo was similar to the Fleet logo, except there was a planet at the guard instead of a star and the wings that rose up behind it were more natural looking. The name, "Harumi 'Jax' Brandt", had been embossed on the back. There seemed to be a small rod imbedded in the metal underlining her name.

"A DNA memory circuit?"

"Yup. We've kind of combined the tags with another Earth Military thing called a challenger coin. That circuit contains everything you've done for the Corps and is DNA signed by me, the Gunny, and Commander Lewis. Anyone in the Corps ever gives you problems, show them that, let them scan it if need be, and it should smooth your way. Makes you one of us."

159

Her throat choked a little as she spoke. "I don't know what to say. Thank you. I'm not sure if I deserve this; I was just trying to survive."

"That's all any of us are trying to do. You've earned it, trust me."

"Thank you." She smiled lightly as she slipped it over her head and tucked it into her shirt.

"Why did the Commander sign it? She's Fleet."

"Yup, but she started out in the Corps. Then Fleet got their grubby paws on her." He gave a wink and a small grin.

"I wonder what the story is with that?" She raised an eyebrow at him.

"Don't know, you'll have to ask the Commander." He shrugged.

"Right. I should let you rest, and I need to get some too before I start my shift again."

"Aye aye, Lieutenant Brandt, ma'am." He gave a salute that was all playful in nature.

"Be well, Varick." She offered out her hand and they shook. "Oh, I need to get your knife back to you. Not sure what happened to it."

"Probably in your security locker in your berth. Someone will get temp access to drop it off, since you were listed as injured. But you keep it. Like I said, it is my second backup and my Dad will be glad it's getting some use."

"Your Dad?"

"Yup. He makes all my knives. He's a metallurgist on Gaia, but he likes to forge knives as a hobby. Don't know what he puts into them, but they always serve me well."

"Yeah, me too. Thank you again, and my thanks to him." She rose to leave. "Rest well, Corporal."

He nodded his head and settled down into his pillows as she walked out.

Moving along the corridor, she found a comfort in the Ares' stark gray walls. Knowing nothing would burst these walls, nothing would be trying to kill her, being here gave her a sense of peace. She felt a vibration, a kind of rhythm, that she hadn't noticed before. She moved easily, giving way to those that came, or moving into space as it was offered. That feeling of fighting to get somewhere on the ship was gone. Even the struggle of moving up and down the stairwells was gone.

The portal to her berth opened as she approached. She slipped in. She heard it close behind her, but she just stood for a moment. Her eyes scanned the room.

It was as stark as the hallway. Nothing personal decorated the room. All her belongings had been lost on the Indiana. Her friends in the Rat Pack had said they might be able to retrieve her personal data from the Indiana and recreate pictures and some personal items, but it had never seemed important until now. She just hadn't really paid any attention to it. She wished she had.

She went to her security locker and let it scan her. The locker was about half the size of the personal chest she had under her bunk for her personal gear. It sat against the wall and she had mostly ignored it. It chimed and opened with a small hiss. A small screen popped out to show her who had accessed the locker before her. B. Jackson, Fleetwalker. Just dropping things off.

Inside, on a small top shelf, was her one personal item. The knife. Such a simple tool, without which she may never have survived. She took it out and placed it on her back, letting her waistband hold it firm.

I may not be able to always carry it on duty, but any other time I can, I will be ready. You always need a knife. She sat on her bunk and put her back on the cool metal wall. Crossing her legs, she stared at the barren wall across from her.

I was just trying to survive. Images of the Screech she killed flashed before her. *How many was it? I don't know. I killed. But they were trying to kill me. I'm still a killer.* She shook her head. Her thoughts wandered to those she had lost. She had to try hard to remember the crew of the Indiana. Some of the details were already going vague. *I have to remember! They deserve that.*

161

Reason O'Connor, Daniel Trucker, Jonathan Camp, Imes, what was her first name again? Thea, no, Teresa, no, Thelma! Thelma Imes. I should remember, it's too important. She realized there would be some names that she just couldn't recall. *Did I even know all of them?*

Each name weighed her down. *I lived, they died. I need to do right by them. Doing what's right, not revenge. The Screech are evil. Right?*

More recent names came to her. Her squad, whom she had barely known, but to whom she owed so much. *Ryan Nelson, Marton Saville, Teagan Thirgood. Those Corps that died would have done right by me if our positions were reversed, I have to do the same. Can I?* She fingered the dog tag under her shirt. *I'm just trying to survive.* Her shoulders felt crushed under the weight of her thoughts. *What am I doing here?*

Her door chimed. Her thoughts registered that it was probably the second time, but she wasn't sure she wanted company. *Just go away.* It chimed again. She let out a sigh. "Open".

The door slid open. Not waiting to be invited in, Lieutenant Junior Grade Rosita Koike stepped in. *Rose. My 'little' sister.* Still in her work fatigues, with her tool vest and belt.

She was older than Jax, but Rose was a little shorter. Rose's hair was also shorter, and she had a better tan, but other than that, they looked so much alike people called them sisters. *My best friend.* "Hi Rose. I don't feel up for company."

"Oh, really? Thought you might want to talk after some of the stuff I've heard about your ground mission." She stood with her hands behind her back, a warm smile on her face.

"Commander Lewis said we shouldn't really talk about it till the Captain gives the okay. Sorry."

"Okay, if you really feel that way," she said it so sweetly that the words practically dripped out of her mouth. "But everyone already knows about Rallic, the little fripper, and there's this ..." She brought her hands around.

Held between them was a small cylinder with just a hint of heat rising from it. The smell wafted into the room and caressed Jax's nose. The loveliest smell that there ever was. A chai tea latte.

"I guess I'll just take this and go."

"You're evil."

"Yup, had MS1 Zakar make it just for you."

"Scum."

"I guess I'll just go then." Rose made as if to turn and walk away.

"Don't you dare. Get in here and give me that." Jax jumped off her bunk and snatched the prize from Rose's hands. She felt the warmth caress her hands as she breathed in the heady smell of the chai. Jax gave a tilt of her head and they both sat on the bunk.

"So, tell me all about it. Don't leave out a thing." Rose's legs were crisscrossed and her head was bent forward. Her eyes were wide with anticipation.

Jax took a long sip of the grand liquid. The talking came slower as she relived her tale. It wasn't long until some weight came off her shoulders.

She talked a little faster. Some thoughts were pushed aside. She had survived and others hadn't. She would try and make peace with it. She would find a way to live up to all the names that rolled through her head.

This is not just my life now, but all of theirs too. I will make them proud.

163

You'll probably think this story is about me, but you'll be wrong. This story is about the Ares.

Chapter 19

Tests

She was early getting to the bridge. *That's never happened before.* It gave her a moment to finish her latte. Drink was allowed on the bridge, but you had to obtain and secure it using foodfab cups. All the pod stations on the bridge had their own. Unlimited caffeine was vital for those long shifts. It just wasn't the same as a fresh cup. Finishing her last drop, she placed the cup into the recycle bin and entered the Command Deck.

A quick glance showed in its direction showed her that the stoplight still displaying red and blue. Battle stations and running stealth. Several days out from the mission to Roost I and still holding the same.

The game of cat and mouse was continuing. The Ares had put many light years between itself and Roost I, but the Screech were relentless. Even this far out, there were three ships still searching. Three ships to avoid, three ships that could call in many more.

The Captain stood at his usual spot, looking intently at the holotable. His large frame dominated the table. The white hair stood out in stark contrast to his dark skin. He wore his Fleet Captain's jacket, open at the front, and the standard officer fatigues. The Captain's jacket looked like old leather, had double-breasted buttons, some kind of white fur lining, and a collar that stood slightly up. The ship was always colder when running silent for long periods of time. Most of the bridge crew wore something similar, including her. She admired the Captain's jacket for a moment, wondering if the fur lining made it any warmer. Her jacket was plenty warm, it just lacked that nice touch of style.

The Captain caught a glimpse of her and tilted his head to call her over. She passed her eyes over the images on the command table. Her space shark was moving in an elliptical pattern around one of the squid like ships of the Screech. The two other Screech ships were running a strange crisscross pattern on the other side of the Ares. Nothing showed that the Ares had been detected, but they were being boxed in.

The Captain waved his hand and a screen slid in front of the Lieutenant. Displayed was a standard input for the ship's course, speed, heading, pitch, roll, yaw, and special coordinates. More could be brought up to command if you desired, such as weapons and shields, but this was simplified. There was also a countdown timer. Initially, she had thirty seconds, but by the time she took it all in, the time was cut in half. Her fingers flew to input her choices. The timer expired and she was only half done. She took a deep breath and slid the screen back to the Captain. He waved his hand again and a screen with his course slid back to her.

Her flight path was similar, but her speed calculations were not. The rest of it, she never got to. On the holotable, the shark avatar started its move along the Captain's prescribed path.

She studied the information before her. The Captain's plan was detailed, and he had delivered it fast. She recognized the classic strategies he was employing. Back tracking and a random change in course, designed to make the Ares hard to find. He was testing her tactical abilities and she had relied on instinct. That instinct had failed. Details and execution matter in these situations. *I can't always 'Jax Way' it.* She nodded her head; *I need to work on details and be fast.*

The Captain gave her another nod to go take her station. From the look in his eyes, she had a feeling more tests would be forthcoming. *Well, at least it won't be a boring shift.*

She made her way around the holotable to the Engineering Station. Most of the Command staff was on shift, currently. Commanders Haddock for Operations, Bard for Navigation, and Moro for Weapons. Only Commander Urud, who hated being on the bridge, was absent. Commander Moro caught sight of her and narrowed his eyes. She paused in her walk and stood tall. *I'm done shrinking away. I'm watching you too.* His gaze broke as he turned back to his duty. *Or is it that he doesn't want to look at me? No matter, I have work to do.*

At the Engineering station, she patted Ensign Sales on the shoulder. Coleman Sales, Cole to his friends, turned his intense gaze from the screens and gave Jax a warm smile. This usually quiet man (*unless he was drunk*, she joked to herself) was a member of the Rat Pack. She was considered by many to be their fourth member.

When running silent you could talk, but superstitions ran hard on ship, so most people didn't. Cole rubbed his bald head, pointed at some screens that he was keeping an extra eye on, and gave her a thumbs up. Jax signaled back the same as Cole left the Engineering Pod and she settled in.

The pod looked like a large, open egg shoved into the side of the bridge. Each pod had room for two, but usually only one officer was on duty at a time. The pods, ENG, OPS, WEP, and NAV, were the central hubs for their divisions. For Jax, that meant all engineering data was gathered here for monitoring. Information on engine operations, internal ship's energy, and repair crews, needed to be checked. ENG was the biggest division on ship.

The Lieutenant let out a quick stretch of her arms before starting down the standard checklists. Most of Engineering hated bridge duty, preferring to be knee deep in wires and grease, but not her. *I like seeing the bigger picture, how everything works together. Captains get to see the whole ship working that way.* That was the dream for her again, to be a Captain. For now, she had to focus on the job at hand.

Finishing her checklist, she glanced over at the holotable to see more course corrections being laid in. The Captain nodded his chin at her. Taking his meaning, she opened a screen for Navigation. Within seconds, a new problem appeared before her. Same countdown as before. Her fingers danced on the screens, putting her solution together.

Finalizing her solution, she sent it off with seconds to spare. A few ENG alerts flashed in front of her eyes. The secondary qave drive was fluctuating and required some residue energy to be siphoned off. Some holoscreens on the Hanger Deck were glitching and needed a repair crew. It would have been a pretty mundane day, if it weren't for the ships hunting them. A message back from the Captain showed her solution side by side with his actual orders. She scrunched up her nose as she studied his solution. It seemed like her focus was a little limited. The Captain had adjusted their course based on things she hadn't considered; some nearby planets and an incoming meteor, to name a few. Also, he had allowed a greater margin of error for the Screech themselves. Her solution only accounted for the immediate surroundings. His thoughts were broader, where they could be and what it meant for the ship. She needed to think further ahead.

Her shift continued and so did the tests. As a break appeared between routines for engineering, a new problem would present itself. *Captains don't get a rest, so why should I? This is what I want, after all.* All her solutions would be shortly followed by corrections and recommendations. Seeing the Captain's decisions carried out in real time on the holotable drove the lessons home. She worked on that longer game strategy.

On the last challenge, her answer flowed out immediately. She sent it out at the same time as an alert popped up in the engine room. Transfer links running from the qave battery to the engines were losing power.

Making sure the repair teams trying to find the issue didn't run into each other kept her hopping. Commander Urud found the problem himself before the work crews could. A simple relay switch had burned out. It was popped out and replaced. Problem solved. So much commotion for what turned out to be a simple problem.

She returned to her other monitoring to find a message from the Captain. *Let's see what I did wrong this time.*

"Your solution was a little better than mine. Nice work."

Her eyes opened wide. She read it again. When she compared her solution to the Captain's, there were only slight differences. The axis coordinates for their flight path formed the largest discrepancy. He liked hers better. She smiled to herself as she sat back in her chair. *Score one for me.*

A few more tests came her way, but she was on point. She was seeing the bigger picture the Captain wanted from her. While not exact, their answers now paralleled each other. Then it changed. The next test asked for a firing solution on the three enemy vessels they were avoiding. *I've never done that before.* Thankfully, there was no time limit on this one.

She switched between staying current with her Engineering tasks and taking the tests. She tried to research what she could and propose the best options. There just wasn't much time for study. There might not be a time limit, but you do not keep a Captain waiting. *My brain is starting to hurt, going to get a headache. I'm going to sleep well tonight.*

A half hour later she sent off her answer. Leaning back in her chair, she tried to clear her head. Grabbing her foodfab cup, she took a long sip of the ship's version of her favorite drink. *I guess exhaustion makes it taste better, this is not so bad. The mental stress might get to me more than the ground mission. Okay, maybe not, but still.* A few moments later, the Captain's solution appeared before her. She wasn't even close. *Well, that's humbling.*

Energy ratings, the number of guns, yield on armed torpedoes, it was all wrong. Comparing hers to the Captain's, well, his was like a master painting and hers was like a scribble drawn by a three-year-old. A small shake of her head. *I guess I have more studying to do.*

The next one arrived, this one with a time limit. He'd given her half the time she put in the first one. *At least with a time limit I can fail faster. No, stay focused, use what you know.* She tried to apply some ideas from the previous test, but sent it back with no real hope she was even close. *Dad always said the best teachers are the mistakes you make. Back to the engineering work. I feel like a yo-yo.*

Energy routing and repair teams dominated the work. An issue with someone in the Hanger Deck wanting to run an engine test on a fighter had to be shut down. *We're running silent, what were they thinking?*

Her next break in work brought her results from the weapons test, and once again, she had failed. She had barely looked at the results from this test when another one appeared. She was only given minutes. She fired off her best. Fail.

Another test, a firing solution for their current position. One-minute limit. She rushed it and missed any kind of torpedo usage in her solution. She attempted several more tests, all with the same outcome. She was clenching her jaw and staring at the screen like she could drive holes into it. At the top of the hour, she was back on her checklist for Engineering. She punched through it rather than tapped. *Deep breaths, they're just tests, and you need to learn. At least my shift is almost over, and I can use my free time to study. I can do better.*

A request from Commander Moro appeared on her screen. He was asking for a bigger power reserve for the WEP station to draw from. She adjusted some energy requirements and gave him what he needed, sending back a single, 'Approved', notification. Then it dawned on her. She turned and stared at the Captain, who raised an eyebrow at her. She scanned over to Commander Moro and then back. The Captain gave a nod, a smirk, and then turned back into laying a new course.

Jax pushed back into her chair, anger at herself flaring. She had been competing against Commander Moro on tactics. She had been losing. *Well, that's even more humbling.* She punched the screens even harder than before. *I guess the Captain's trying to teach me more than one lesson. I don't like it.*

"There's our opening!" The Captain's exclamation on the silent bridge startled her. "Helm, bring us to thirty-seven degrees starboard, minus forty-two relative depth, and increase speed to one third qave drive."

Commander Bard responded, "Changing course and increasing power." Her voice always projected as if trained to do so. On her small navigation screen, Jax saw the Ares swing around and accelerate.

Everyone on the bridge seemed to stop. She looked up from her screen and stared at the Captain. His iron gaze burned into the holotable. Her space shark was moving through a gap in the estimated sensor sweeps from the Screech.

Moments passed before his deep voice called out again. "Ops, confirm we are clear of Screech flight paths and scanning." With the Captain's proclamation, the Lieutenant looked to see the Screech heading off in a different direction. *We're slipping right through their fingers.*

"Running scans." Working Ops from the holotable, Commander Isaac Haddock opened several screens. The scans ran and everyone waited.

"Status confirmed we are clear." A toothy smile crossed the Commander's face. It looked out of place on the muscular man. No one seemed to care since the results were the same. A cheer rang out across the bridge.

"Good job, everyone." The Captain straightened his back and relaxed his eyes. "Stand down from combat alert and cancel silent running." The Captain and Commander Haddock patted each other on the back. Even Commander Moro's usually grim face broke out in a thin smile.

Each station confirmed the orders, OPS, WEPS, ENG, and NAV. The Lieutenant started the procedures to bring the ship back to normal operating levels. Power dampeners cycled off. Energy returned to all non-essential areas. Hanger Deck was given the green light to start operations again. For the first time in days, the Ares was running normal.

She sat back in her chair and glanced at the clock. Only minutes left in her work shift. *That shift went by fast, but it doesn't get much better than that.*

"Captain, we have a message coming in from Gaia Military Command. It's Admiral Koonce," Commander Haddock said.

"Put it on the table, Commander."

"Aye aye, sir."

The Commander waved his hand and the upper torso of Admiral Koonce appeared on screen. He looked old to Jax's eyes. He had dark hair, but it was receding. His cheeks and eyes were sunken, giving him the look of a man who hadn't slept. His dark blue uniform, while neat, showed years of use.

"Ichabod, please tell me you're headed back." His voice crackled as if he was forcing the words out.

The Captain raised an eyebrow. The lack of formality had surprised him, she thought. The Captain answered anyways. "We just cleared our pursuit, Admiral. We're clear to set course."

"Then you need to hurry. We've decoded part of the information you got from Roost I. It might already be too late. The Screech are heading for Highguard."

CHAPTER 20

Ominous

The Ares was flying. The Captain had wasted no time cutting the Admiral off and laying in course. Battle stations were resumed, but all stealth protocols were forgotten. The stoplight just burned red.

Jax was supposed to be coming off shift. The alarms went off. The Captain made an announcement and she got a message from Commander Urud telling her to stay put. He was staying in main engineering and putting all his best people where they were the most help. Since most of engineering would rather avoid the bridge, she would be staying on duty. *Fine by me, I am good here and the Commander knows it.*

The first thing she needed to do was to reinstate all the power requirements back to WEP and OPS. She took the gained energy from shutting down silent running and dumped that into WEP also. She wondered what Commander Moro would think of that. *Stop being petty, Jax*, she chided herself. *We have bigger concerns.*

Time seemed to drag. The faster they went, the longer they seemed to wait. Long range scans didn't pick up anything. Ops posted continuous updates, most of which amounted to, nothing to report.

The Captain paced uncharacteristically around the holotable. Occasionally, he would stop at each station, and ask some minor question. He'd give an update or clarification, a word of advice, a simple command, all of it to kill time. Eventually, the Lieutenant realized it was also to keep the bridge focused.

Did I do the same with my crew? No, I thought I had all the time in the world. I wasted it when I could have been making things better. It was all just fun and harmless. We thought we would explore the universe in peace. The reality was so much different.

Commander Haddock called out from Ops. "Long range scans have detected possible Screech ship energy signatures."

"Can we confirm numbers and probable course?" the Captain asked.

"Working on it."

The bridge went silent again. Hope built in those precious moments, only to come crashing down again when Haddock said, "We have confirmation on Screech energy signature. Three ships leaving Screech space, heading indicates a direct path to Highguard Station."

The holotable updated with the information, zooming out to show the Ares and the Screech racing across space. Little red triangles marked the Screech.

"Can we identify possible ship types?" the Captain asked while studying the flight path.

The Lieutenant knew what the Captain wanted to hear. She wanted to hear it too, everyone on the bridge did. Something small like a scout or even a drone. Something we can overtake, something slow. Something that showed they were not attacking. Highguard was Earth's crowning achievement in space, and like all Earth vessels, it was completely defenseless. It carried no offensive weaponry and no defensive shields. *How long ago was it that I thought that was a good thing? We come in peace, but the rest of the universe comes to war. We should have known better.*

"Power levels indicate Screech frigate class ships."

Hearing that was all they needed. There was no mistaking their intentions now. The Screech didn't send frigate class ships for scouting. Highguard was in trouble.

"Estimated time till they can reach Highguard? And our intercept?" the Captain asked, turning to Commander Haddock at OPS. The whole

173

bridge crew turned from their screens to look. To focus on him. His brows were pressed together, sweat beading down his forehead as he ran the numbers.

"Screech will reach Highguard around 0-7-30. Ares best time to Highguard is at 0-8-10," the Commander said as he lifted his head from the screen. His eyes and shoulders slumped; sorrow drenched his face.

The Captain's large fist slammed into the holotable. The explosive sound reverberated around the bridge. "NAV, give me all you can, push the engines to critical, make up that time. We'll drop out of qave drive here." A mark appeared on the holotable, close to the location of Highguard. "Maintain max sub-light speed, there will be no room for error. Commander Moro, targeting solutions on all hostiles." As the responses came in, the Captain barely registered them; his eyes were locked on the table.

Time stretched on on the bridge, every thought frozen on their objective. The image of Highguard loomed on the table, a harbinger of despair. Jax's heart sank. Real time images of Highguard were now being shown on the command table. The Screech had started their attack. Highguard was burning. The greatest space station of humankind was alight, plasma launching into the darkness. Shattered pieces broke off and tumbled away. It was rocked by explosions that echoed only silence into the depths of space.

The Screech were merciless. The station was destroyed, yet they continued to fire. The Ares watched in horror. Highguard launched lifepods and the Screech wiped them from existence. Each blip disappeared from their screen, never to return. Watching and waiting were all they had. The final seconds ticked down and finally they could act.

The Ares came out of FTL on top of Highguard Station. The flashes of plasma and debris from the battered station danced off their shields. The space shark had arrived, and it was ready to hunt.

The first Screech ship was only fifty meters off the port bow. The portside energy weapons laced into the ship with a broadside pass. The alien ship's energy shields lit up in defiance of the attack, only to be overwhelmed and fail. The rear torpedo tubes launched four missiles that streaked out and all hit home. A blossom of light and energy erupted from the target. The Screech ship blew apart, adding to the remains of Highguard.

Energy beams bounced off Ares' shields as it rolled to its next course of attack. The Lieutenant watched OPS closely. Commander Haddock adjusted their shields to meet the attack. A symphony was happening on the bridge, and for the first time, Jax was playing a part. She fell into the rhythm of working, listening for commands, reacting, and anticipating. The Captain would speak or wave his hand, to send a command, and the bridge would follow. The individual words or motions became meaningless as they moved in harmony together. Course corrections, changes in firing patterns, all of it embraced her.

The remaining Screech ships had separated and circled out, trying to create a crossfire in which to catch the Ares. The Captain never liked dog fights with the Ares. Its strength relied on stealth and hitting hard. Still, the ship was designed to handle any situation of war and master it.

The Ares rounded and closed fast on one of the Screech ships. It was an aggressive move to bring the ship out of the crossfire. The warship's arsenal was concentrated on the one target.

They passed over the top of the alien vessel, exchanging blow for blow. The Ares's base-mounted TBWs ripped into the Screech's shields. The creatures' top shields flashed and gave way. The Screech rolled, bringing its base shields around for protection.

As Ares cleared the alien vessel, the other ship came swooping in. The aliens' blue and green high-energy beams focused in, its own missiles letting loose.

The beams hammered the shields. Counter measures were launched and intercepted all but one of the alien missiles. The missile ignited like a mini sun. The shields held, but the force of the blast pushed the Ares around, its tail whipping out of control.

"Energy spike on starboard shields, power drop to twenty percent," Jax called out, sending notices to OPS, WEPS, and the Captain.

"Changing shield configuration, updating energy allowance," Commander Haddock, the OPS officer, called back.

"Helm, bring us to seventeen percent port, increase twelve percent vertical pitch. WEPS, prepare to fire." The helm and WEPS positions replied instantly to the Captain's orders; the Ares was off like a shot, heading nose first into the second Screech ship. It was like they were playing a cosmic game of chicken. Energy from both ships burst into light, breaking off their shields, testing their might.

The alien ships failed. Beams punched through as they passed each other in the dark. The Ares' High Energy Lasers cut deep into the opponent's hull. Explosions hemorrhaged from deep inside the alien vessel as it broke up into space.

In a last desperate attempt, the last ship turned to ram the Ares. The Captain was ready. "Displacement roll, bring us back and 180 degrees on target." The Ares elevated and flipped while turning back to its starboard side. Commander Bard handled the Ares like a fighter, rather than a warship.

The enemy ship passed through where the Ares should have been. A slight flight correction and the enemy came into sight. A combination of energy beams and torpedoes left it looking like nothing more than an extinguished spark in space.

"Ares is clear Captain. All hostiles accounted for." OPS was quick on the scans. Cheers went up but were subdued amidst what they had lost.

"Have all hands stay at action stations. Begin scanning for survivors," the Captain said, trouble lacing his usually solid voice.

"Aye, Captain. All hands at action stations. Scanning for survivors," OPS replied.

Jax sat back in her chair. She began checking through the damage to the ship. The shields, still holding, had taken a pounding. They were hanging on a ledge, too much of a push and they would fail. Parts of the outer portside hull had taken damage from the blast, its intensity pushing through the shields. It would need repair or outright replacement. Work teams had already been dispatched by Commander Urud from Main Engineering. The efficiency of the Engineering teams left little for the Lieutenant to do. She monitored and made her reports, but other thoughts weighed on the bridge.

She brought up the external scans on her station. No doubt all those working in command pods had done the same. She kept the screen small, but like everyone else, she had to know. *Please let there be survivors. Please let there be survivors. Please let there be survivors.*

They combed the wreckage with sensors, sent out ships to visually inspect every centimeter. Time marched on. Her legs ached from sitting in the pod, so she transferred her station to the command holotable. At least, that's what she told herself she was doing. In reality, it was easier to see the search efforts from there. Everyone on the bridge held out hope for something, but a grim mood had settled over them all.

She had to stifle a yawn. The double shift—or was it triple?—was taking its toll. Every piece of debris was checked, no chance taken that something could be missed. A grim feeling was not only felt but seen in the faces of everyone on the bridge. She wouldn't leave the bridge. She sent a message to Commander Urud saying she was fine, no replacement necessary. It didn't matter how long the shift was. It didn't matter what the truth was. There had to be survivors.

The Lieutenant kept herself distracted, checking through ENG updates. Commander Urud was with a team fixing the shields. There was some secondary damage they had initially missed. The whole process was taking longer than their first estimates. As they took systems offline to fix, she made sure backups came into play to cover the outages. It was mundane work, but it gave her a small distraction from the more horrific scene outside the ship.

Hours passed, or maybe it was days. Time was ceasing to have any meaning. The Captain made the call that no one wanted to hear. The Screech had been brutally efficient.

There were no survivors. All hands lost.

A hundred thousand people extinguished from the universe. They never had a chance to fight back, to defend themselves. Jax's stomach was queasy just thinking about it. *Earth needs to change.*

With that blow, she received notice that her shift would be ending. Commander Urud was sending someone up. Time for her to get some rest. Then the warnings started.

From deep inside Screech space, pathjackers sounded off. One after another, the alarms turned from a trickle into a flood. The data poured into the Ares and an image formed on the holotable before their eyes.

It looked like the Nest from Roost I, but it was flying in space. There were extra attachments on it, four large cones that lit up space like mini stars and propelled the spire forward. The scans gave it size and shape. It was enormous, almost ten times the size of the Nest. Around it, flew smaller ships like a flock of birds. Four of them were classified as destroyers. Six of them, were frigate class, like the one Ares had destroyed. Finally, a dozen of the smaller ships, like those that attacked the Indiana came into view. They were classified as combat ships.

It was a caravan. The telemetry showed that it was moving on a direct path. The usual wavy flight path of the Screech had been abandoned. There was only one possible destination for them on that path: Earth.

She leaned in and her whisper echoed loudly across the bridge. "Well, that's ominous."

Chapter 21

The Plan

The Captain did something Jax had never seen him do before. He went into the Captain's Pod. Unlike the rest of the pods on the bridge, the Captain's pod only had one seat and no way for anyone else to view in. She knew it had full holo integration with the ship. Sitting in that pod, the Captain could become the ship, issuing commands or physically moving the ship as you would an arm or a leg. Jax longed to try it.

Another function the Captain's pod had was a direct comm connection to Gaia Military Command (GMC). Normally the pod would close, a panel moving to shut it off, giving the Captain privacy. However, Ichabod Moss was larger than the average Captain. He hated being in the thing, let alone sealing it. So, it stayed open.

Once in, the shouts and bangs echoed out of the pod. Admiral Koonce, and whoever else from GMC was brave enough to be on the other end, were getting an earful. Something was not to the Captain's liking.

Jax knew the Captain was a two-star Captain. It wasn't a rank used in old Earth military. In the Gaia Military, it made Captain Moss equal, almost, to an Admiral. It let their best Captains stay Captain, get promoted, but still stay active in the field. Jax doubted a lesser Captain could get away with the ruckus Captain Moss was making.

It lasted close to an hour. She was tired and ready to give in. Her shift replacement, an Ensign Tock, had arrived some time ago. The emergency situation meant two engineers working the bridge was fine. She tried to hold out. Commander Urud had commanded her to get some rest, but she had to know what was going to happen. Tock couldn't force her to leave, and no senior officer mentioned it, so she stayed.

She was about to give in when Captain Moss climbed out of the Captain's pod.

The Captain stretched out his back as he bellowed, "Command staff, meeting, Briefing Room One. Now." Jax figured that was the end of it; Commander Urud would be on his way. She started to make for the exit, but the Captain held his hand up to stop her. "Lieutenant Brandt, Commander Urud is stuck fixing the shields and might be late to the meeting. He says, if you are here, you can speak for ENG, so you will join the briefing."

"Aye aye, Captain." *Since when can I speak for Engineering?* She followed the Captain out. *Maybe I should have made for my quarters earlier. No, focus. The ship needs everyone doing their best. Be a Captain. There's no rest when duty calls.*

When they entered the briefing room, Commander Lewis was already seated. The Lieutenant moved to the far side of the table, passed a couple seats, and took the chair usually occupied by Commander Urud. She stuffed another yawn into her jaw. *No time for that, you're at the big table now.*

Commanders Haddock and Moro entered next. Isaac Haddock moved his muscular frame into the seat next to her. He gave her a quick nod and a small welcoming smile.

Commander Moro paused at the portal and his faced pinched when he saw her. Despite her fatigue, she sat straighter and steeled herself. *I belong here, I am a Captain.* Terrance Moro almost bared his teeth as he took his seat to the left of the Captain.

Commander Bard was the last to enter. The skinny NAV Commander walked in with a stiff back and sat across from Jax with equal rigidity. An aura of formality always seemed to surround her.

Now that the staff were gathered, the Captain wasted no time. He waved his hands and the holotable sprang to life. "Here is the problem you know."

The Screech convoy populated the table. Each ship was shown in miniature detail, as clear as if they were really floating in front of them. The Lieutenant marveled again at the array of ships. Destroyers, frigates, combat ships, and at the center of it all, what was now labeled a Colonization Lander.

"This is something the higher ups have speculated at, but until this moment, have never seen. We believe this to be a kind of planetary engineering ship. Once at its destination, it will enter the atmosphere and embed itself into the crust of a planet, much like a kinetic missile." The image in front of them shifted. The convoy was closing in on the Earth. "Besides the damage created by such an action, it will give the Screech an instant stronghold from which to colonize or invade a world."

The holo image shifted, to show the Colonization Lander breaking into the Earth's atmosphere, impacting the surface of the planet. A mushroom cloud rose up. Ripples of earth rolled away like waves hitting the beach. Coils unfurled from the structure, wrapping the surrounding landscape in its embrace. Screech ships and soldiers came pouring out.

Jax glared around the room. All the Commanders were sitting back, hips pressed deep into their chairs. Eyes wide, they couldn't tear them away from the images playing in front of them. The Captain dismissed the screen and stayed silent. *He wants everyone to process what they just saw. It was the end for Earth.* Earth couldn't fight the Screech from space, they had no battle ships. On the ground, they had no military. Only a First Responder Brigade for emergencies, and then the Peacesmiths Co-Ops. Nothing equal to the task before them, even if they knew it was coming.

"What's our course of action, Captain?" Commander Moro asked.

"Well, that leads to the problem you don't know." He planted his hands on the table as if to stable himself. "Gaia Fleet Command and the leaders of the Humanistic Commonwealth have informed me that all potential support for intercepting the Lander is too far away to get here before the Screech reach Earth."

"Even the other Ares class ships? With their speed, surely they can join us?" Commander Moro asked.

"Unfortunately, with the use of the pathjackers, we have covered more space than we ever have before. With that coverage comes new findings. Active Ares class ships have been dispatched to investigate those findings. We thought the Screech would be looking for us and ignoring Earth. We thought wrong. We have been spread too thin."

Her stomach lurched. It wasn't her fault, she knew, but the idea had been hers. The pathjackers. It had seemed so great at the time, but now it was going to cost them. *So, what do we do now? The Captain must have something.*

"Can we notify Earth? Get them to evacuate?" After she threw it out there, she looked at the faces surrounding her. A mix of sympathy and horror highlighted them all.

"Any transmission of an alien invasion would be treated like a hoax. Even if we flew right up to them and announced ourselves in the Ares, it would take them weeks to wrap their heads around it. Months to plan and execute such an evacuation. That is time we just don't have," the Captain said.

"And that is what we have to fight for, isn't it, Captain?" Commander Moro's words were full of spite. "The Earthers that are too proud to see the truth, too lost in their Utopia. That is what you are leading us to understand, isn't it?"

"Yes, we have been ordered to stop the Lander at all cost."

At all cost? What does that mean? At all cost? So, a suicide mission? Surely that can't be right? The Lieutenant searched the room, hoping that someone's face would reveal something she had missed.

The briefing room door opened. Everyone was momentarily startled as Commander Urud joined them. His usual cheerful face had dropped into a morbid expression. She was sure the Captain was relaying this meeting to him on a private channel.

Jax stared at him for a moment while he hovered in the doorway. Maybe he can add something. *There must be something.* In that moment, she realized, *I am sitting in his chair, I need to let him handle this.* The Lieutenant made as if to vacate Commander Urud's chair, but he gave a slight wave of his hand for her to sit. As she settled back in, he took one of the auxiliary chairs on the wall behind Commander Lewis.

"So, we prepare all stations for one fight of our lives." The Navigator Commander's voice echoed through the room. She didn't speak often, but when she did, it always carried weight. She was a professional, even when facing the end. "We all know why we are out here and the challenges that brings. Let us not try and avoid the darkness."

"Correct. All stations start preparations. We have little choice but to meet them head on and do what damage we can. If we can't stop them, then at least let's slow them enough till reinforcements can arrive." The Captain's eyes surveyed the room as he spoke.

This was the plan? This was the something he had to offer them? This is a crappy plan. The whole idea of, 'at all cost', continued to rattle in her head. *There has to be a better option.*

"We'll make it more than a good fight." Commander Moro was sitting straight, his head held high. "Earth may not be worth it, they may not appreciate it, but for the High C and the Gaia Fleet, we shall make it a day to remember."

The Captain almost rolled his eyes. "That we will, Commander. If there is nothing else, all stations will begin preparations. I want us ready early, so no surprises. Let's get to work."

While everyone began to rise, Jax was glued to her chair. *Is this where everything had led her? Surviving the Indiana. Becoming a part of the Ares. Surviving the ground mission on Roost I. It had all led to this? At all cost. Run straight at the Screech and sling it out. The Captain has said over and over, we don't want to be in a dog fight. So why are we going into a dog fight?*

It was a crappy plan. From the Indiana to here and this was it? Can't let this be it. Time to be the Captain. "I have a plan." She said it before she registered what she had done.

The room froze. The Captain was already standing, and the Commanders were in different stages of rising.

"A course of action has already been decided, Lieutenant. I suggest you follow orders." Commander Moro practically snarled the words.

"I have a plan." She spoke each word clearly, precisely, as she locked eyes with Terrance Moro.

Before the Commander could continue, the Captain raised his finger. "I'm assuming, Lieutenant Brandt, that this will be worth our time to reconvene. You should have voiced your opinion before we dismissed."

Her face softened as she turned to the Captain. "I have a plan. I apologize for not speaking sooner. Long shifts are slowing me down."

"Make it good, Lieutenant," the Captain said, motioning for the Commanders to resume their seats. All eyes turned to her. *Now, do I actually have a plan? I am tired. Maybe I should have kept quiet.*

"We are waiting, Lieutenant." Annoyance crossed the Captain's face.

I need a little more time. Work it out. Find the long view. "You have said over and over the Ares should not be in a dog fight. Attacking the Lander straight on does not play to our strengths. I think we should attack from the back of their convoy, where they have limited protection."

"Of course it would, Lieutenant. But to circle around would take too much time and they would detect us before we could engage. With their velocity moving away from us, we would be ineffective." Commander Moro spoke without looking at her.

"Unless we let them fly right past us. We can use a standby protocol to enhance our stealth capabilities. Hiding in the wreckage would also give us more coverage." While she talked, she began laying the pieces into her personal holoscreen. *I do have a plan. I can see it now.*

"We don't have a standby protocol." Moro dismissed her like a child he didn't want to deal with.

"I know a team in Engineering that I'm sure could put one together." She brought her eyes up and locked them with Commander Urud's. He studied her for a moment, his eyes rolling into his head as if to think. A slight smile creased one side of his lips when he gave a slight nod.

Commander Moro sighed. "Be that as it may, there is not enough wreckage left of Highguard for us to hide in."

"That's why we're not hiding in Highguard, we're going to hide beneath the Indiana."

Jax transferred her work to the main holotable. The wreck of the Indiana came into focus, its hull shattered in the middle with one of the Screech ships protruding out like a sore thumb. A monument in space to one of the greatest tragedies of her life.

She steeled her heart and triggered an image of the Ares that flew into place. "The Indiana is just sitting there, waiting for us. For our purpose, it's perfect. The qave drives from both engines will still be leaking energy. That energy should be able to mask anything the standby protocols miss. Also, since it poses no threat, the Screech won't give it a second glance."

When she looked to the commanders' faces, she found agreement starting to register on all of them, except for Terrance Moro's. His face was pinched as if he was grinding his teeth. She continued. "Once they pass, we can come up to speed almost instantly. Then we move in and use the rail guns to target the ship." The holo image played out her scenario.

Commander Moro scoffed. "Besides other things, your lack of experience is showing. For the rail guns to have the necessary effect at these velocities, we would have to be a lot closer." He moved his hands for a moment and then waved them to the table. The image of the Ares firing on the Lander updated, with the Ares almost two thirds closer than it had been. She was taken aback by the realization. *This is still the plan. We can still make it work. Work the plan.* She pushed forward.

"Thank you, Commander Moro, for that correction. I still believe our flight team can handle it." She turned to Commander Bard. The skinny, stiff-necked Navigation Officer was quick to nod her agreement.

"And we have the best weapons team around." It was both a statement and a challenge as she turned back to Commander Moro.

He paused and ground his teeth some more before he replied. "Of course. However, this is no guarantee they will go that route. Once past Highguard, they could approach Earth from many flight paths. They are not known to fly in straight lines. We are still better engaging them directly before they choose a path we cannot predict."

"They will go here." She pointed at the Indiana.

"Unless you can provide something more substantial, Lieutenant Brandt, then I agree with Commander Moro. We can't risk them circling off while we hide and wait," the Captain said.

I know they will go here, but why do I know? I can feel it, see it. I need to focus. I'm so tired. Captain Moss had been trying to teach her to lay it out, to rely not just on her instincts, but to know why it works. *Show them why it works.*

"Lieutenant? We don't have time for debate. If you're going to make your case, you need to get to the point," the Captain said, pushing her on.

The point. The Screech are always on point. That was it. It all came together. "They'll come here because this is what the Screech do any time they attack; they dive straight in. With the Indiana, they circled around until they decided to come at us. On Roost I, they circled us constantly until they committed. They did the same at Highguard, as well. Circle, observe, and be evasive until they attack. Then they hold nothing back." She was speaking fast, the words flowing. "It's more than just a pattern, it's a part of who they are."

186

She looked from the image of the Indiana at the faces around her. Startled surprise stared back. "Can we verify this?" The Captain spoke to Commanders Bard and Haddock.

The room went silent while the two Commanders collaborated. Jax stifled a yawn and willed her eyes to stay open. *I could use a nap. I had better be right, I don't think I have anything left.*

The two Commanders nodded at each other and Commander Bard spoke. "There are other instances in our files that back up Lieutenant Brandt's hypothesis. Our encounters at Talos 4, Hyperion, and Maysworld are the most convincing." The Captain took a deep breath and sat back in his chair. Jax had no idea about any of those references. *More homework for me. Wonderful.*

"Captain, surely you can't be considering this based off such circumstantial evidence? A hypothesis by someone who has barely been in this conflict?" Commander Moro looked almost ready to burst.

The Captain splayed his hands on the table again. It was a slow and careful movement. No one dared talk. Taking a deep breath, he closed his eyes. When they opened, his steel gaze shone with the decision he had made. There would be no more discussion.

"Head to head, we might slow them down. We might not. With the Indiana plan, they might not go that way. Then we've missed our chance. The choice made today will either mark our valor or condemn us as fools." The Captain's eyes surveyed the room. He met each face with a look of cold determination in his eyes. "Our fate will be decided with the Indiana. Commanders will begin preparations to enact Lieutenant Brandt's plan. I want action reports in my hands in one hour. Dismissed."

As one, the Commanders rose to depart. Commander Moro was the first out of the portal. He swept away like a storm. The thunder of his boots stomping the ground could probably be heard all the way to the engine rooms.

187

The Lieutenant had started to rise when a look from the still-seated Captain glued her down. Within moments, they were alone. The Captain spoke. "When I told you to be a Captain, I didn't mean to physically take over."

"My apologies, Captain. I didn't mean to." She gulped the last words down.

"I know, it's the only thing that saved you. Military protocol may be bothersome, but you will learn it and respect it. Am I clear?"

"Yes, Captain."

"Captains can decide how their ships run. On my ship we are formal, especially in meetings such as this. When I give commands, they are to be followed, not countered after the fact. When you have your own ship someday, you can make the choice, but for now, you will follow and keep your insubordination in check. Your constant disregard for proper protocol will hurt you at some point. Mark my words." The Captain pulled his large frame up and started for the door.

"Yes, Captain."

"As it is, I'm sure Commander Moro will have a complaint on my desk by the time I make my quarters." He turned before he crossed the threshold and pointed a thick finger at her. "I hate dealing with complaints, Lieutenant Brandt."

"Apologies, Captain. I'll do better. I promise."

He turned back to the door. "Yes, you will." He stepped out and paused once more, throwing her a small glance over his shoulder. "Oh, and Jax? Good job." The Captain left and she sat there, stunned. She leaned back in her chair and tried to take it all in. Eventually, she allowed herself a slight smile.

Chapter 22

Monsters

Everyone on ship was living off caffeine, including her, although she still couldn't bring herself to drink that nasty thing known as coffee. Thankfully, MS1 Zakar had done some magic and added more caffeine to her chai. It was glorious.

She sat in the wardroom, reviewing screens of all the ENG work. Sipping tea. Taking nibbles at food. Hopping through checklists. Getting little to no rest. The last couple days had been a blur. The trip to the Indiana had given them some extra time, but they would need every second they could get.

Engineering had hit some walls creating a standby protocol. While the Ares was designed for stealth, running at standby was proving itself to be a different beast altogether. Systems like shields and weapons just weren't designed to run while powered down. Work arounds became the best options; multiple engineering teams were installing energy shielding and power dampeners where none were supposed to exist.

I keep causing the engineering teams more work. I'm sure they'll make me pay for that at some point. Her work was regulated to the organization of work teams and communicating with other divisions. While she could get her hands dirty, the truth was, she would be in the way of the more experienced Ares crew. They had a limited amount of time and that meant putting the best people where they could do the most good, pronto.

Commander Urud was in the main engine room handling things there. The Rat Pack, led by her 'little sis', were busy in engine room two. It was all controlled chaos as they raced the clock to implement her plan. Captain Moss had made it clear this was her responsibility. He had also stressed that she needed to not only be heard but seen. So, she couldn't just manage from the bridge, she had to get out and see it done. She had been all over the ship. *All that running is finally paying off.*

She ticked off another report of finished work. Took another long draw on her tea. Then she started to gather her tray to leave. These breaks were mandatory, by order of the Doctor, but no one wanted to take longer than necessary. *I'll take ten and say I did twenty. Got to keep the Doc happy. Sit, eat, and get back to work.* At least, that was the plan till Commander Terrence Moro walked in.

He held his head high like he owned the place. His shoulders were squared back like the fatigue of the past few days had had no effect on him. The weapons teams had been just as busy as engineering, double checking the energy weapons and getting torpedoes ready, running gun checks, drilling scenarios, and doing everything else that WEP did. Yet, compared to how disheveled she felt, he looked sharp and fully rested. *Scum.* He stopped halfway to the counter and tilted an eye towards her. He stiffened back up, planted a toe, and did a crisp turn. He marched over to her.

Looking down his nose, like he couldn't be bothered to drop his head and look her in the eye, he said, "Do you have a problem, Lieutenant?"

"No, sir. Just working while I eat. Sir."

"I don't want any of your issues to negatively affect this already deranged plan." He was practically spitting the words through his teeth. "So, if you have something to say, let's hear it."

Technically, in the wardroom, you didn't have to stand when a superior officer is talking to you. The Lieutenant wasn't going to give him anything to complain about, though. She stood and straightened her back. "I have nothing to say to a superior officer, sir."

He stared off over her head as the silence stretched out between them. "I see. I hear that you converse better without so much military formality. So perhaps we should speak freely."

She raised an eyebrow at him. *What's he up to? He never does anything without proper military protocol. How far can we push this?* "Freely and off the record?" she said tilting her head at him.

He looked down at her and said, "Fine."

"You sure you want others to hear what I have to say?" She gave a small jerk over her shoulder. Commander Moro's eyes moved around the room. Several small groups of junior officers had stopped their breaks to watch them. *Probably waiting for me to hit him again. Sorry to disappoint them.*

His throat grumbled as he said, "Clear the room."

The room came to life. It was like someone had paused a holovid and had just now started it playing again. The junior officers moved, racing one another for the portal. Only the Commander and Lieutenant remained.

"Satisfied?" he said through clenched teeth.

"Very," she said, realizing he was already agitated. *I can push more.* "It pains you to just drop all the pretense and just talk to someone, doesn't it?"

"You don't know anything about me. It pains me to talk to people like you, who make a mockery of us."

"I've never mocked you. You've had some kind of problem with me since I've gotten here. I've put my life on the line the same as any member of this crew. How is that a mockery?"

"They are trained. You are only here by happenstance. Each day you get something right, it's an accident, not by design. You act like you know what you're doing, you talk like you know what you're doing, but it's a lie. You think you can do better than those of us who are trained for this. You mock us with every action you take. You will get us all killed for nothing."

191

"Us? Us? You keep saying that like I'm not a part of this crew."

"This crew is for Gaia. For the Humanistic Commonwealth. For the Gaia Fleet and the Terrain Corps. Not for you. Not for Earth."

"You pompous ass. Most of this crew is from Earth."

"They knew the choice before coming here. They chose to honor Gaia and leave the ignorance of Earth behind."

She tried to swallow her laughter, but a chuckle still escaped. "They didn't leave Earth behind. They came to protect it. Same as me. They understood that Earth isn't prepared and wanted to do something about it. They gave up their lives for the good of all humans, Earth and Gaia alike. So did I. But that's not what you're about is it? You don't care about Earth or human beings as a whole, do you? For you, it's all honor and glory, all for Gaia. You just want to be looked at like some kind of hero."

"You wouldn't understand. Too bad your father never explained to you what it means to serve. To dedicate your life to your people, to have to carry their honor and their grace."

"My father? He was hated by the people he protected."

"You lie. Your father was the greatest General Earth ever knew. He was revered."

"I never lie about my father!" She had just wanted to antagonize him, but now she could feel her anger growing. She stepped into him and was pleased to see him step back. "Oh, you know the history books. The Keres Incident. The great victory. That all happened just before I was born. But as I grew up, I saw a different story. What I know is that people would spit at him as we walked by, they would move seats to get away from us in restaurants. Leave rooms just so they didn't have to be near him."

"I don't believe you."

"Believe it. The history books remember his fifteen minutes of fame. It was gone in the blink of an eye. I lived with it. The only place he was revered was on base or when he was home. Anywhere else, he was a villain."

"I'm sure you were too young to understand, but the Keres incident made him a hero for all time. If you aren't lying, then your memories are flawed."

Her eyes flared. "My memories of my life are just fine, thank you very much. I knew my father. We had many long talks about all this, simple ones when I was younger, a few deeper before he died. Keres, the way people treated him, all of it. As a kid I didn't understand. Why did people hate my daddy so much? Why did they fear him?" She stretched her neck and locked eyes with Terrence Moro, not really expecting him to answer. "He said, 'I don't do it for their recognition, I do it because they need me. They need me to think about the monsters, so they don't have to. They need me to fight the monsters when they come. They hate and fear me because I'm a reminder that there are monsters out there'."

Moro scoffed. "Monsters? Something you tell a child. If he were alive today, he would tell you differently. There is nothing wrong with gaining glory protecting your people. People worthy of the protection will give an equal worth back. I'm a reminder to Gaia that they are protected. They thank me for it. Earth is lost and understands nothing, maybe someday you'll understand that. I doubt it."

"No, I understand it more today than I ever have. I wish I would have understood it sooner. He was talking about humans, but aliens count too. The Screech are monsters. Humanity may not understand it, but it needs to be protected from such threats. It's also why I hate you so much. You're a monster just as bad as the Screech."

"Excuse me?"

She was talking faster. She couldn't put it in words before but there it was. Now that she had said it, the realization rang true. *I know what I hate about you.* "The Screech attack humanity, they kill without provocation. They seek to destroy us. But so do you."

193

"That's absurd," he said, his cool demeanor breaking slightly.

"Is it? Every time you talk about Earth versus Gaia—the weak Earthers, they're not strong enough, not good enough, we shouldn't be protecting them—you tear us apart. You encourage others to do the same. Us versus us instead of all of us versus them, just like Rallic."

"I had nothing to do with Private Rallic."

"Yes, you did. With every word, you encouraged him. Made it okay for him to see an Earther dead. As long as it's for the good of Gaia."

"That's absurd. I would never jeopardize a member of this crew."

"But, according to you, I'm not a part of the crew and I'm from Earth. So, it's okay if something happens to me. You say things like that all the time. You might as well command it."

"You are out of line. I would never command such a thing."

"You don't have to command them. You enable them to do it on their own. The hero of Gaia, their grand champion, your words alone inspire them. Your words lead to their actions. You're just a Rallic through words instead of action."

"That will be enough."

"They can justify it because they think that's what you really want. Gaia first and Earth can die on its own."

"I said that will be enough!"

"How many more want to let Earth die, let the humans there die, because Terrance Moro says so?"

"Lieutenant! That is enough." Each word was barked out. His eyes targeted hers like laser beams.

The Lieutenant snapped to attention. "I guess speaking freely is over. Permission to be dismissed?"

The Commander was shaking as he sought to contain his rage. His jaw was clenched so tight the lines on his face contorted with each breath. Even his tan skin couldn't hide the red that flushed his face.

194

The Lieutenant stood cool and proud. Inside, her heart raced, but she had control. *Maybe I pushed too far. Maybe. Right now, I just don't care.*

"Dismissed, Lieutenant." He spat the words while containing his rage.

She planted her right toe and turned sharply on her heel, marching to the door with her back straight, and her eyes forward. As she entered the doorway, she stopped and turned. Commander Moro was like a statue, his gaze never breaking from hers. "I know we're on the record now, so I want you to know I'm not afraid of you. I'll follow your orders, but I will also hold you accountable for them. Prove you're not a monster."

The Lieutenant turned and left. She could hear him yelling at her, but at this point, Jax just didn't care. She walked on. *I'll pay the price for this later, but right now, it's worth it.*

Chapter 23

Target

They waited in silence; the air was thick with anticipation. People were still scrambling around the ship, finishing any last thing they could. It was busy work, they were ready, and they just had to wait.

The Lieutenant was standing at the holo command table. Working from there wasn't as efficient as working from the pod. *Efficiency isn't what I want right now.* It gave her a better view of the tactical displays. *I want to see what's happening. I need to.*

OPS was feeding constant information from the pathjackers into the holotable. Their own active sensors were shut down, so that left only the pathjackers and passive monitoring. They were waiting for light and energy to reach out to them from the darkness. The Screech convoy was still too far away. Once it entered that range, they would have less than hour before contact.

Commander Haddock's muscular frame hovered outside the OPS pod. Two of his best were working within it. It wasn't often OPS had a full staff on the bridge; it spoke volumes about their situation. Isaac Haddock's head swung back and forth from the pod to the command table. They didn't want to miss a detail. Everything had to be accounted for.

The Captain stood like a statue at the table. So unmovable that, sometimes, you forgot he was there. He waited, he listened, he would occasionally issue a command. No matter what, his eyes never left the displays. His steely gaze was unwavering.

"Screech convoy will enter our passive scan range in 5, 4, 3, 2, and 1," the OPS Commander said, his high-pitched voice sounding at odds with the weight of the situation. He paused, his hands waving, his eyes connecting with his holoscreens, verifying data. "We have passive scanner contact. Estimated time of arrival is forty-two minutes."

The Captain's response was instant. "Batten down the hatches, prepare for the storm."

It was an odd command to the Lieutenant's ear, but the meaning was clear. *It was time, no turning back now.* Across the bridge, everyone sprang into motion. Only ENG and NAV had their normal staffing. One engineer on the bridge to coordinate, was enough; engineering wasn't done on the bridge. NAV rarely needed more than a pilot and co-pilot on duty. The weapons stations were full with Commander Moro at the table and two of his best gunners staffing the pod. Even the Captain had some Fleetwalkers standing by to assist him. They were entering data, tracking stats, and taking care of a dozen minor things, all so the Captain could focus on the bigger picture.

The Command table zoomed out to show the Indiana and Ares in relation to the Screech. It was hard for her to look away from the Indiana. Her first command, her first great adventure in space, now hanging there, lifeless. Nestled underneath it, the Ares looked equally dead. She couldn't tear her eyes away. It was so hard to look at, even if it was the exact look they wanted.

Time was moving way too fast, twenty minutes gone.

"How long until we are in the normal Screech sensor range if we were under silent running?" the Captain asked.

"Five more minutes until we enter their bubble," Commander Haddock replied.

A countdown appeared on screen. Five more minutes to see if this plan will work or if we are nothing more than a target. *Come on, Screech, stay the course and have a blind eye.* A cold sweat was passing over her. Across the bridge, other officers were wiping their brows.

"Entering Screech sensor range." The entire bridge held its breath as Commander Haddock spoke, or maybe it was just her. Moments ticked away. "No change in course or speed from any ship. Currently we are clear."

"Yes!" The exclamation came from the unusually formal NAV officer, Commander Bard. Jax turned to look, but she was tucked away in her pod. Instead, she caught the eye of Commander Moro. He had his chin up and gave a huff and turned his attention when she looked his way. *Well, I guess there'll be no credit coming from that side.*

"Stay strong, people," the Captain intoned. "We are not there yet. OPS, if there's no change, I want verbal updates every minute and then continual updates when they are within ten."

Time ticked on. With the updates from OPS, each station focused on their duties. The Lieutenant flipped through screens. It was wasting time; Engineering was on point and left her with nothing to do. She took moments to look at the weapons plans being laid out by WEPS. *I have so much I need to learn.* The attack plans had redundancies upon redundancies, secondary options to cover successful hits and failures, options attached to flight plans and options independent of them. It was staggering to see the amount of information that was being laid out.

Watching the NAV station was also insightful. I thought I knew how to pilot, but this is beyond me. Waiting to be used were pre-planned attack patterns. The patterns were live simulations that constantly updated off the real time data from the Screech advancement. Commander Bard and her co-pilot, listed on screen as a LTG1 Boxmeer, were also planning for one-on-one fights, retreating and even ramming other ships. *Let's hope it doesn't come to any of that.*

The timer on the command table ticked down to the minutes. "NAV, I want both exit course and attack patterns ready to go. If they spot us, you have leave to initiate as needed."

"Aye aye, Captain. NAV is ready and standing by," Commander Bard said. The oldest Commander on the Ares, she was even older than the Captain. Jax had asked the XO why she wasn't the Captain of her own ship. Commander Lewis had chuckled at her and asked right back if she had looked at Lilly Bard's flight record. She hadn't had the time. It seemed obvious now that she was just too valuable as a pilot. *When you're the best pilot, no one wants to take you out of that position.*

The bridge settled again into its rhythm. Anticipation ran high as the timer counted down and Commander Haddock voiced his updates.

Her job was almost too easy. *I almost wish something would break just so I had something to do. No, don't think that way, find something to occupy your mind.* She focused more on her beautiful space shark, nestled under the "rocks" of the Indiana, and the Screech convoy floating smoothly toward them. She swallowed hard as the images began to parallel each other. Her gaze was so intense she no longer heard the workings of the room around her. Her hand moved briefly to wipe her brow.

The Screech destroyers, each one the size of the Ares, came first. Their rounded edges flew in perfect formation. Their tendrils floated out behind like strange space jellyfish.

Next came the Lander. The Lander floated smoothly in space, passing the Indiana and the Ares. The size of it was staggering. She had known it was big, but seeing it like this sent chills down her spine. *My shark now looks like a minnow.*

Cold sweat was matched by the thump of hearts throughout the room. Superstition took over. Each move was carefully made to limit sound. It seemed right, even though in space, it did not matter. The Lander was moving at a rate just over the Indiana's top speed from so long ago. Its passing still felt like waiting for the sun to rise during the darkest night.

The trailing ships faded in. First the frigates and then the combat ships, a crawling parade before the Ares. Each of them just a smaller version of the destroyers. They have a design they like, and they stick to it.

Across the bridge, people started moving again, coming to life as if they had just awoken from hibernation. The Lieutenant pulled her eyes from the screen to run her checks for Engineering. The Captain's voice boomed across the Command deck. "Cancel standby mode, but keep us in silent running. Initiate intercept course, guns to the ready. Let's go hunting."

From their hiding spot, nestled under the Indiana, the warship swung out and came into line with the Screech. "Standby mode has been cancelled, Captain. All systems are back to silent running and ready to go," the Lieutenant called, relief lacing her voice. She double checked all her screens, making sure there were no surprises from standby mode. Her board was green. *Well, at least that part of the plan worked as needed.*

"Excellent, Lieutenant. Commander Haddock, time to intercept?" the Captain asked.

"Fifteen minutes to intercept, but we are inside their bubble, if they're looking, they can detect us."

"Well, let's hope they're looking the other way."

The technical readouts on the table showed the Lander was still gaining speed. At the current rate, it would still take months to get to Earth. But it was accelerating. The best estimates showed that, by the time it was done, it could cut that time to weeks. It was now or never.

They made it five minutes before the Screech reacted.

"We have movement from the trailing squads." Commander Haddock was rushing his words. "They're circling off, massive increase in velocity. Never seen spikes that high from that kind of ship before."

"There's an opening. Track those ships, but that's what we were hoping for. NAV, full speed ahead. WEP, how long till we are in range?"

"Five minutes, Captain. Railguns one through eight are go," Commander Moro said.

"Captain, the ships that peeled off are still increasing. They're lining up, never seen the Screech use this kind of formation before," Isaac Haddock called out.

"Keep monitoring, Commander, we just need to make our shot."

"Aye aye, Captain." Commander Haddock's hands started waving, his head swinging from side to side. He called something to his officers in the pod and then turned back to the table. "Wait. Captain. One of the front destroyers has veered off. Its course suggests it's coming around. We also have panels opening on the Lander."

"Weapon ports?"

"No. We have incoming ships. Massive launch!"

The command table zoomed in on the Lander. The Lieutenant watched as hundreds, possibly even thousands, of small ships were propelled out of it. They looked like smaller versions of the combat ships following the Lander. *Are those fighter craft? What good are fighters going to do versus the Ares?*

"They're on a ramming course," the Captain said as if to answer her thoughts. "Reinforce front shields. WEP, open fire all energy weapons. Commander Bard, evasive maneuvers but keep us on target!"

The answer from each station came as one. The Lieutenant had already transferred the energy from non-essentials and silent mode. *Don't need that anymore.* WEP was using it all as fast as she could release it to them. She watched as the Ares lashed out with its PBMs and TBWs. The small avatar on the holotable showed red beams cutting the enemy away, searing lines through the small ships, but they couldn't stop them all.

"They're insane, they're throwing ships at us like missiles." Commander Moro spit the words out.

The Ares began a deadly dance, weaving through the suicidal ships. Commander Bard once again handled the massive warship like a fighter.

She banked and weaved causing the small fighters to miss their mark. The Ares would angle so other ships were deflected off the shields instead of hitting square. They were still looking for a clean shot on the Lander, but they couldn't find one.

"Captain! Incoming! Three combat ships! Port-Aft, thirty-five degrees, X-axis. How did they get around like that?"

Commander Haddock's eyes were wide as he gripped and leaned into the holotable.

"Target those ships! Target those ships!" the Captain thundered, but it was too late. The image of the Ares exploded into light.

Chapter 24
Captains first

This wasn't possible. The crew standing at the command table were flying in the air and being battered from side to side. Only the hand railing running around the table kept some of them from being thrown about the room. The Captain's two Fleetwalkers weren't so lucky, they were slammed against the hull.

The lights on the bridge flickered. Another impossibility. Even if both qave drives were to go down, the bridge and each individual station pod had independent power supplies that could keep them running for months. *This is bad, this is very bad.* The pods all went into lockdown. Hatches closed over the inhabitants. Like large lifepods, each one was secure in their own little bubble. Even if the bridge found itself breached into open space, the pods would keep working.

Artificial gravity should have kept them grounded no matter how the Ares turned or rolled, yet they felt it bucking again as their arms strained to hold on. The room settled. The Captain sprang into action. "What the frip was that? All stations report," he bellowed as he helped the Fleetwalkers off the floor. They were bruised and shocked, but otherwise okay.

"Weapons are active, but we've lost a lot of energy. Running on secondary power only. All beam weapons are reduced. Port and rear torpedo tubes are not responding." Commander Moro was sharp to reply.

"Navigation is now stable, maneuverability down forty-five percent. I'm also showing secondary power supply only. Qave drive is down over fifty percent!" Commander Bard said.

OPS was next. "They came in three in a line, Captain. On their trajectory, we should have passed them by, but they pushed their engines to critical, flattened their arc. Speeds they normally couldn't get. First one overloaded our shields, the next two exploded on the hull. Bastards. I should have kept a better eye on them."

"Take blame later, Commander, we're still in the fight. NAV and WEP, handle those fighter craft and keep us safe till we can assess damage. OPS, don't lose that Lander, we are still taking it down."

"Aye aye, Captain." The stations responded in unison, the sound echoing from speakers outside of each sealed pod.

"ENG, what's our status? I need a damage report."

While they had been giving their reports, the Lieutenant had been engrossed in checking her readings. *This just can't be real.* Multiple red lights blazed on her screen. New ones popped up one after another, but no matter how many appeared, they all paled in comparison to the warning she couldn't take her eyes off. The only warning that really seemed to matter.

She took control of the main holotable. She knew it was a breach of etiquette, since that was usually the Captain's prerogative, but they had to see this to believe it. The image of the Ares took up the whole table and rotated around to show the impact of the Screech ships.

"They hit right at the main engine room. The third ship breached the hull." She swallowed the lump in her throat. "I think everyone in engine room one is gone." Commander Urud, all those engineers, so many names, so many faces. *This shouldn't be possible.*

The command team all turned to her in dead silence. She kept talking, she had to or risk shutting down. "Main engine is still intact, its enhanced shielding and reinforcements held." *Mom always said they were tougher than the*

204

ships they powered. "However, the section of the Spine that feeds out of engine room one here—" The Ares spun and zoomed in as she pointed. "—Is damaged. We can't get power from there till it's fixed. It's also causing other disruptions throughout the ship. Internal communications, power regulators, artificial gravity, everything will be impacted." For the first time, she dared to look up from the screens at the people around her. She was greeted by nothing but grim faces. The Captain wasted no time in breaking the silence.

"Can we get ahold of engine room two to fix the damage?"

The command table returned to its normal space view. The Ares rolled and turned hard to starboard, avoiding an attack. The command crew felt the movement as they were pulled sideways. Hands clutched the guard rail. Beams lashed out from the Ares and the target disappeared in a ball of light. Commanders Bard and Moro were a lethal combo. Jax talked quickly. "Negative. Engine room two went into automatic lockdown when we were hit. No one in or out. Plus, with the communication problems, we'd have problems talking to them anyways." *My friends are in there. Please stay safe.*

"Can we use a repair drone to do work on the Spine?" The Captain said, one step ahead of her. Repair drones were used outside of the ship. Mostly, they worked on the hull when sending a live person wasn't a possibility. While the Ares traditionally shied away from using any kind of robot or artificial intelligence, they weren't ignorant of the fact that sometimes it was just a better option.

"Yes. A repair drone should have the tools necessary to make the repairs. Two issues, however. First off, with comms the way they are, we can't program and launch a drone from here. We'll have to go to drone bay four and activate it manually." She had paused for a moment to double check herself. *Which drone bay was nearest the problem?* She had wanted bay number six. *Lucky number six.* But it just wasn't the best option. *Don't get caught up on silly superstition, stay on task.*

"And the second problem, Lieutenant?"

"The drone can't perform the calibration needed to bring the Spine back online. And that calibration has to be done from the repair site. Someone will have to go out there and do it manually," she said as her mind went to work. *I'll have to figure out how to reprogram the drone. I've never worked with those. I'll have to run, far end of the ship. Always seem to be running. What else will I need?*

The Captain's voice snapped her back into focus. "Very well, Lieutenant. XO?" Commander Lewis turned sharp eyes to the Captain. "Protect the ship first but keep us on a pursuit course. I want that Lander. As soon as I've restored the Spine, full speed ahead, don't wait for me to get back to the bridge."

Wait. What? That just sounded like the Captain is going out there. That can't be right. It was the XO, Commander Lewis, who voiced her thoughts first. "Captain, I object. Your place is on the bridge. Lieutenant Brandt is the engineering officer on station and should be the one to go. That or at least a senior officer."

"Objection noted, XO. But, last I checked, none of the senior officers came up through engineering. You came up through security by way of the Corps. Commander Moro through officer school and tactical. Commander Haddock is linguistics and intelligence. And Commander Bard is a flight jockey. Right now, we need everyone where they can do the most good."

"Then send Lieutenant Brandt, sir. Standard ops dictate that the Captain does not leave the bridge," Terrance Moro said.

"With all respect to Lieutenant Brandt's capabilities, I doubt she has been on ship long enough to know anything about a repair drone, let alone to know the proper instructions to have it repair the hull and Spine under such conditions."

The Captain looked at her, the question clear in his eyes. Her mind raced for a solution, but the Captain was already there. He knows the answer; *he's just waiting for all of us to catch up to him.* "That's correct, I've never worked with them, or the hull for that matter."

"That leaves me the only available engineer, so for the good of the ship, this Captain is leaving the bridge. XO, you have command, keep us safe and keep us on the hunt. I'll make the best time I can and get us back up to power. Stay sharp and stay focused and we can still take these bloody birds down."

The XO's face was icy cold. "I can't fault your logic, but I don't like it."

"You can put in an official reprimand later." He flashed a big, toothy grin at her. But we don't have time now. I need to get going." The ship turned again, their feet coming off the ground. The holotable was a mass of Screech ships and beams of all colors. While they debated, the fight outside waged on.

"Captain, wait." The Lieutenant jumped into the conversation. *This isn't right, it should be me. I need to do something.* "Let me go with you. Engineering jobs all require two people for safety. I may not know the drone or hull repair, but I do know how to calibrate and work with the Spine. Plus, who knows what you'll encounter with the hull damaged; an extra set of hands could be useful."

Commander Lewis backed her up. "I agree, Captain. If you have to go, take back up."

"Who's going to run ENG while you're gone?"

"ENG is running itself at this point."

"We'll still need someone on the bridge to reactivate all systems once the Spine is repaired. Best if you stay here to activate the startup protocols ASAP."

"Can't do that until we know it's fixed. If I run it too soon, we could blow out the whole system, fry it beyond repair. With comms down, you'll need to come back to the bridge for that to happen. I'm just taking up space here, better to put me where I can do the most good," she said, not letting her gaze drop from his for even a single second. "You're the Captain, those are your words, let me help."

He gave her an evil eye, but she could feel he was all out of excuses. "Very well. Lieutenant, you're with me. XO, you have the bridge. Keep us safe, but make those frippers pay for what they did to our ship."

"Aye aye, Captain." Commander Lewis moved into the Captain's spot at the command table.

"Well, Lieutenant Brandt, shall we run?" He waved his hand gracefully to the door.

She nodded her head and returned the gesture. "Captains first."

And they were off.

Chapter 25

Captains' Run

They were running. Their first stop was repair drone bay four. From the bridge, that was less than half a kilometer away. Their footfalls thundered down the halls. At first, Jax thought it would be easy to pace the Captain. She was in good shape. The Captain wasn't fat, but he was thick, with years of hard work layering his frame. Being that big, he couldn't be that fast. She was wrong. Ichabod Moss could move. His large frame sped down the corridors, eased into turns, navigated stairwells as if born to them. This was a man who knew his ship.

As they rounded one of the last turns to the drone bay, she caught a glimpse of his face. He was smiling. And was that laughter? Yes, it was. A deep guttural laugh that just couldn't be held back. She almost missed a step with the realization. Here they were in a fight for their lives, enemies all around, the ship damaged, and this man, this Captain, was having fun.

As they entered Drone Bay Four, he turned to her. "Good. I didn't lose you. Is there a problem, Lieutenant?" His head tilted sideways as he read what must have been bewilderment on her face.

"No. It's just I've never seen you like this. Given the situation, I'm a little shocked by your approach."

"I see." A half grin crossed his face as he took a seat at a workstation. The ship heaved under their feet as if to remind them they were still under attack. The small, clean station lit up and came to life. A bay window across from them also lit up. On the other side were ten rows of repair drones, stacked five high. There was a small walkway between the window and the pods for a technician, but it was currently empty. His fingers flowed smoothly over the controls. "We'll have to change a drone arm to a precision laser welder. All these are outfitted for bulk hull repair. Go change out drone three. I'll start the prep work."

"Aye aye, Captain." She moved to the left and the access door to the walkway slid open. A quick jog and she was at drone three. Tapping the control panel, a warning beep began to sound as the drone glided out on its rails. The Captain's voice echoed from an intercom into the walkway. "Repair routines are loading into the drone. Swap the work arm out. The replacement should be just under the window in the cradle."

She glanced over her shoulder. In the window, the Captain was pointing down. Her eyes dropped to see a small rectangular box about a meter long with a green light flashing. "On it." She moved to the side of the drone. Each drone was roughly egg shaped with two rotating cylinders on each side. The eggs were about two and half meters long and the side cylinders were half that. The cylinders could be rotated and had a variety of modular arms for different tasks. As she started to spin it, looking for the heavy welder, the Captain's voice echoed again. "So, why do you think I was enjoying the run down here so much?"

Amazing, here in the face of danger, working to save the ship, he wants to have a casual conversation. The ground under feet rumbled, once again reminding her the ship was on the move. She was shaking her head as she found the arm and gave it at turn. It unlocked and came loose in her hands. She held it in both arms as she walked back to the cradle. With the work, her mind settled into that welcome rhythm she so cherished. That's when she got her answer. "To put me at ease, so we can focus on the job."

"Close enough," he said as she dropped the heavy welder arm into the empty slot. "A Captain has to be what the situation needs. Calm and collected. Loud and scary. A diplomat or willing to smash someone in the face," the Captain said, with a hint of a laugh.

210

She shivered a bit at that last line. A quick memory of punching Commander Moro in the face flashed into her mind. She grabbed the replacement arm from the other cradle. Size and weight were similar, but at the tip, was a much smaller welding head. The welding assembly had two three pronged hands that were about the size of her fist. The left and right hands could grab and clamp whatever the drone was working on. *Let's hope that's good enough to get the job done.*

As she placed the arm on the drone, she let her thoughts run aloud. "I've lost so many. I'm sure you have too. How do you throw that aside and allow yourself to laugh? Even if it's necessary, it seems so grim."

The arm clicked in. She pushed a few buttons, and the drone slid back into its place on the rack. As she came back into the control room, the Captain looked her straight in the face. "I never throw them aside, Jax. Never. I morn them in my heart, but we honor them by living. Not by sinking into dread at their passing." She swallowed hard and nodded her head. She would have to think on it, find a way to practice it, but it made sense. *Can I do that?*

"Good work, Lieutenant." The Captain returned to the console. "Launching drone now." Lights flashed red on the drone side of the bay window. A portal opened and number three drone glided into it.

"Launch will run itself from here. Let's get on the next objective."

"Aye aye. Lead the way."

They didn't have far to go, but they were still double timing it. Minor quakes echoed their steps, like the ship was pushing them on to hurry.

A straight run past a few more bulk heads and they entered a sub engineering station. They both knew the protocols for Engineering and going outside the ship. Beside the door was a small shelf with lens boxes. The Captain grabbed a box on the go, held it to his eyes, and replaced it, all in one smooth motion. The Lieutenant stopped for a moment to hold hers up. A small beep and flash and the box inserted the ENG contacts in her eyes. She blinked a few times as the HUD came alive. She eyed

211

through a couple of menus and had the Spine specs queued up and ready to go. She looked over and the Captain was halfway into his EVA suit. *Even getting dressed, I'm a step behind, amazing.*

She stepped into the suit. It was a dull white color, bordering on gray, much like the Earth counterparts she had worn before. It was also much slimmer than the combat gear she had worn on Roost I. The smart suit adjusted to her size, the same as it had done for the Captain's bigger frame. The whole thing had the feel of a full body leather jacket. While they grabbed head gear and equipment vests, the Captain continued their running conversation. "You know we're making this all up as we go."

It only took her a moment to realize he wasn't talking about their current situation. "I heard something similar from Corporal Chambers after our ground mission."

The Captain barked a quick laugh. "The Terrain Corps has it easy. Humans have been fighting with their feet on the ground since they walked on land. Even though Earth shut down their militaries, re-creating them for Gaia is easier. We have a framework to pull from. Fleet is different. We might model ourselves after old Earth Navy or Air force, but space combat is not the same. Out here, when we break the rules, we're actually setting a new standard. We're years away from having any kind of set playbook to follow, no matter what we tell ourselves. It takes a dynamic mind to just survive." He pointed a thick finger at her for a moment, till he tilted his head indicating they needed to get moving.

Down the hall and past one more bulkhead, their feet started to float with each step; the artificial gravity was giving out the closer they got to the danger zone. Before them a hatch was shut and outlined in red. They had arrived.

The Captain stopped at the portal and checked the hatch controls. "We have a vacuum beyond this point. We have a good seal. This corridor is secure for now."

The Lieutenant activated her wrist holo and started scrolling through screens. "This close, we should be able to access the corridor cameras beyond the bulkhead. Let's see if they're active. Got it." She transferred the image to their contacts and gave them a real time overlay. It wasn't as nice as the images from the combat helmets, you could still see the hatch and wall, but the screened images were just as impressive for what it showed.

They spoke in unison at the sight before them. "Well, that's not good."

Just a meter past the hatch, the hallway disappeared. A large mass of burnt, twisted metal circled an opening into the darkness of space. The blast area easily covered over fifty meters, with a deep depression at its center. It burrowed through the decks, to the heart of engine room one. Emergency shields sparked repeatedly as they worked to seal off exposed corridors. Several of the small Screech ships zipped past, red fire from the Ares flashing after the targets. The Ares rolled. The light gravity beneath their feet caused them both to shoot a hand out and stabilize off the wall.

The Captain stayed focused on the job at hand. "There's the spot where the Spine is exposed." His finger pointed while tapping the bulkhead. "Where is the repair drone?"

"Give me a sec." Her hands raced across her holoscreen. "Got it."

A small green circle appeared on the image before them. While drones had basic thrusters to maneuver in open space, they also had retractable legs to attach and crawl along the hull. Drone number three was crawling near the breach like a spider on a web. It looked so small compared to all the damage around it.

"We'll seal that back hatch and use this corridor as our airlock."

"On it." She ran back down the hall. When she hit the door controls, they slid shut with a boom. Hatch locked and sealed, she returned to the Captain. "Door secured. I'm thinking we should use physical tethers rather than the energy straps. There's lots of chaotic debris out there that could disrupt the straps."

The energy straps were the same as the ones that held her trusty NEW24; a combination of qave battery and anti-gravity technology. As long as you had enough energy, they had no real length, couldn't get tangled and held strong. They could, however, be disrupted as she had found out the hard way. "Right," the Captain replied, nodding his head. "We can tether here." He indicated one of the handholds located on the wall. They were just as standard on the Ares as they had been on the Indiana.

She pulled a cable from behind her work belt. The physical tether was extremely thin, not even as thick as her finger. The micro carbon fiber could get tangled, but the thin line could handle metric tons of force, making them close to unbreakable.

They clipped their lines to the handholds, the Captain positioning himself by the door. "Hold tight. Once I open the door, for a moment, it will feel like we're in a hurricane. After that, follow me. We'll climb onto the hull and work our way up to the Spine. Maintenance ladder should still be there. I think that's what the drone was using. We check the drone's repair work, fix anything necessary, calibrate, and get back in. Focused and fast. Ready?"

"Aye aye, Captain." She grabbed the handhold with her left and saluted off her helmet with her right.

"That's the attitude. Let's hope the XO can keep her stable while we work." He gave a big grin as his hand hit the hatch release.

She gritted her teeth and held on with both hands as the air was sucked from the room. The Captain let out a roar.

They floated out the hatch and began a climb to the outer hull. Two Screech ships zipped by, their blue and green energy beams fractured off the Ares' shields. One ship scraped and bounced away as the Ares rolled. Their suits automatically activated magnetic locks to keep them stuck to the hull. Even with that, Jax's arms screamed as she fought to hold on. "That was unpleasant. I think I like staying inside the ship better."

214

"Agreed. Then let's move faster, so we can get back inside."

Turning off the magnetic locks, they started their climb over the damage and up to the outer hull. The maintenance ladder was waiting for them. Rungs pressed into the ship designed for work crews needing to transverse outside the ship. Parts of it were speckled with debris from the impact, but nothing that would hinder them. Hand over hand and foot after foot, they began to work their way down to the Spine. The Ares would turn, their suits' magnetic locks kicking in and holding them in place. As the warship stabled, they would disengage and start moving again. An uneasy pattern, but they were making progress.

They were halfway to their goal when the shields flashed and broke into a kaleidoscope of color. They never saw the ships that launched the shots. No sound reached their ears in the vacuum of space. The Captain turned and looked back at her, his eyes wide behind the faceplate. "Shields are down! Move!"

Her arms and legs tensed to push forward. She looked up, desperate to move forward, that's when she locked eyes with the Captain. He was flying straight at her. *He's going the wrong way!* No time to brace, she felt his mass bowl her over.

She yelled out more from surprise than fear. She tumbled and turned away from the ship. Lights flashed off her face plate as she tried to stabilize herself. Spinning with nothing to hold. The tether hit its limit and snapped her body back. She doubled over at the waist as it jerked, her teeth grinding.

"Captain! Captain!" She didn't need to shout for him to hear, but instinct took control.

Her HUD should locate him if she could just get him in view. She turned to scan. The Ares rolled. This time she screamed in fear. The tether pulled tight and she was wrapped towards the hull. As she was pulled into the damage crater, she tried to angle her body as if for a fall. She failed. Her left shoulder slammed into the wreckage. The pain erupted

215

from her lungs. Pulled along the jagged wreckage, it cut deep through the suit and into her arm. She yelled in pain. Her EVA suit gushed oxygen. Her HUD lit up with warnings, alarms blasting in her ears. Safety foam automatically deployed, filling and sealing the ripped suit. Medical nanites went to work on her arm and shoulder, dulling the pain. Thankfully, they don't hold back like the combat suits.

Within the wreckage, she found a grip. Pulling tight with her right arm and securing herself, she traced the path of the tether to orientate herself, her since of direction lost in the spin. Assured of her direction, she pulled herself up and started climbing the tether. She struggled to hold on with her left hand, fighting both the injury and the safety foam. She was climbing and constantly scanning, calling for the Captain. Overhead, a quick flash caused her to jump when the Ares' shields activated. In that moment, she saw it.

The Captain's tether. Twisted out and into space, a snake without its head. Its end was burnt. The Captain was gone.

Her heart raced. Her grips locked down hard, her entire body tightened. *No! No! No! No! No!* The one word echoed in her head as a thousand options flipped instantly through her mind. One option screamed above the others.

Mourn later.

She moved. Hand over hand. One foot after another. The painkillers handled her arm, or they didn't, she was lost in the moment. Her focus was absolute, all her emotions pushed to the side. She stopped for only a moment when the drone broke off the hull and went tumbling into the void. She pushed forward again. Everything around her was lost, there was nothing except her goal. The mission. The ship.

She arrived at the Spine. She had crawled down off the hull to rest upon it. She didn't remember that. She checked the welds. Each one looked solid, clean. There was only one way to be sure. She pulled the calibrator out. It felt loose in her left hand. She willed it to stay. *You have one chance. No more time.* She didn't even bother to activate the engineering contacts. The numbers flowed through her head.

She was smooth, smooth was life, rushing was death. 3-1-2-7-6, the sequence started. Twenty numbers. No mistakes. 9-3-2-3-8-4, the sequence ended. The calibration tool displayed a small message of her victory.

Calibration complete

Joy crossed her thoughts; a smile crossed her face. Time and her surroundings flowed back into her. Warning lights blinked on her HUD. Alarms blazed. Oxygen was almost gone. Her arm throbbed with pain. She blinked, her eyes flying through menus. *Where was it? Where was it? Where was it? Got it!*

She eyed the recall on her tether. A hum that indicated it was working sounded in her helmet. She was whipped backwards. She tumbled. She rolled. Her left arm burned again as she skidded off the hull. She was floating through the damaged crater of the Ares.

My great space shark. I fixed you. She was pulled back into the door where her excursion had begun. Her lungs burned as she screamed one last time, her body pounding into the wall. Despite the pain, despite everything, she managed to close the hatch. She pushed against the wall. She closed her eyes, waiting for the seal. Waiting for the pressure and the oxygen to return.

She passed out.

Chapter 26

Teeth

She didn't remember waking up. She didn't remember taking her helmet off, or her right glove. The left was sealed with the medical foam and was hugging her stomach. She didn't remember running, but she had. The bridge lay before her. She staggered into the control room. The XO, Commander Gemma Lewis, was the first to see her.

"Jax! Oh my. Are you all right? Where's the Captain?"

The XO scooped her up, coming in under her right side and securing her about the waist. Jax's head was shaking the whole time. They stumbled as the XO found her footing, the Lieutenant's weight collapsing against her.

"He didn't make it. Got the Spine fixed. Need to get to my station." The words were forced from her mouth. Rough and jumbled, she pushed them out. Her body felt numb and her lungs were on fire. Once the XO had taken her weight, her legs had ceased to move.

She couldn't look at anyone else on the bridge as the Commander walked her, carried her, to the ENG pod. She sat hard and her whole body seemed to let out a grunt. Her good arm went to work. She zoomed through the standard checklist. Integrity – check. Power flow – check. She couldn't really read what was in front her. Instinct took over. Next item. Check. Next item. Check. *Now restart, you fabulous beast. Restart.*

"Is it working?" The XO leaned in.

"Almost got it." The list was finished but nothing happened. *This has to work. It would work. Please start working.* The screen in front of her started to flip. Red lights moved to green. Some changed to yellow and some stayed red. In the end, she got what she needed as the qave drive kicked in and the power flowed. "We are a go. I don't know if it will last. Make it count."

The XO gave one sharp nod and went to work. "Give me full power to engines and shields, anything else goes to WEP. Helm, flank speed, let's get back to target."

"Attack plan, Captain?" Commander Bard paused before she said, 'Captain'. It was tradition on ships, if you were in command of the ship, then you were Captain, even if it wasn't official rank. For all the respect they had for Gemma, it would not come easy.

"We're going to fly straight at them and unload every piece of ordnance we have right up their ass. Commander Moro, prepare all weapons systems, empty the holds, nothing is to be held back. Time to finish this match."

Lilly Bard shook her head as she turned back into her pod. She might have responded but it was lost to the Lieutenant's ear.

"Aye aye, Captain." Terrance Moro responded. His voice was loud but there was a tint of anger in its usually professional tone. "Rail guns one and three are offline, all other weapons are hot and ready for your command."

"All right then, for Ares and Captain Moss."

All eyes turned toward the new Captain and the crew responded together. "For Ares and Captain Moss." In her head, Jax added more to it. *For the Indiana. For Reason O'Connor. For Daniel Trucker. For Jonathan Camp and Thelma Imes. For Ryan Nelson. For Teagan Thirgood and Marton Saville. For all that I have lost, that we have lost. Let us finish this.*

They were professionals, they went back to work. *Mourn later.* The Lieutenant shifted in her seat. She grabbed her left glove, twisted the lock, and pulled it away. Pain wretched her arm, but she wanted both hands free.

Safety foam flaked and fell off in chunks. She used her right hand to clean her fingers and stretch them out. She used her ENG contacts to activate the EVA suit's medical nanites. A blink and she gave herself another dose of painkillers. She had to keep going, whatever it took. The medicine flooded her system. Even with that, it wasn't enough; the pain stilled pulsed throughout her body. *You are not hurt, she willed herself. If I can mourn later, then I can feel pain later too.*

There was still a lot of red on her board. So many warnings screaming for attention. She dismissed most of them with a few waves of her hand. Got to stay focused on the plan. *Keep working what we need and let the rest wait. Later.* Right now, everything seemed to be later.

The ship's internal communication was still splotchy. She couldn't talk but got messages to engine room two and got them up to date on the ship's status. The damage to the Spine. The Captain. The repairs. Their plans now. Her mind entered a zone of pure focus. *Mourn later. This is the plan. Work the plan.*

She received a confirmation from LTG1 Koike. Rose. They understood and all was ready in engine room two. They had been in lockdown since the ramming of the Ares but had continued their work. Jax's heart lighted a little knowing at least some of her friends were safe.

They had lost ground, but with both qave drives online they were gaining fast. The last of the few Screech fighter ships were left far behind. While Jax and the Captain had been fixing the Spine, the command crew had been busy. All the combat ships trailing the Lander had been destroyed. Two of the Destroyers were also gone, having dropped back from their lead positions to protect the Lander. The Ares still packed enough punch with one active drive to handle them. The last one had landed a blow that disabled the shields. The Lieutenant would never forget that moment. More damage to the starboard side. Some of the fighters had broken through. Impacts littered the hull. Still, the Ares fought on.

Only the Lander and the last two destroyers maintained their course for Earth. Straight as a laser, they pushed forward, the loss of ships seemingly having no effect on their goal. *Do they feel the loss as we do? Do they care they have lost friends or family? Do I care anymore? No. I just want them to die.*

"One of the lead destroyers has broken off and is moving around to intercept," said Commander Haddock. His voice seemed rougher than its usual light tone.

"Entering weapons range," Commander Moro added.

"Hold weapons till we're closer. Keep eyes on that destroyer. Right now, it's not a target. Its intercept arch is too great to cut us off at these speeds. I doubt if that ship can pull the same stunt as the combat ships." The XO, the Captain, were leaning into the holotable.

"Aye aye, Captain. They won't catch us wanting again," Commander Haddock said through closed teeth. Pain washed over his words as his eyes kept vigil on the screen.

The Lieutenant looked over. The Lander was large in front of them. Her space shark was easily gaining ground at this point. Before, the Lander had looked insurmountable, so huge that there was no way the Ares could take it. Now, with most of its convoy destroyed or left behind, it looked like a target. No more ships launched from it; all the hatches were closed. They had spent everything trying to stop the Ares and they had failed. *Now it's our turn.*

"Two minutes till firing range for the rail guns, Captain," Moro said.

"Prepare to fire all railguns. Prepare for full barrage on follow up. Weapons, standby."

"We're getting some fluctuations from the Spine patch. I don't know how long it will hold," the Lieutenant said.

"Make it hold, Lieutenant. We're almost there. Make it hold."

"I don't know if I can break off at these speeds, Captain. We are on a ramming course." Lilly Bard said, with no worry in her voice. It was more matter of fact.

"Hold true, helm, we are not breaking. We have one shot. Hold true."

Jax's eyes were going back and forth between the Command table and her workstation. She had adjusted what she could, putting more strain on engine two, pushing it past the warnings, and past its known limits. She had adjusted the power relays, shutting down everything except what was needed. Instinct guided her hand. It was all she could do. It would either hold or it wouldn't. Fate would decide.

As much as she listened, she didn't hear the call to attack. She felt it, the vibrations of the ship, the rhythm that came from being in tune. All of it screamed in her mind as the teeth of her space shark came into play. Railgun two launched. Railguns four to eight all launched. *Lucky number six.* The beams were white hot as they lanced out from the Ares. Six super dense projectiles propelled by quantum wave technology pushed beyond the light speeds achievable by sentient races. It achieved infinite mass and slammed into the Lander, devastating its shields. It punched right through the Lander. The beams ripped holes wide open, but the Lander continued on. Then the barrage started.

Jax's eyes were locked on the spectacle. Every beam on the Ares lashed out, turning her space shark into a burning, multi-pointed star. Small sparks, waves upon waves of them, shot forth. Every torpedo tube spat missile after missile. Explosives bloomed like flowers in space. It would be beautiful to watch if the intent behind it wasn't so deadly. Any kind of protection the Lander might have had was gone. The beams, the torpedoes, ripped the hull of the Lander apart. Pieces shattered and drifted off into space. An opening appeared.

The full barrage of the Ares continued as they flew straight into the Lander. "Keep firing! Full shields!" the XO, the Captain, continued to shout. The whole bridge was shouting. It was fear, it was exhilaration, for some, it was all their mind could register to do as they traveled into the belly of the beast.

The Lieutenant pushed everything to shields and weapons. In this moment, nothing else mattered. Her board lit up with red; there were no longer any systems working within safety parameters. Alarms blazed. The bridge rumbled with vibrations, a growl that shook the crew to their bones.

The Ares rammed through, bucking and turning as it shredded the guts of the Lander. Debris cut through the shields of the warship as they began to flicker. Gashes burrowed deep down the length of its hull. Still, the Ares would not fall. In that last moment, when the shields were almost gone, when the patch of the Spine started to give way, when the ordnance was spent and only the beams remained, the Ares at last broke through.

The Lander's hull fractured outward. Behind the Ares, secondary explosions rippled across the Lander. The small explosions multiplied. Then they multiplied again, growing in intensity, growing in size. The Lander went nova. For a moment, in the middle of space, a star was born. The Screech destroyer, still leading the Lander, listing as if it was hit by the rail guns, soon followed. The shockwave bellowed outward and wrecked anything in its path.

On the bridge of the Ares, the Command crew braced for impact. They were strapped into pods, braced on the holotable rails. Warnings blared. The Ares' velocity carried it on. Its engines failed and only its momentum was left to drive it forward. The Ares started to list when the wave hit.

There was nothing the bridge crew could do. Their world went dark. Their lives were in the hands of the Ares.

Chapter 27

Limping into the Sunset

The Ares was dead. Her body was dragged along by the shockwave of the exploding Lander. She was floating aimlessly, with no defenses, a slow-moving, artificial comet. There was, however, hope.

The bridge power flashed back on instantly after the explosion, its independent back-up power kicking in. The Command team went to work, gathering crew, organizing repairs, rushing to breathe life back into this wonderful space shark.

It took hours to get basic functions back up and running. Freeing the ENG crew from the lockdown in engine room two was the biggest help. The best engineers left on the ship were let loose. To patch and bypass the necessary systems. Thanks to their capable hands, the energy flowed like blood in the veins. The engines pulsed like a heartbeat. The Ares lives.

There was still one enemy destroyer in the area. In the aftermath of the Lander's destruction, the Ares lost track of it. Was it hunting them? Did it retreat? Was it damaged? Too many unanswered questions. They weren't up for a fight, so they looked for a place to hold up. A place to be safe. The engines rattled. There were jumps to maximum speeds, followed by lulls to sub-light. It was like riding a roller coaster in space. Desperate days passed before they found a temporary haven.

It was a small, unnamed solar system with three planets. One, a small gas planet, hung near the sun. The middle one was little more than a big rock in space. The last planet, though, was the size of Mars with rings that radiated thousands of meters out from the center. The system was within human space but lacked anything worth noticing. It seemed like a good place to hide.

They parked in orbit with the unnamed planet's rings hanging above them, hoping that the ice, iron, and other particles of the rings would mask them visibly, and from active scans. They had launched pathjackers to act as scouts. An early warning system. So far, they had been safe.

Jax walked the halls. Well, limped might be a better description. Coming back in from fixing the Spine, she had damaged herself more than she realized. The Doc had fixed her up. He had bandaged her arm, given her nanites for her hip, and anti-inflammatories and painkillers for the rest. He had tried to make her stay in sick bay but there was too much to do and every hand mattered. *Even banged up ones like mine.*

Communications were still spotty throughout the ship, so she limped around, organizing work crews, checking on repairs, and delivering messages. Every little bit helps. Commander Lewis—*acting Captain Lewis,* she reminded herself; it was a hard adjustment to make—*she's amazing. She's going to make a great Captain. She is a great Captain.*

That's where she was headed now. To give report to Captain Lewis on the state of things. *As long as nobody attacks us, we'll be okay. That's pretty much what it all bordered down to. Just okay. With so many lost, so many dead, so much damage to the ship, what else could they be?* She tried not to think about it. Commander Urud. Captain Moss. So many names in the engineering crew to think about. It could be crushing to the core to dwell on it. *Mourn later.*

The halls were busy. People rushing, carrying supplies, knowing that, each minute, their lives were on the line. As an officer, usually enlisted fleet members would give way to her. She was slow, their work was more important, so she gave way. Still, those whose hands were free saluted as they passed, heads held high. *I've never been saluted this much, what is up with everyone?*

"Excuse me, ma'am." She hadn't seen him come up behind. His sharp voice startled her, and she stumbled into the wall. Her left shoulder hit and her whole face pinched. She felt his hand catch under her right arm.

"Fleetwalker Percy. You scared the crap out of me."

"I'm so sorry, ma'am." He said, a look of horror crossing his face. "I just wanted to see if you needed any help."

"I'm fine, Percy. Really." She shook off his arm. "I'm sure you have more pressing orders to follow up on anyway."

"No, ma'am. I mean, yes, ma'am. I just, well, I just wanted to thank you. You saved us."

"We all did our part. I don't deserve any special thanks."

"If you say so, ma'am, but that's not the story I've been hearing." His words race through her mind. *What story is that? How the Captain died, and I lived? How I passed out and almost doomed us all? Not sure I want to know what stories are going around. I need to get out of here.*

"I'm fine, Fleetwalker Percy. I have to meet Captain Lewis. You should get back on task."

"Aye aye, ma'am." He snapped to attention, fired off a salute, and was on his way.

She took a moment to steady herself and to clear her head. Stretched her bandaged shoulder and adjusted her arm. The Doc had had her in a sling when she left the MedBay, but she had ditched it. *I need to use both hands right now. Maybe not my best decision. Perhaps I can get a replacement? I don't need a 'Doc lecture' right now; I'll go by when he is busy, get a corpsman to help me instead,* she chuckled to herself. *Stay focused and keep yourself on task.* She walked on, angling for briefing room one.

Usually the Captain would be on the bridge, but this wasn't a usual time. With communications down, people were running messages by hand. People coming and going constantly to keep everything updated. The constant parade through the bridge was a distraction to those helming the ship. So, the Captain had moved command to briefing room one for the time being.

Getting people in and out of the Briefing Room was easier than going through the bridge. That, plus the fact that briefing room gave them more space to get organized. Ship repair, charts, checklists, and more. The Captain was monitoring everything from briefing room one.

The bridge was running a skeleton crew. Someone on helm and someone on watch for problems. Usually, that meant Commanders Bard and Haddock. They had lost so many of the engineering crew that all hands were needed for repairs. Pilots from the Hanger bay, all the Corps, and even all the bridge Commanders pitched in. To her surprise, Commander Moro had been one of the first to jump at the chance to help repair the ship. It was almost as much of a surprise when he walked out the portal ahead of her now.

She hadn't really seen him since the Screech attack. Since the Ares had moved off for safety and repairs. Since she had gone off on him. She moved back a step, both to make room and to stabilize herself. Her stance was as formal as she could make it. *I really need to go see the Doc again, this hip is killing me.* She hugged her damaged arm to her side and worked hard to stay out of his way.

He would pass her by and that would be that, just give it a second. He was talking before she realized it. "Lieutenant. You look miserable."

"Yes, Commander. I've had better days." *Was he really going to start something here? Now?* Commander Moro eyed her up and down. She felt like he was examining a piece of meat. His jaw clenched and moved like he was chewing his tongue.

"Your service during the attack—" He paused and looked away from her. "—Was acceptable." He walked away. She stood there with her mouth open. *What was that? Should I have said something back? Good job, maybe? Oh my. Let's put that in with, mourn later.* She shook her head and walked into the Briefing Room.

227

The meeting table was aglow with holoscreens, each one detailing what was happening on the Ares. Major problems, like engines, shields, and weapons, dominated the largest screens. Secondary items, like repairs for comms and the hull, floated around the edges.

There just weren't enough people to work on everything. It was a bit overwhelming seeing the entire table occupied. Captain Lewis was seated at her normal XO position. Leaving the 'Captain's seat' empty. She nodded her chin for Jax to take a seat. In front of her, she cycled through some screens that looked to Jax like weapon readouts. Probably updating information based off whatever Commander Moro had brought her.

The Lieutenant took her seat and felt the relief of taking pressure off her hip. She smiled slightly at the sensation. As she stretched her legs, her eyes continued to scan the screens. A small screen jumped out, isolated and floating on its own just off Captain Lewis's left side. Casualty Report.

Small because it just wasn't important right now. *Mourn later.* So close and kept clear of other problems because it was so important. A small lump built in her throat.

The acting Captain stopped and cracked her neck. The sound gave the Lieutenant goosebumps. "How's my acting ENG Commander?"

"I'm getting along fine. Still trying to figure out how I got to be the acting head of engineering. Wouldn't Rose, LTJG Koike, be a better choice?"

"Probably, but when I asked, she said to give it to you. So did everyone else in ENG for that matter, so it's yours. Get used to it."

She barked a small laugh "They're getting back at me for all the work I've been giving them, or they just want to avoid the bridge. There are better people for the job,"

"Probably, but that's life aboard a warship." A small grin was on the Captain's face. "So, what news from the ENG group? I could use something positive."

"Well, mostly positive. Rose should have Spine repairs done

within the hour. She figures another hour to make sure the shields and hull are stable, and we should be able to get on the way. She thinks communications will stabilize with the Spine but can't tell yet. We may have to keep running messages by hand. She'll update when she knows more."

"That is good news. I'm ready to head home."

Home. The word caused her mind to drift. *What a great word that was. What will it be like back on Earth after all I've been through? I could use a proper vacation. Maybe somewhere tropical. Hawaii would be nice. What am I thinking? Home is not Earth anymore. So where is my home?*

"Jax? You okay?" Jax's eyes snapped up to meet the concern leveled at her.

"I'm fine. Just wondering about home. Not really sure what that means right now."

"You have friends here and you have a place with us. When we get to Gaia, we'll get you some general quarters to start with, until you can find a place of your own. Once your personal stuff arrives from Earth, that should help too."

"What? Doesn't Earth think I'm dead? How am I getting my stuff?"

The Captain shook her head. "Sorry we didn't explain this better. We usually don't orientate people on ship." Gemma Lewis leaned back in her chair to gather her thoughts. "You've probably been listed as M.I.A. at this point. It might be a year or more till Earth gets a salvage crew out to the Indiana. Investigating the wreck, looking for bodies, that kind of thing. It should be interesting what they make of the Screech ship." The Captain chuckled slightly before continuing. "Anyways, being M.I.A., they'll pack up all your stuff and place it into a storage container somewhere. We have agents on Earth who will find it and then arrange to have it transferred somewhere for some reason. It will go missing, and a short time later, you'll have your stuff."

"That's amazing."

"Gaia may still be figuring out some things, but others they have down to a science."

"I still don't get that. Keeping Gaia a secret, all the subterfuge. What good does it do?"

The acting Captain shrugged. "Some people don't like to hear it, but Gaia is not as self-sufficient as we would like to think. We still need supplies from Earth. Certain building materials, manufactured goods, some foods. You ever try Gaia coffee?" Gemma stuck out her tongue.

Jax chuckled and said, "I don't drink coffee."

"That's right, you have a chai obsession," Gemma said, smiling. "All that, plus the people we recruit. We just don't have the institutions to train some groups of people yet. Doctors, engineers, and others. We even sneak some native Gaiaians back to Earth to go to school."

"That's crazy. But why keep it all secret?" Jax said.

"Earth government has sold the idea that any intelligent race exploring space is enlightened. They will come in peace," the acting Captain said as Jax leaned back in her chair.

She was going to shake her head at how stupid that sounded. Before she could say anything, she cut herself off. It dawned on her she was just like that such a short time ago. *My great space adventure. How foolish was I?*

The acting Captain continued. "So, anything counter to their message is considered invalid and is suppressed, even if it is generally known. Think of the kinds of political battles that would be waged trying to get war machines built. How long would it take them to even approve of an Ares kind of ship? If they knew Gaia was out there doing what we're doing, they could cut off our supply chain. That would hurt us badly. So, we operate as the Klick-Klick. That lets us run ships that people don't relate to humans. If they're seen, it just adds to the rumor mill that there is life out here. Plus, it looks mean, so that adds some fear into it. Keeps them looking in the wrong direction, but hopefully thinking in the right one."

"Wow. All this to fight the Screech." Jax mused, while shaking her head.

"Not initially. When Gaia was founded, they didn't know about the Screech. But it was founded with the idea that a species like the Screech could, and probably did, exist. A good thing they did."

"I agree with that. I keep thinking I understand it and then I learn a little bit more," Jax said, shuffling in her seat, trying to stretch her hip. "Seems crazy to me. Probably above my pay grade to really get all the complexities of it."

The Captain smiled. "Mine too."

"In one way, I do get it. I was one of those people. I thought I knew myself. Thought I had it all figured out, exploring space. Find life. Have an adventure." She turned her eyes from Gemma and looked at all the screens. "If you told me an alien species was going to try and rip my guts out, I would have laughed at you. Then the Screech came into my life. And the Ares. And all of this." She waved her hand across the table. "I thought I had worked so hard. I was ready for anything. I was so wrong. I wasn't prepared at all. It's made me doubt if I should really be here. If I can handle it all. Maybe when you offered me to stay, I should have chosen to go back to Earth."

Jax saw Gemma lean forward and wave all the screens aside. She placed an elbow on the table, pointed a kindly finger at her. The gesture reminded her of Captain Moss. "Don't take away your old accomplishments just because you've learned something new. Use what you had and let it be your base to grow into something different. You made the right choice, the one of knowledge over ignorance. If it makes you feel any better, I was the same when I got recruited."

"You? I don't believe it."

"Yes, me. I was a Judo gold medalist with a head full of conspiracy theories. I thought I could tackle them all. Then I got thrown in with the Terrain Corps. My first mission made me realize I wasn't going to be able to handle that kind of service very long. So, I switched to Fleet. I've come to grips with it since then, but it's still a part of me. I still have nightmares sometimes."

"Worse than Roost I?"

"Not even close."

"That's a story I'd like to hear one day."

"Sure. As soon as you share the story of your middle name." They both paused for a moment before they started laughing. Jax held a hand up as a sign of surrender.

"That's what I thought," the Captain said. "We've gotten sidetracked enough. If you think you can manage it, please let the bridge know our current timeline to be underway."

"Aye aye, Captain. I'm getting good at limping around." She gave a friendly salute as she rose.

"You're a good person, Jax, remember that. Captain Moss was proud to have you as part of the crew. And so am I," the Captain said, standing and holding out her hand. Jax shook it firmly.

"Thank you. That means a lot to me."

They nodded their heads and separated. The Captain took her seat and brought the holoscreens back into play. The Lieutenant turned and headed to the bridge.

Thankfully, the bridge wasn't far, as she limped her way there. With only Commanders Haddock and Bard on duty, it was strangely empty. She gave her report with no interruptions from the two Commanders. They just nodded their heads and smiled slightly. When she had finished, Commander Bard waved her hand for her to come over. Using the rail on the Command table to steady herself, she worked her way over to the NAV pod. The NAV pod, by tradition, was always located closest the nose of the ship. It seems farther away than normal. She limped on.

"Good timing, Lieutenant," Commander Bard said. "Would you like to see something spectacular?"

"I could use a little spectacular."

"Good. Stand over there." She pointed to a spot at the end of the Command table. "Eyes that way." Her hand moved back to the nose. "Been trying to get the Captain to come take a look. Got to enjoy the little things." A big grin crossed Lilly Bard's usually business-like face.

"Okay. What am I looking at?"

Commander Bard raised a finger as she turned back into her pod. In a moment, the walls around Jax started to melt away. The Observation Deck had been engaged. She was standing in space. The rings of the unnamed planet hung above her head. This system's sun shone bright above the planet's edge. The Ares' orbit allowed a clear view as the sun began to set.

It was nice, but she had seen space sunsets before. She was about to ask what was so spectacular when it happened. The sun was just a quarter hidden when its light started to refract and bounce through the planet's rings. The prism effect was like a thousand rainbows exploding into space. They seemed to expand and envelope her, bathing her in cosmic light. She had never seen anything so amazing or so beautiful. Her eyes lit up with excitement.

Now this is what exploring space should be. This is what I came out here for. The wonders of space that are here, waiting for us to find. She stood there till the end. All her cares, for just a moment, went missing from her mind. The sun set and the universe around her faded to black.

This ends Warship Ares
Captain's Fate Book 1

NEXT

The story of Jax and the Warship Ares continues in
Book 2 of Captain's Fate:

WARWORLD GAIA

Coming Soon!

From the Author

Hello wonderful Reader!

Thanks for taking the time to read this, my first novel. I hope you enjoyed reading it as much as I enjoyed creating it! If you could please take just a few minutes of your time, I would love a review. Reviews are the life's blood of self-published authors. Even a short review of a few words will help me reach new readers and encourage me to continue to enhance my craft.

I thank you for your support!

-Skip Scherer

About the Author

Skip Scherer lives in Washington State with his lovely wife, daughter, two dogs and an immortal fish.

Before he started writing, Skip got a degree in computer graphics and design. After working as a freelance artist for many years, Skip made a huge life change and opened a martial arts school. That career choice lead to a way of life for over two decades. He continues to run that school to this day, writes at night and continues to take on new challenges.

If you want to know when Skip's next book will come out, please visit his website at http://www.skipscherer.com, where you can sign up to receive an email when he has his next release.

You can also join him on social media:

https://twitter.com/skip_scherer
https://www.facebook.com/WarShipAres

Made in the USA
Las Vegas, NV
08 November 2021

34003174R00143